A Dandy Little Game

Bill McCulloch

For Donna,
   Something for the
trip to Vancouver.

Bill McCulloch

For Carolyn,
a loving partner
who accepts my *mishegas*

1

Veteran bookie Frankie Aiello stopped taking Johnny Sharansky's markers—what the gamblers call IOUs—on the first weekend in July. Johnny was irate, of course. It never took much to set the guy off. But Frankie wasn't about to change his mind. "Believe me," he told Johnny, "I'm doing you a big favor. You think I'm an asshole—go ahead, think whatever you want."

Within twenty-four hours, every handbook controlled by the Accardo organization, meaning all of the handbooks in Chicago and a handful in Cicero and other western suburbs, got word that Johnny Sharansky was running up big losses and should be considered a high risk to welsh on any markers.

No longer able to place bets on credit, Johnny started carrying more cash. In theory, this should have been a good thing because it limited Johnny's losses to whatever he had in his pocket. Trouble was, he was out gambling almost all the time now, and his pocket was always heavy with cash—we're talking extremely long green. In Johnny's way of looking at it, his luck was about to change, but if he wasn't gambling, and gambling big, how would he know?

In other words, the losing streak was making him crazy.

His thinking had gone so haywire that he put three grand in his kick on a Wednesday afternoon and took a cab out to The Dome, an Accardo casino on Irving Park Road, west of the city limits. This was dumb on several counts. For one thing, three grand was more than the average working stiff made in a year—*a year*. For another, it represented a big chunk of Johnny's dwindling cash reserve. And for another, anyone who flashed that kind of money in a casino or a cabaret was liable to flash "easy score" to some street tough.

Usually, Johnny wouldn't be caught dead in a casino unless he was trying to impress a dame. But he hadn't had a real date in two years, and he'd been losing big on ballgames and the horses. The payoff on a winning roulette number was looking like a fast way to recoup some of the lost money and confirm a change in his luck.

The change was just around the corner. He could feel it.

In more normal times, Johnny would have dismissed that kind of thinking as *meshuge*. But normal times had taken a holiday.

The Dome casino, operating in the basement of a red-brick building with the small sign "Irving Park Athletic Club," had recently reopened after being raided and boarded up the previous fall. All the criminal cases had been quietly "nolle-prossed" by the state's attorney a couple of months after the raid. Nobody knew why. And except for the *Chicago Tribune*, nobody cared.

With a fist full of twenty-dollar chips, Johnny began by standing at one of The Dome's three roulette tables, waiting for a number to suggest itself. After watching a couple of spins of the wheel, he played two chips on twenty-four black. The bet came up a loser.

He tried a hunch play—the day of the month, five red. Four chips this time. Another loser.

He thought he heard a voice telling him to play his age,

but the voice must not have known that forty-three doesn't exist on a roulette wheel, so he placed a bet on shortstop Lennie Merullo's uniform number instead: eight chips on twenty-one. The ball dropped into thirty-six red, the highest number on the wheel.

"I should have played this when I was younger," he said to no one in particular.

"Hey, don't I know you from someplace?"

Johnny turned to his left and met the gaze of a middle-aged man, grossly overweight with close-set pig eyes, wire-rim glasses, and hair flying in all directions. He was perched on a low stool rendered almost invisible by his bulk, and was wearing a short-sleeve white dress shirt with prominent sweat rings under the armpits.

"Yeah, I know you," the man said, squinting. "I see you and your brother all the time at that bookie joint in the Loop—the one on Wabash."

"I've been there," Johnny said cautiously, his eyes narrowing. "But that's not my brother. I don't have a brother. And I never saw you there."

"I remember now," the fat guy said, snapping his pudgy fingers and pointing at Johnny. "It's Joe—that's your brother's name. And you're Johnny."

"I just told you, I don't have a brother—Joe's a friend. Known him since I was a kid."

The guy offered a clammy handshake. "Name's Marv," he said. "It's an honor to meet you. I heard you guys are big-time players, like for twenty years. So where's your friend?"

"He took a powder a week ago," Johnny said. "More than a week maybe. He'll be back—he's just taking a little time off."

"Smart guy," Marv said. "It's like I always say—you can't lose money if you keep it in your pocket."

"What the hell's that supposed to mean?" Johnny shot back.

"Nothing personal," Marv said, drawing slightly back

from Johnny's glare. "But it's not exactly a state secret you guys were on a bad streak. Hell, everybody knows Frankie Fats cut you off."

"Christ," Johnny sputtered, one hand coming up, palm toward his face. "Why does everybody have to know my fucking business? I can't believe that asshole."

"Hey, hey, take it easy, pal," Marv said. "I didn't hear it from Frankie. He doesn't talk about business. But you know how it is. Other people talk."

"Well, don't believe every goddamned thing you hear," Johnny said, his face still flushed. "See, there's a phrase I been using all my life: You never know the next person's business. You think you know something about my business? Forget it. I can walk into any handbook in this city right now and bet a grand, two grand, whatever I feel like."

"Yeah, but you can't sign a marker, right?"

"That's a temporary thing," Johnny snapped, giving his hand a dismissive flip.

"Not if you keep on doing what you're doing," Marv said. "Mind if I make a suggestion?"

Johnny looked away, his mouth hardening into a straight line. He took a breath, two breaths. "What kind of suggestion?" he said without looking at Marv.

Marv leaned forward, trying to see Johnny's face. "Stop playing the longest odds on the table," he said. "Go for the best odds—you know, red-black or odd-even. Whatever comes up on the wheel, let's say it's black, bet black again, and the same amount. Except if you lose—that's when you raise the bet and switch to red."

Eyes blazing, Johnny gathered his chips and arranged them in a single neat stack, tapping the stack with his fingertips to align the chips. "That's your system, eh? Tell you what—I need a drink. You want one? I'll get it."

"Hey, thanks." Marv leaned back and smiled. "Make it a bourbon on the rocks, Cabin Still if they got it. Except tell the bartender you want stab and kill. Stab and kill. Get it?"

He broke into a high whinny.

Johnny went to the bar, ordering a bourbon for Marv and a Canadian and water for himself. He stayed at the bar a minute, seemingly lost in thought, then muttered, "What the fuck," and walked back to the roulette table.

He put the bourbon next to Marv and took a drink from his own highball. "OK, I'm going to let you in on something." Johnny went into a slight crouch and his hand came up in front of his mouth again. He leaned in closer, but avoided eye contact, instead glancing to the right and left as he spoke. "See, I been doing this for a long time— over twenty years, just like you said. I know every goddamned system there is. And here's what else I know. You can put your money on a number or you can put your money on red or black or odd or any goddamned thing you want. It's all the same."

"No it's not." Marv drew himself back, his tone indignant.

"What, you think you're past-posting the house by betting odds and evens? Go ahead, knock your brains out," Johnny said. "But I'm giving it to you straight: No matter where you put your money, it's all the same as far as the house is concerned. The only difference is, I got a chance to walk out of here with maybe five or six grand, plus whatever I've still got in my kick, and you're going to be sitting here waiting for the wheel to come up the same color twenty or thirty times in a row."

Marv took a slug from his drink and placed a five-dollar chip on red. "All I know," he said, "is you must have dropped two or three hundred bucks since you walked up to this table, and I'm—let's see," he leaned forward, head tilted, to eyeball his stack of chips, "I'm forty bucks to the good. I'm sticking with the short odds."

"Fine," Johnny said. "In fact, you're right. Whatever you say is right, mister. You go ahead and play your ... your system. I'm going to try a different table." He had already taken two steps when he turned and came back. "Here," he said, flipping one of his twenty-dollar chips onto the table in front of Marv. "Put it on a fucking number, for Christ's sake."

After dark, when Johnny left the Dome, he had eighteen dollars in his pocket.

Thursday morning he sat in his North Side hotel room, glancing through a three-day old *Tribune*, when he saw an ad for one of the area's dog tracks. He stopped and looked out the window toward the lake. "The dogs," he muttered. "What *mishegas*." The losing streak might be making him crazy, but not crazy enough to bet on the dogs. Not yet.

He spent the day sleeping.

A line of squalls rumbled from west to east across the city late Friday morning, dousing the summer heat for a couple of hours. Roused by the thunder, he had tea and a sweet roll in the hotel grill, then spent the early afternoon studying the next day's entries at Arlington Park, looking for something—a familiar name, a funny name, anything—that would help him break out of the slump.

About sundown, he went to the closet and pulled a hatbox off the top shelf. For most of Johnny's adult life, the box had been his kitty. He knew that only chumps kept their money in banks—the Crash in '29 taught him that, and then several times since. He took a hundred dollars in small bills out of the box, took note of the paltry assortment of bills that remained, and replaced the box.

After showering and shaving, Johnny put on a pair of white boxer shorts and a sleeveless undershirt, then returned to the bathroom. Combing his brown hair straight back, he stopped to look at himself in the medicine cabinet mirror. His face, round and boyish-looking not that long ago, was showing signs of age—wrinkles radiating from the outer corners of his blue eyes, faint frown lines creasing his forehead, deeper lines drooping from the corners of his mouth. Tired.

He dressed, choosing a dark-blue suit from the crowded closet. Pocketing the hundred dollars, he walked to the Wilson Avenue station, and took a southbound "L" to Chicago Avenue. A short cab ride took him to the Rush Street nightclub district where he had the prime rib dinner special at Club Alabam—$1.75 on Fridays. Normally, if he and Joe were together, they would stay for Club Alabam's floor show. But Johnny left shortly after paying his dinner tab. He had two more stops to make, and he wanted to be well clear of the nightclub before three young enlisted men, getting drunker and more obnoxious by the minute, started a brawl.

"I got business to take care of," he explained to the *maître d'*, who professed great disappointment that Johnny was not staying for the show.

He went out into the night air still heavy from the rain earlier in the day and walked to a three-story brownstone on Erie. A middle-aged woman wearing a housecoat and too much makeup opened the front door: "Johnny, where you been? We thought maybe you'd died or something."

"Yeah, I've been real busy," he said, removing his hat as he stepped into the entry hall. "Is Helen, ah ...?"

"Upstairs—she's all yours, blue eyes."

Now in her early 30s, Helen was a big-boned blonde, a good two inches taller than Johnny and twenty pounds heavier. She had large breasts, wide hips, big thighs—even her feet were big.

She had come to the city from Iowa in 1937 or '38, and had first encountered Johnny when she was working as a hatcheck girl in the Loop, something she did for three years before drifting into her current line of work. She thought Johnny was a screwball, but usually in a way that was non-threatening. And he was cute.

Johnny, intrigued by Helen's bigness, used to kid her about being his *zaftik* farm girl, although he had no idea if she'd ever been near a farm because she didn't talk about her past. That was fine with Johnny.

Helen flashed a half-smile when she saw Johnny quick stepping across the second-floor sitting room in her direction, holding his black fedora by the side dents in the crown: "Hey, crazy man, long time no see. What's the rush?"

"You know me, Baby—I'm busier than FDR."

"FDR, eh? Well, Mr. Busy," she gathered her robe about her and rose from the plush settee, "I'm guessing we're going to have to postpone that candlelight dinner again. Sounds like another fuck and run."

"No, not tonight," Johnny said, his expression taking a turn for the serious. "We've got to change the routine, Baby—really. I need something different, a new angle."

Helen squinted suspiciously. "If you think I'm taking it in the keister, you got another think coming, fella." She crossed her arms under her breasts and looked away, plopping backwards onto the settee.

Johnny held his arms out wide and flashed a smile. "Hey, *zaftik* girl, you know me—that's not my *shtik*."

She gave Johnny a smirk. "Let me guess—you want to peep in my heater."

"Hey, Jews don't do that, Baby," he said. "It's not kosher. I'm talking just a little bit different." He looked around at the other working girls in the sitting room and lowered his voice. "Maybe we take a little longer, you know, do it with you on top. Or you, ah, smoke my cigarette, if you catch my drift—just something to change my luck. Okay?"

"Aha," Helen's eyebrows arched, "so Mr. Busy has been having a rough time of it? Is that what I'm hearing?"

"Rough time? For Christ's sake, Baby, I've been living in a nightmare. Twenty-three years and I never had a bum streak like this. I can't pick a winner!"

Helen arose from the red velvet settee and languidly moved toward one of the sitting room doors, motioning Johnny to follow. "You been hanging out with gypsies or something?" she asked over her shoulder. "Maybe some gypsy lady put a spell on you."

"Yeah, that's what it feels like," Johnny said, falling in behind Helen. "Like a curse—and no matter what I do, it's always following me around." He glanced over his shoulder and waved a hand behind him. "Shoo, get away from me," he said.

"Like the guy with the rain cloud in Li'l Abner."

"In what?"

"The comics—you know, Li'l Abner?"

"Lady, there's no comics in the *Racing Form*. But you got the idea. That's why I'm looking to change things."

"OK, little man, I'll be your witch doctor," she said, closing the door to the small bedroom. "And since you're not like most of the crumb-buns who come in here, I'll do what you said—both ways, take it nice and slow. Regular price. You just lie down and relax."

His face brightened. He held his hat flat against his chest and rolled his eyes toward the ceiling. "Oh, Baby—I can feel my luck changing already. But I don't want any favors. I'm going to pay extra. That's the way I want it. OK?"

"The customer is always right," Helen said, removing the robe and freeing her swaying breasts. "If your luck doesn't change, you can always come back. You should come around more often anyway. I got lots of ways to get rid of gypsy spells."

2

*"H*ey, gorgeous, how old's your boyfriend?"

The beer-slurred question came from one of the three Army privates sitting at a table near the Club Alabam's dance floor. Margaret Turner rolled her eyes. She had been through this before—strangers making it their business to find out why her male companion was wearing civvies.

"Buzz off," she said, crushing a cigarette into her ashtray.

She had no intention of explaining that her fiancé, currently in the lavatory, was unfit for military service because of knee problems dating back to his days as a football lineman at Amherst. Explanations would only invite argument.

"Hey, come on, Baby, no need to get sore. We're just curious, is all."

"Mind your own business," Margaret snapped. "And I am not your baby."

The talkative G.I. drew back, eyes wide. "Uh-oh, I'm in big trouble now." The soldiers guffawed.

At twenty-six, Margaret was four years out of Smith College. She had once hoped to travel in Europe after graduation, accompanied by her roommate and best friend, Gabrielle d'Audeville, a redhead from Cherbourg, but Hitler scotched those plans.

Gabrielle had cut short her senior year at Smith, flying to Portugal and then home to France at Christmas break as German forces were preparing for what became the invasion of Norway, Denmark, and the Low Countries. She had sent a letter to Margaret reporting her safe arrival in Cherbourg. Since then, nothing.

Margaret had graduated, and had returned home to suburban Evanston, her life descending into gray tedium relieved only by titillating novels and an occasional movie. In December of '42, she attended a Christmas reception at her father's LaSalle Street law firm, where she was introduced to Brantley Cheswick Adams III, a thirty-two-year-old tax and trusts attorney from Winnetka, an affluent bedroom community two train stations north of Evanston. He was a shade over six feet tall, with thinning hair, a youthful face, and a biting brand of humor. They had been seeing each other once or twice a week—on dates in the city or over dinner at the Turner home in Evanston—ever since the Christmas party.

While Margaret had welcomed the diversion of regular evenings out, she accepted Brantley's attentions with a certain detachment. She sensed that this was the man—or at least the kind of man—her parents wanted her to marry. But she wasn't sure Brantley was what *she* wanted. When Brantley had proposed in June, she had hesitated.

A good lawyer, he had pressed his case: "I'll be in line for a full partnership at the firm in another year or two, maybe sooner if we're married. I can give you a very comfortable life, the kind you've always known. And I promise you, I will never so much as look at another woman."

Margaret had come to feel affection for Brantley. If it wasn't love she felt, it was at least fondness. She wasn't getting any younger, as her mother kept reminding her, and there were no other prospects. After an awkward pause, she had accepted his proposal.

"What the hell's going on?" It was Brantley, brow furrowed, walking back to their table and looking back and forth at Margaret and the soldiers. Full of the kind of bravado that one seldom saw in combat veterans, they had studied his walk from the men's room to the table and were quietly sharing their observations, heads together.

"Nothing," Margaret said. "Just some imbeciles trying to make the evening a total loss." She had twice sent her prime rib back to the kitchen, complaining it was cold and inedible. The cabaret chanteuse she had wanted to hear, Genevieve Val, had been canceled for laryngitis. And now this.

"I'll talk to the manager," Brantley said.

"What good's he going to do?" Margaret said, giving Brantley an impatient look. "Maybe we should just forget the rest of the show. It's not what I wanted to hear anyway."

"If you're feeling lucky, we could go upstairs. I heard they've got gambling up there."

"Not anymore," she said. "The roulette tables were taken out three years ago. The police raid was all over the papers—didn't you read the stories?"

The soldiers at the nearby table were still sizing up Brantley. "Hey, fella, where's your uniform?"

Brantley shot an annoyed glance in the direction of the soldiers and waved off the question, then turned back to Margaret. But the most aggressive of the three G.I.'s wasn't giving up.

"What are you, some kind of farmer? Naw, too soft."

"Let's settle up and go to some other club," Brantley said. "This is ridiculous." He held one hand up, index finger raised, and tried to catch a waiter's eye.

"Or maybe you're one of those limp-dicks who says he doesn't believe in war—eh?"

Couples at other nearby tables were now taking note of the taunts, flashing annoyed looks in the direction of the

G.I.'s. From somewhere, a man's voice said, "Hey, knock it off, soldier." Somebody else yelled, "Eighty-six those kids!"

The soldiers laughed and slapped each other's shoulders, apparently delighted by the disruption they were causing.

Margaret leaned closer to Brantley, looking him in the eyes. "This is humiliating," she said. "Aren't you going to say something—stand up for yourself?"

"We're leaving," Brantley hissed.

"Oh, for God's sake," Margaret blurted, getting up from her chair and turning toward the soldiers. She jabbed an index finger in their direction to emphasize what she was about to say, but as the words were forming one of the club's bouncers stepped in front of her, grasped her wrist, and gently lowered her hand.

"We'll handle this," he said quietly. "No need for you to get involved."

Margaret looked irritated. "In case you haven't noticed, I'm already involved," she said. "Those idiots over there have been extremely insulting to me and my fiancé."

"I said we'll handle it," the bouncer repeated. "Please, just take your seat."

A second bouncer was now looming over the table of G.I.'s, explaining what the consequences would be, even for men in uniform, if there were further disruptions.

Margaret was breathing hard. She watched the little drama at the nearby table, noting the immense size of the bouncer and the instant respect he commanded from the boisterous G.I.'s.

Musicians were filtering back onto the bandstand after intermission.

Margaret leaned toward Brantley, who was now holding his wallet, and still trying to get their dinner tab. "Is there a decent hotel within walking distance," she asked, "somewhere we can get a room?"

"Maybe not tonight," he said. "I've got some work I need to finish. Waiter!"

As they stepped out onto the crowded sidewalk in front of the club, Margaret clutched the sleeve of Brantley's suit jacket. "Did you see that?" she said in a low voice.

"See what?"

"That man in the straw boater, going into the club. I think it was Jake Guzik."

Brantley stopped and gave Margaret a patronizing smile. "My dear," he said, "I can't think of a single reason why a hoodlum from Cicero would be walking around, all by himself, on Rush Street on a Friday night? And even if I could think of a reason, Who cares?"

Margaret scowled and looked away, pouting like a scolded child. "I still say it was him."

3

After settling up with Helen, Johnny took a cab to the South Side. At 43rd and State the driver, a middle-aged woman with a union button pinned to her cap, pulled to the curb.

"Hey, this isn't the address," Johnny protested. "It's four blocks east of here."

"This is as far as I go, mister," the woman said over her shoulder. She tipped her head to the left. "Too dark once you get off State. Know what I mean?"

Johnny cursed. He paid the fare on the meter—"You don't get a tip for half a ride"—got out on the corner, and began walking east on 43rd Street.

As usual on a summer night, women and old men lounged on the front steps of the tenements lining 43rd. Bottles of cheap hooch, mostly white port and other fortified wines, were fueling arguments on several stoops as Johnny walked by. A few children, the ones who'd been given a reprieve on bedtime, played games in the dark.

A white man in a blue suit walking on 43rd Street late in the evening—he was bound to draw silent stares, but Johnny didn't notice. This was one of the neighborhoods, far removed from his own tenement in the Nineteenth

Ward, where he had felt safe on days when he was ditching school—and that was a shitload of days.

As an accomplished truant, he often spent mornings in saloons and hotel lobbies near 35th street where he could run errands and do small favors for ball players. His preferred afternoon destination was Comiskey Park; he paid his way in with the tips he'd made in the morning. During the winter or on days the White Sox were out of town, he had come here to 43rd Street—a neighborhood studiously avoided by truancy officers.

With his luck about to change, Johnny needed to find the most reliable tout he could think of. That would be Noah "Eight Count" Carter, a one-time racetrack groom and club fighter, who now ran one of the South Side's five numbers rackets. A determined card player with a vile temper, Eight Count—a nickname that only someone with a death wish would speak to Carter's face—seemed to have connections all over the city, though he rarely left the Negro neighborhoods flanking South State Street.

Entering Jeremiah Johnson's pool hall at 43rd and South Prairie, Johnny glanced around the room, looking for familiar faces, noting the empty chair near the entrance door. Usually Johnson would be sitting there, but the chair was empty. Johnny figured "J.J.," as regulars called him, was either taking a leak or had turned in early.

In the center of the room, a boisterous group of almost two dozen men pressed around one of three pool tables. They weren't playing pool, of course—not at this hour. They were shooting craps, yelling and cursing and exchanging money on every roll of the dice. Until one of them spotted Johnny. Then the group fell silent. Heads turned. Johnny felt the stares.

Beyond the pool hall, the back room at Johnson's contained three round tables, each illuminated by a light suspended from the ceiling, and a mismatched assortment of chairs for the twenty-four-hour card players and kibitzers who inhabited the room. Joe had spent countess nights in this room back in the early '20s. If there had been a graduate school for card players, this is where Joe would have earned his Ph.D.

Two of the back-room tables were empty. At the third, Carter, well dressed and prosperous-looking at 63, with a black patch over one eye, was about to deal a hand of five-card draw to four middle-aged *shvartzers*—all of them wearing white dress shirts with French cuffs. Alerted by the wary looks around the table, Carter removed a soggy cigar stub from the corner of his mouth and turned slightly, squinting into the haze of smoke with his one good eye to see who had entered the back room. His eye widened.

"Great googly-moogly, look what the cat dragged in! Relax, y'all, this cat's not the law—known him since he was a pup. Ain't that right, Johnny? Taught you how to shoot dice when you was a school boy. So where the hell you been, man? I was supposing you got too highfalutin for the old neighborhood."

"Hey, you're my people—I still love the little people," Johnny said, spreading his arms to include the card players in his beneficent declaration.

One of the men snorted, the other three just stared at Johnny.

"Grab some matchsticks if you want in," Carter said, returning the cigar to its place in the corner of his mouth. "Easy pickings tonight—these cats are beating me like a cheating wife."

"Are you kidding? You couldn't pay me to sit in here and do this. No, I'm looking for a horse. You got one?"

"Maybe," Carter said cautiously.

"What do you mean maybe? Don't fuck with me, Noah. Either you got one or you don't."

"My, aren't we all het up tonight," Carter said, starting the clockwise deal. "The losing must be getting to you, J-man. Jacks or better to open, y'all."

"So you heard."

"You know me," Carter said, placing the un-dealt cards on the table in front of him and collecting his hand. "I try to keep up."

"I don't get it," Johnny said, turning his palms up and adopting an injured expression. "The other day some asshole I never seen before calls me by name and says he heard I can't sign markers. Since when did my business become public property?" His face was reddening.

"Take a deep breath," Carter said without expression. He nodded at the player to his left, "Can you open?" The player shook his head. Carter nodded to the next player. "You and Joe-B," he said to Johnny without taking his eyes off the card players, "you're kind of like movie stars. Not down here, of course—I'm talking 'bout up in ofay-town. The players know y'all have lasted a long damn time. So they talk. Where the hell is Joe-B, by the way? He'd bring a little class to this godforsaken table. Nothing personal, niggers, but y'all have been off your game in the repartee department this evening."

"Joe's visiting one of his sisters," Johnny said. "He'll be back in action pretty soon. And, yeah—the fucking bookies are killing me. Thing is, I got a feeling. All I need is one good tip, one winner. And if anybody's got a horse, it's Eight ... it's you. That's what Joe and me always say."

"OK, J-man, since I seem to be running a motherfucking charity tonight, check the entries at Arlington." He pointed without lifting his left hand off the table. "Razor, it's four dollars to you—you still in?" Then back to Johnny: "You're looking for Constant Aim, a three-year-old. Tough to beat at a mile-and-an-eighth. And a sleeper. That's your ticket."

"I love you, man. Constant Aim. I might even take the train out to the track tomorrow afternoon, make a day of it, you know?"

Carter put his cards face down on the table and shook his head. "Forget tomorrow. If the horse runs, it'll be Monday."

"Monday," Johnny's hand shot up to shield his mouth. "For Christ's sake, Noah, I need something for tomorrow. Don't fuck with me, can't you see I'm dying here?"

Carter was glowering now. He folded his hands on top of the cards as if he might be about to offer a prayer—except he wasn't in a praying mood. "That's all I got," he growled. "Now you best be on your way before I get up from this table and kick your ungrateful ass."

Johnny returned to the front room. He made a point of paying respects to J.J., who had returned to his usual station to the left of the street entrance, a vantage point that allowed him to give the once-over to anyone coming in.

J.J. confirmed that he, too, had heard about Johnny's run of bad luck. "Maybe the Lord be telling you to quit before something bad happen," he said. "You and Joe-B both."

"Hey, nobody loves a quitter. We got to keep pitching, me and Joe."

Johnny pulled the slender roll of bills out of his pocket, peeled off a single, and held it out to J.J. "How much to get into the game over there?

J.J. took the bill. "Hasn't changed—still two bits." He dug into his pants pocket for change.

"Forget the change," Johnny said. He turned and drifted over to the animated group playing craps around the pool table in the middle of the room. His brief chat with J.J. having established his bona fides, none of the players gave him a second look now. Still holding the roll of bills, he watched for about three minutes. Keeping his hand low, he looked down and made a rough count. After the dinner, the curse-breaking session with Helen, the "L" fare, the contribution to J.J., and a couple of cab fares, he still had close to fifty dollars.

"Now or never," he said out loud. He peeled two singles off the roll for another cab fare, and was about to put forty bucks on the pass line—a chance to double his money in a matter of seconds—when the din in the room was pierced by two shrill rings, each about two seconds long, from a small bell mounted on the wall above the curtained front window.

The bell had been activated by a "blind man" stationed, with stool, white cane, and tin cup, on the sidewalk outside. Instantly the room went quiet. Gamblers picked up their money and dispersed to the other pool tables or the sides of the room. The dice were picked up. With J.J. supervising, two patrons and the blind man lifted the three-sided craps setup off the middle pool table and carried it to a storage area behind the room where Eight Count was playing cards. The whole operation took less than half a minute.

Within a few seconds, Johnny knew, a police patrolman, or maybe a couple of plainclothes dicks, would stroll into the pool hall, acting like they owned the place. The cops might be looking for someone—a pet stoolie, a guy who had skipped a court appearance, a neighborhood *shmuck* who'd just roughed up his old lady. Or the visit might be routine—a little reminder that cards, craps, and unlicensed liquor sales would be tolerated only as long as J.J. continued to send a paper bag containing a sawbuck and a bottle of Cutty Sark to a certain district captain on the first day of each month.

Whether the cops were looking or hassling, Johnny wasn't interested. He'd played this little game before.

Striding toward the storage room, where he could exit through an alley door, Johnny returned the bills to his pants pocket. Before entering the back room, he turned and gave a wave to J.J., who had joined the craps players and kibitzers now standing around the periphery of the room, trying a little too hard to look like they always stood around doing nothing at Jeremiah Johnson's pool hall.

"I'll tell Joe you sent regards," Johnny called.

J.J. gave Johnny a questioning look and held up the

dollar bill.

"Keep it," Johnny shouted over his shoulder. "I'll be back."

Saturday morning, Johnny stood on a chair in the walk-in closet behind the Murphy bed in his room and again pulled the big hatbox off the top shelf. He sat down on the bed and emptied the box onto the bedspread.

It was a dismal scattering of bills—mostly ones, twos, and fives. He gathered the bills and began counting, placing each denomination in a separate pile, always turning the bills so they faced the same way.

A month ago the box had contained over thirty thousand dollars. As far back as he could remember the cash in the box had never totaled less than two grand, and at least once, before the Crash, the box had held close to ninety thousand dollars.

He counted twice. The total was the same both times: seventy-eight dollars. Including the cash he'd tossed on the dresser when he got back from J.J.'s, he had just over a hundred and twenty-four dollars to his name. Before heading downtown to Frankie's handbook, he considered setting fifty bucks aside, just in case the session with Helen hadn't changed his luck. But that would be an admission of weakness, and that was bad. "Scared money always loses," he muttered.

He folded the bills, and put the wad in his pocket, then clapped his hands and pushed up on his toes. "This is it," he said. "Everything changes today."

4

*J*ohnny pushed the stack of rumpled bills across the counter—large denominations on the bottom, singles on the top.

"Give me the five horse, Code Mentor, sixth race, Detroit," he said. "A hundred twenty-three bucks. To win."

A clerk wearing a white dress shirt with black sleeve garters licked his thumb and began counting. He went through the stack of bills twice. The count done, he snatched the pencil propped behind his right ear and jotted numbers on two slips of paper, talking out loud as he wrote. "One hundred twenty-three dollars, number five, to win, sixth race, Detroit." He pushed one of the slips across to Johnny.

With the slip tucked in his left front pocket, Johnny turned and shouldered past four men shuffling toward the counter to place their own bets. He walked to the center of the windowless, high-ceiling room, tipped his hat back, and waited.

He patted his chest and took a deep breath.

Middle-aged men, maybe twenty-five of them, all

wearing hats, milled about the handbook. Most of them, like Johnny, kept to themselves. They jotted notes on folded copies of the *Daily Racing Form,* listened to the race results coming in from City Sports Service, and checked the handwritten sheets hanging on the wall opposite the betting counter.

Before the war, it would have taken two boys, working as fast as they could, to post scratch sheets. But these days, with so many tracks closed or converted to military use, one elderly clerk could do the job without breaking a sweat.

As usual, most of the men standing around the room were chewing cigars or smoking cigarettes. Not Johnny, though. He'd smoked a little when he was a kid, partly to be like the ballplayers he encountered on the South Side, but mostly to piss off his old man. Smoking had never become a habit—he just couldn't see the point. Right now, the foul-smelling haze hanging in the room made his eyes sting, but he was used to it.

This was his world, or a big part of his world—the other parts being fight arenas, cabarets, brothels, and the city's two ballparks. He knew the lingo here, knew a lot of the characters. And, as noted by Eight Count Carter, most of them knew him.

One of the cigar smokers, a thick-set man known to most here as "Bowtie," caught Johnny's eye. Bowtie was wearing a dark fedora, dark pinstripe suit, and—what else?—the bowtie, purple today. "Hey, how you doing, little man? Where's your shadow today? The smooth talker."

"Joe, he went on holiday last month," Johnny said, trying his best to avoid pointless chitchat. "No big deal, he'll be back."

"You fellows related, by any chance?"

"What?" Johnny's attention had already moved on. "You say something to me?"

"Just making conversation," Bowtie said. "I asked if

26

you was related to that guy, like cousins or brothers."

"Friends," Johnny said, "from the Nineteenth Ward. Hey, that reminds me, you know a guy named Marv comes in here?"

Bowtie scratched his chin and squinted at Johnny. "Fat guy? World's greatest expert?"

"That's the guy."

"What's the deal? He owe you?"

"I wish he did."

Bowtie snorted: "No you don't. You'd still be waiting for your money come Christmas."

"Figures." Johnny bounced on his toes and glanced around the room. "I can spot a loser a mile away."

"Hey, I got to get a bet down," Bowtie said. "I'll see you around—you and your friend."

A chunky black p.a. speaker hanging from the loft railing in the handbook emitted an audible pop, the usual signal that a result was arriving from City Sports. Most of the men stopped what they were doing. "Here is the finish in the sixth race at Detroit. The winner, Stell, the three horse, paid eighteen-forty, seven-eighty, and six-twenty ..."

The monotone recitation continued, now competing with exclamations of triumph or disgust from a handful of bettors. Johnny stood silent for several seconds, his mouth agape, then crumpled to his hands and knees, looking like some poor mook who had just been kicked in the stomach or gut shot by a .38. His back heaved up and down as he gasped for air. When he finally had enough breath he uttered a cry so anguished that it froze every movement in the room.

The wail roused Frankie Fats from his desk in the loft above the room. Frankie waddled to the loft railing, body hair protruding from his shirt collar and covering his podgy white arms like a sweater. Sizing up the scene below, he frowned and shook his head.

Bowtie walked through the circle of gawkers around Johnny and touched Johnny on the back of the shoulder.

"What happened? You OK, little man?"

"Hey, don't worry about that dummy," Frankie yelled at the faces now turning to look up at the loft. "There's nothing wrong with him. He's just trying to find where his luck went—ain't that right, Johnny? And the old Sicilian warned you, didn't he? Tried to slow you down. But, no, you knew better."

To Johnny, it sounded as though Frankie Fats was far away, yelling from the far end of a tunnel. He pushed himself up to a kneeling position, wiping his hands on the front of his trousers, but pitched forward again, arresting his fall with outstretched hands.

"No, no, you can't stay like that!" Frankie barked. "Don't make me come down there, Johnny. Just get the hell up off my floor and leave. Be a man, for God's sake!"

Later, in a phone booth in the back of a drug store north of the river, Johnny extracted a nickel from the few coins in his pants pocket and dialed a North Side number. He took deep breaths, trying to remember how he had gotten from the Loop to the drug store. The phone rang once, twice, three times, "Hello."

"Joe, it's me. You busy?"

"Johnny, good to hear your voice. I been thinking about you all day—since I got back from my sister's. No, I'm just sitting here listening to the radio. What's up?"

"I ... I hardly know how to tell you this I'm so balled up right now. Remember what we used to say when we started this racket, how it could end someday?"

"Of course," Joe said. "What are you saying? You went bust?"

"To my sorrow."

"Oh, no. That's bad news, my friend, very bad. I mean, like you said, we always knew we were beating the odds ... and the losing streak was killing us. But I figured we'd pull out of it, just like we always did before. How much cash did you leave yourself?"

"None."

"None?" Joe's tone was incredulous. "Did you say *none*?"

"It's all gone, Joe. I blew my last C-note this afternoon."

A long silence ensued. "What the hell were you thinking?" Joe said. "I thought we agreed we'd always keep a little something on the side—like two or three hundred, at least. We never talked about going to zero. That's just plain stupid."

"I know, I know," Johnny croaked. "But I had this feeling, Joe, I really did. It was even stronger than the feeling I had before the Braddock-Baer fight. I really thought ... no, I *knew*, my luck was going to change today."

"Jesus," Joe said. "You mean to tell me you couldn't win shit for, what, almost a month? And then you woke up this morning and said, Hey, I'm going to bet my last hundred because I have this ... this really strong feeling I'm going to win today? What *mishegas*. How many times have we said it? Never try to ..."

"Yeah, yeah," Johnny interrupted. "Don't remind me."

"And that's not my rule, it's *yours*," Joe said, his voice rising. "Never try to guess when a good team is going to lose or a bad team is going to win, and never bet against a streak. That's what you told me right after we started this racket. What the hell happened? Did you think Congress repealed the laws of probability?"

"I don't know, Joe. I made every sucker play in the book, broke all our rules. I'm thinking maybe I can't help it. I don't know, it's hard to explain."

"What's to explain?" Joe said, his voice weary. "What you're really telling me is you can't be left alone. If I'm not keeping an eye on you, everything goes to hell. Did you think I'd bail you out? Put you back in action? And we'd just go on gambling like nothing happened?"

"Honest, Joe, I wasn't expecting anything," Johnny

pleaded. "I mean, we always said we'd look out for each other—but that's if one of us got sick or something. It never applied to gambling."

Joe exhaled with an audible sigh. "OK, let's get down to cases. How much do you figure you need to tide you over, you know, while you're looking for a job?"

"A job," Johnny repeated. "Jesus, Joe, I don't know if I can do that."

"You *have* to. How much?"

"I'll think about it, call you in a couple of days," Johnny said.

"What about now? Where are you? You want me to come get you? Bring you some food, take you home or something?"

"No, thanks, I still got forty, forty-five cents. I can get home. I might even walk home, for Christ's sake. It'll give me time to analyze my fucking case."

"What about rent? You need a place to stay?"

"No, I'm paid through August."

"Well, that's one good thing" Joe said. "Hey, how about your sister? I almost hate to mention this, but if something bad happened, and I wasn't around to help, would she be able to give you a little money?"

"No dice," Johnny said. "I give *her* money."

"Jeez, I had no idea. How long have you been doing that?"

"Years," Johnny said. "Since she was sick."

"You're a good brother," Joe said, "even when you're a stupid gambler. One more thing, if you don't mind my asking. Did you bet that C-note on the Cubs game?"

"I wish. No, it was a fucking horse. I made the bet at Frankie's place. And of course that dago prick had to rub it in. But I don't want to talk about it now. I need ... no, wait, the Cubs—what happened today?"

"They lost to the Giants."

"Figures," Johnny said. "They stink. I should've gone to Wrigley instead of that bookie joint. Hey, Joe."

"What."

"It could happen to anyone."

Joe chuckled. "That's another one of your rules, my friend. But I'm not so sure this could have happened to anybody except you. Anyway, call me."

"Yeah, OK, Joe."

He stood on the corner in front of the drug store. The sun had been down for less than an hour, and muggy heat still radiated off the pavement and nearby buildings. He fished a quarter, a dime, two nickels and a penny out of his pants pocket and stared at them in his open right hand. Traces of grime from the handbook floor still darkened his palm's life, destiny, and love lines. Johnny returned the coins to his pocket and started walking north on Clark Street.

5

*W*alking quickly, head down, hands thrust into his pants pockets, hat brim pulled low over his eyes, Johnny went straight north, looking up occasionally to check an address or glance around for a familiar landmark. He was drawing a bead on Wilson Avenue, a couple of blocks from the lakefront.

He walked past nightclubs—Upper Crust, Chez Louie, Happy Daze—where he would have been welcomed, called by his first name, given the eye by attractive dames. But only until they found out he was flat broke.

He and Joe could still go to the clubs, same as always, except now he'd have to ride on Joe's ticket. The hatcheck girls and bartenders, the head waiters—they'd know; they'd not treat him the same. And gamblers would avoid him like a swamp. They'd know he was a loser, and nobody wants any of that to rub off. Even worse, they'd dismiss him as a nothing guy.

He couldn't buy a decent meal for himself, much less a round of drinks for the bar. He didn't have money to give his sister. He couldn't go see Helen or one of the other working girls he favored. He couldn't even take his suit to the cleaners.

In Chicago, a fellow with no dough, no prospects, and a rumpled suit was a nothing guy.

Now he lay on the Murphy bed in his room at the Chelsea on Wilson Avenue. The Chelsea was one of dozens of apartment hotels across the city. It had a few rooms for transients, but most rooms were let long-term for rates as low as $5.50 per week. Johnny was one of a handful of gamblers who lived there. Other residents included cabaret singers and musicians, bartenders, call girls, and, lately, women working men's jobs in war industries. During the summer months, the Chelsea was also home to unmarried Cubs players.

Johnny had lived at the Chelsea for eight years because it was only two "L" stops away from Wrigley Field, provided weekly linen and housekeeping service, and had a 24-hour café off the ground-floor lobby. The Chelsea also had a small parking garage that Johnny had used before he sold his car to avoid gas rationing. Johnny always paid his rent in cash several months in advance. At his request, the rent receipts were never made out to him personally, just to "tenant, #517."

Dawn was about an hour away. An oscillating fan, rattling in its metal cage, stood on a table under the east-facing window pushing stale summer air toward one corner of the room then the other, one corner then the other, over and over, intermittently ruffling the pages of a *Daily Racing Form* on the dresser. Every now and then, the Sunday morning stillness was pierced by the distant squeal and rumble of an "L" train.

He lay motionless on his back, hands at his sides, still wearing the same clothes he had put on the previous morning: blue dress shirt and pale yellow silk tie; lightweight suit pants, tan, with dark smudges at the knees from his encounter with the floor at the handbook and less obvious smears near the pockets where he'd wiped his hands; tan hose; and brown wingtips. His hat, a light brown Dobbs with a black band, lay on the floor next to the bed. The suit jacket was on the floor near the door, where he had shucked it when he entered the room.

He flickered off to sleep several times, but awoke with a start each time. As humiliating as it was to be tapped out, it was even worse to know that every member of his family would say, "I told you so." All had warned him his gambling habit would be his ruin, sooner or later.

His father had been dead for twelve years, but in some ways their relationship remained as contentious as ever. How many times had Johnny sat at a family *seder* and silently endured his father's scorn while his sister and his aunt stared at him, nodding their heads?

"Don't be a *yekl* all your life," his father scolded, over and over. "There's no future in gambling—that's why they call it gambling. It's not a living, it's just gambling already."

The words were engraved in memory, always available to piss Johnny off, as if he had just been subjected to one of his father's tiresome harangues:

"You keep going like this, you're going to wind up on West Madison Street with all the other bums. And when that day comes, don't expect any help from me, your father who told you to get a real job. God forbid you should get a real job. Look at me—all my life I put in a day's work for a day's pay. What's so terrible about that? Just think how your mother would feel if she could see what you're doing with your life? May she rest in peace."

Johnny still derived grim satisfaction knowing his father, the man who pointed to his own life of hard work as a model for his ne'er-do-well son, lost everything in the city's bank panic of '32 and wound up killing himself. The death had been ruled a "third-rail accident" by Chicago Elevated Railways and the Cook County coroner. But the official version was a load of crap. Any guy with over thirty years' experience as a transit worker knew damn well to stay far away from that 750-volt rail—unless he wanted to croak.

Johnny stared at the ceiling, dimly aware that the first light of day was seeping into his room. He felt a tear trace a line down the left side of his face and drip into his ear.

It was daylight now, but still early. Except for one trip to the bathroom to pee, he hadn't moved from the Murphy bed. He had just twenty-four hours before the start of the workweek—*the workweek, for Christ's sake*—twenty-four hours before he would have to get out early and start looking for a job, just like Joe said.

Tears welled in his eyes again.

"Rags ..."

He stared at the crazing in the white paint on the ceiling, noticing the intricate little patterns, like road maps. In some places, the patterns formed identifiable shapes—a face, a rabbit, a fiddle with no neck ...

"Rags ..."

The clop of hooves on pavement penetrated his consciousness. Turning to look at the alarm clock on the nightstand, he wondered what a street peddler was doing in this neighborhood at 8:30 on a Sunday morning. He turned back to stare at the ceiling.

A moment later he convulsed, going taut as a spring. He swung his feet off the edge of the bed and stood, blotting his eyes with a shirt sleeve and steadying himself on the nightstand as a brief wave of dizziness threatened his equilibrium. When his head cleared, he stood straight and blurted out loud: "Fuck me! I ain't dead yet."

He took five quick steps to the open window on the alley side of the room, and yanked the sash up so he could lean out.

"Hey, hey," he shouted down.

The driver of the horse cart raised his head, searching.

Johnny waved: "Up here."

36

The driver reined the slow-moving draft horse to a stop and shaded his eyes, looking up toward the fifth-floor window.

"Wait there," Johnny shouted. "I'll be right down." He went to the door of his room and opened it, then went back to the walk-in closet behind the Murphy bed, placed his arms around as much of the clothing as he could, squeezed and lifted. The hangers, some wood and some wire, came up off the bar. He backed out of the closet. Using a rear stairway, he took the garments down to the alley and heaved them onto the back of the rag picker's wagon.

"There's more," he said, "I'll be right back."

It took three trips to empty the closet. He brought everything: suits, jackets, overcoats, shirts, shoes, hats. When he entered the alley with the third load, he saw the rag picker loading clothes into the large scale hanging on the back of the wagon.

"Hey, Dutch, what the hell are you doing with my stuff?" Johnny demanded.

"I weigh."

"You weigh. Then what?"

"I pay. Two cent a pound. Very good price—high. Because of war."

"Two cents? Two cents a pound?" Johnny's face and neck flushed. "Why don't you just hold a fucking gun on me and take all my goddamned clothes, for Christ's sake? Do you have any idea what I paid for some of this?"

The peddler shrugged: "Same for all. Two cent."

"Let me tell you something," Johnny said. "I'm giving you a chance to make some real money here. Look at this suit." He tugged at a gray, pinstripe sleeve in the pile on the back of the wagon. "Italian silk. Two hundred fifty dollars brand-new. Hardly ever worn. You got a real opportunity here, for Christ's sake. What are you going to do? Sell it to the government for chicken feed? Or sell it on Maxwell Street? Shit, you could get eight, nine dollars

37

for a suit like this on Maxwell Street. Easy."

He had the rag picker's attention. "How many suits?"

"Shit, there's at least eleven. And you got dress slacks in here, too." He rummaged in the pile of clothing. "Sports jackets. Silk shirts. And don't forget the shoes ..."

"OK, forty-five dollar, whole shebang."

"Make it a hundred—and you're still robbing me."

"Forty-five. Very fine price."

"Fuck."

Pat Peiper, the field announcer, was already giving the starting lineups when Johnny came up the ramp on the Sheffield Avenue side of the bleachers and walked into the sunlight. He surveyed the grandstand, right field to left and shook his head. A full house. And the Cubs were in last place.

He turned and scanned the section of the bleachers that rose toward the scoreboard in center field, looking for familiar faces. He still couldn't get used to seeing so many unescorted women at ballgames when it wasn't Ladies Day. There were groups of them all over the bleachers— and a few, here and there, who appeared to be alone. Give the credit to Prohibition, Joe always said—the Eighteenth Amendment got everybody, including women, into saloons because people felt a civic duty to demonstrate what a bird-brained idea Prohibition was.

After that it was only a matter of time before women, classy women, started showing up at other traditional male strongholds without dates or husbands. Joe conceded that the Nineteenth Amendment and the war were factors, too. But Joe was sure the liberation had been launched by Prohibition.

Johnny ascended the aisle on the left side of the center field bleachers until he reached the top row, under the massive scoreboard. A grizzled gnome of a man wearing a Panama hat looked up from the small notebook in his lap.

"Johnny, how you doing?"

"You know me, Izzy—still fooling 'em. You?"

"I'm getting by."

Isadore "Izzy" Abramowitz was one of the senior members in a group of more than three dozen gamblers and bookmakers who sat in the top row of the bleachers during every Cubs home game—moving down a couple of rows only on chilly days in April and September to escape the wind blowing in off Lake Michigan. They made and took bets on any game in the Majors. They also made bets on anything that was likely or not likely to happen in the course of the game at Wrigley: whether the home team would score in a particular inning, whether the guy at the plate would hit a grounder or a fly ball, whether the shortstop would adjust his cup before the next pitch. And when they ran out of things to bet on, they argued over baseball minutiae.

Izzy tipped his head to one side to see around Johnny. "Where's Joe?"

"He went to visit family. He'll be back." Johnny turned and glanced at the field, noting the skinny right hander warming up in the Giants bullpen. "What can I get on the Cubs in game one?"

"You can't get shit, Johnny, you got to lay three to two. What happened to your pants?" Izzy waved his pencil in the general direction of the dark stains on Johnny's knees.

"The floor was dirty at my church. How is it I got to lay three to two on a club that's already, what, twelve, thirteen games under five hundred?"

"Thirteen," Izzy said. "They stink. But so do the Giants. And the Giants are starting a nothing guy in the first game. Hansen. Chipman's going for the Cubs."

"Jesus. What about the second game?"

"You can't get odds there, either. It's six to five, pick 'em."

"Who's pitching?"

"Passeau and Voiselle."

"Jesus, the two frogs. That's going to be a helluva

39

game. No wonder it's a full house. What if I take the Cubs to sweep?"

"Yeah, you can get odds on that. But I'm not handing out any Christmas presents today. If you're so sure the Cubs are going to win both ends, you're better off taking it a game at a time. As you already know."

"Yeah," Johnny looked distracted. "What if ... what if I take Passeau to pitch a shutout in the second game?"

"Holy cripes, you want to make a proposition bet?"

"Hey, don't act like it's a big deal," Johnny shot back. "All you mopes do out here is make prop bets. All day long. I seen you guys bet on what inning the blonde in the second row is going to go to the lavatory. So what can I get on a fucking shutout?"

"Passeau got his brains beat out by the Giants two months ago, you know. Gave up a pile of runs."

"Doesn't mean a goddamned thing. Every day's a brand-new ballgame, mister, what can I get?"

"On a side bet, it's fifteen, maybe eighteen to one. Something like that. But why don't you wait until after the first game. If you've still got cash, we'll figure it out. You do have cash on you, right? No offense, but there was a rumor going around ..."

Johnny dug the rag picker's bills out of his pocket. After buying an "L" fare and a bleacher ticket, he still had forty-four dollars. He put the money into Izzy's hand. "You want to hold the scratch, that's fine. There's forty-four dollars on the Cubs in game one."

Izzy gave him a pained look. "You're laying three-to-two with forty-four dollars? Is there any way you could make it more complicated?"

In front of a crowd of 38,434, the Cubs escaped the National League cellar, at least temporarily, by winning both games. Chicago took the first game 5-2, and Claude Passeau beat Bill Voiselle, 1-0, in the second game. Johnny left Wrigley Field with three hundred and forty dollars.

Johnny walked east on Waveland Avenue to Halsted, then turned north. He scanned the first-floor lobby at the Eastgate Arms, an apartment hotel in the 4100 block, and spoke briefly to the desk clerk: "Abe Lindgren been around today?"

"Yeah, he was in about noon, reading a paper right over there. But I haven't seen him since then."

Farther north, he stepped into the Players Lounge, a bar on Broadway near Wilson. "Anybody seen Abe Lindgren today?"

"Never heard of him," the bartender said.

"Hey, quit the comedy. Do I look like a cop?"

"Haven't seen him since yesterday."

Abe Lindgren was a Swedish bookie, which made him at least unusual, if not singular, in a line of work dominated by Italians, Jews, and Irishmen. He was what Joe called a "vest-pocket bookie," circulating regularly through certain taverns, eateries, and hotel lobbies in the neighborhoods around Wilson Avenue, recording bets with a fountain pen on a small pad of paper, using public pay phones, and always paying off winning bets in an inconspicuous envelope.

He had been Rogers Hornsby's bookie during the four seasons the great second baseman played for the Chicago Cubs. He provided a similarly discreet service for at least two of the current Cubs players who lived at the Chelsea. And that's where Johnny found him, sitting at a table in the Chelsea's first-floor grill, reading the Sunday *Tribune* and smoking a thin, foul-smelling cigar.

"Abe, I got to get some money on a horse."

Without looking at Johnny, Lindgren carefully folded the newspaper and placed it on the table. He rested the small cigar on the edge of the glass ashtray, fished a small notebook and a pen out of his shirt pocket, unscrewed the cap of the pen, and placed the cap on top of the folded newspaper. Finally, he looked up. "OK, what's the horse?"

"Constant Aim. Running at Arlington tomorrow."

"Yeah, I've heard of the horse. Three-year-old, listed in the seventh race. What's up? You doing OK?"

"Everything is hotsie-totsie. Couldn't be better."

"If everything is so good, maybe you'll get your pants dry cleaned, eh? So how much do you want on this horse?"

"Three hundred forty to win."

"That's a pretty heavy play, Johnny. You sure about that?"

"What the fuck is this? Of course I'm sure, why wouldn't I be sure?"

"I don't know. I just heard some talk, you know, somebody saying you were going through kind of a rough patch ..."

"Let me tell you something, mister." Johnny went into his usual agitation mode: slight crouch, one hand shielding his mouth, eyes glancing furtively around the café. "You never know the next person's business. What I'm saying is, people can talk and talk, but they don't know my business. People *think* they know my business, but look here." He pulled a roll of bills out of his pants pocket and shook it in front of Abe Lindgren's face. "See, I got the scratch right here in my kick. You want to hold it?"

Abe smiled. "That would be nice." He raised the fountain pen and carefully wrote a series of small symbols in the notebook. "Three hundred and forty on Constant Aim to win, right?"

Standing in the deli, Johnny suddenly became aware of how hungry he was. He hadn't eaten anything since Saturday morning, and the seventh race at Arlington wouldn't go off until late afternoon on Monday. He thought about keeping a buck or two so he could get something to eat, but quickly dismissed the idea and placed the roll of bills on the table next to the newspaper. "What do you think the horse'll go off at?"

"I have no idea," Abe said, opening the roll and fanning the bills below the level of the table top to make a rough count. "All I know is most of the money's going on Chief Bud. Hey, you hear about the Cubs? They took two from the Giants this afternoon."

Johnny looked away. "Yeah, I heard something about that."

6

*J*ohnny was delirious with hunger when he checked the front desk at the Chelsea shortly before 10 on Tuesday morning. He hadn't shaved in four days. His shirt and stained trousers looked as though he'd slept in them, which he had. "Did Abe Lindgren leave anything for me?"

The young clerk turned to scan the mail slots on the wall behind the desk. "Let's see, that's four-seventeen, right?"

"Five-seventeen."

"Right. Yes, sir, Mr. Sharansky." He pulled a thick envelope from one of the slots and slid it across the counter top.

Johnny hefted the envelope a couple of times. It contained mostly twenties and fifties, he guessed, and it was heavy. "Hey, loan me a nickel," he said to the clerk. "I got to make a phone call. You know me, I'm good for it."

He quick-stepped to one of the phone booths in the lobby, near the entrance to the café, and dialed Joe's number. He kept shaking his head, trying to clear the hunger fog.

"Hello."

"Joe, it's me."

"Johnny! Jeez, am I glad you called. I've been worried about you, my friend—I thought you might do something ... you know, *meshuge*. So how are you feeling?"

"Everything is hotsie-totsie."

"Don't kid me."

"I'm kidding on the square, Joe. I really am. Listen to this—I can hardly believe it myself: I'm back."

"Back—back where? Not back in action?"

"You got it: back in action."

"Just like that?"

"Yup, just like that."

"What happened? Don't tell me you got one of those loans from the good guys."

"No, no, nothing like that," Johnny said. "Let's just say I got lucky." As they talked, Johnny pinned the receiver against his shoulder with his chin, and used two hands to tear open the envelope. Without removing the money from the envelope, he began walking his right index and middle fingers through the sheaf of bills, checking the denominations. "Right now, Joe, I'm looking at twenty-six, twenty-seven hundred dollars, easy. Maybe twenty-eight. And I'm thinking we ought to celebrate, maybe go down to the South Side, catch a show at Colosimo's or some place like that ..."

"That's great news," Joe said. "But I just want to be sure ... you didn't do some screwball thing to get all this cash, right? I mean, let's face it, you were ... well, you weren't thinking too clearly there for a while."

"Joe, believe me, my stupid days are over. Never again."

The line was silent for a moment. "Humm," Joe said.

"What the hell?" Johnny's voice sounded hurt.

"Hey, I've been watching you for almost thirty years, and phrases like 'never again' don't seem to apply," Joe said. "Do I have to make a list?"

"Not now, I haven't got that much time."

Joe laughed. "OK, I'll spare you. But you're right, considering that you've ducked gainful employment—a narrow escape, I might add—we will definitely celebrate. How about the Loop? There's a guy I really want to see at the Palmer House."

"Suits me. Who's the guy?"

"Victor Borge. From Denmark. Got out ahead of the Nazis. Now he's here. Started out as a classical pianist, but he does comedy. I've heard him on the radio—funny as hell."

"Believe me, Joe, I could use a few laughs. So what time?"

"I've got a dinner date, so let's do the late show. Make it about nine or nine-thirty at the Empire Room. Unless you want to start early. We could meet somewhere for lunch right now."

"Naw, I've got to go shopping, buy some clothes."

"Clothes? Jesus, you've got clothes coming out of your rear end. What's the occasion?"

"I'll explain later. It's kind of a long story."

He sat in the phone booth, his eyes closed, anticipating the tickle of giddiness that always followed a big score. He waited. For once, there was nothing.

7

*M*argaret Turner was in a foul mood.

For openers, she had been insulted by the elderly cabbie who took her to the Palmer House from the Chicago & North Western Station. The cabbie had volunteered a comment about the Democratic Convention, saying he was disappointed Roosevelt wouldn't be coming to Chicago to accept the nomination. "But the man can't do everything," he had said. "The war has to come first."

Margaret hated Roosevelt, couldn't stand the sound of his voice on the radio, couldn't fathom why so many people thought he walked on water. She had known she ought to ignore the driver and keep her mouth shut. Instead, she had repeated her father's assertion that Roosevelt was the most dangerous man in America, a far greater threat than Hitler.

The cabbie fell silent. Only after she had paid her fare in front of the hotel did he speak again.

"Rich brat," he snorted as she was stepping out of the cab. "Is that what you call a tip?"

"Drop dead, Bolshie," she snarled back.

"Fuck you, lady."

As if the exchange with the cabbie hadn't been upsetting enough, Margaret arrived at the Empire Room and was given a message that Brantley would be unavoidably detained—as he almost always was when they had a date. Based on past experience, she assumed he was working late. Of course, he would be abjectly apologetic when he finally arrived—he always was—but that didn't make his chronic tardiness any less irksome. Especially on this night.

They had agreed to celebrate the one-month anniversary of their engagement with a late dinner at the Empire Room, where they could see Victor Borge, then talk about which friends, family friends, and associates absolutely had to be invited to their wedding the following May. Margaret's handwritten list was in her clutch purse.

She went to the almost deserted bar at the back of the Empire Room and ordered a Manhattan, straight up.

"Any special whiskey?"

"Make it Canadian," she said. "Oh, and I'm waiting for a gentleman friend."

The bartender nodded, correctly decoding the information to mean she didn't want to be identified or treated as an unescorted female.

Before taking the first sip of her Manhattan, she pulled a silver cigarette case from her purse and removed a Chesterfield king. She tamped each end of the cigarette on the case, then placed the case on the bar next to her drink and lit the cigarette with a small silver lighter. Calmed by the little ritual and the familiar rush of nicotine, she surveyed the room beyond the bar—the gold ceiling with its enormous center chandelier, the French Empire crown moldings, the green plush draperies filling the spaces between pilasters, also in gold, the bandstand backed by a glittering silver curtain. A living memorial to bad taste, she thought.

For all its rococo glitz, the Empire Room felt comfortable to Margaret. If the room was outrageous, well, she could be, too. She and Brantley had come here to see song-and-dance man Ray Bolger in their second month of dating. After two straight-up Manhattans, Margaret had decided that she wanted more than evenings out with an engaging male charm bracelet. Hiking one eyebrow, she had suggested that perhaps it would be a good idea to take a room upstairs.

Brantley, caught off guard, but only for a moment, had smiled, "What a clever girl—why didn't I think of that?" Within ten minutes they were engaged in foreplay in a room on the ninth floor. From then on, their dates habitually included such assignations—habitually being the operative word, since their lovemaking never deviated from the routine they established that first night at the Palmer House. Margaret always initiated. Brantley almost always assented—the exceptions being nights when he said he had work to do. The lovemaking was always in missionary position.

Brantley was solicitous during sex, wanting to be sure she'd reached orgasm. On the rare nights when he'd had too much to drink, he was less considerate. On one of those nights, he had broached the idea of anal sex.

She had flashed him an apprehensive look, saying, "You're kidding, right?"

And that was the end of it.

She lifted the cocktail glass from the bar and took a sip, feeling the sweet sting of the Manhattan trace a warm line from her lips to her empty stomach. She wondered if maybe she should not have given the bartender a signal that she was to be left alone; maybe Brantley would start being more attentive and more punctual if he found her in lively conversation with another man the next time he arrived late.

Margaret glanced at her Girard-Perregaux watch, then

turned her gaze back to the main room, searching for someone famous or, better yet, infamous. She often did so to pass the time while waiting for Brantley in a downtown club or restaurant. She was always hoping to recognize one of the swarthy, expressionless faces she had seen in police mug shots in newspaper stories and in old reports from the Chicago Crime Commission, whose publications were on file at the Evanston Public Library.

Some people were thrilled by public sightings of movie stars or prizefighters. Margaret wanted to see crime figures.

Her fixation on mobsters had been sparked by the 1930 assassination of a newspaper reporter named Lingle, killed in a pedestrian underpass on the east side of the Loop. Margaret, not yet thirteen, had been titillated by the raw brutality of the murder—a single shot fired into the back of Lingle's head, in front of scores of onlookers, by a gunman wearing gray silk gloves he discarded at street level as he walked nonchalantly from the crime scene.

Margaret had clipped a newspaper photo of a police detective holding one of the silk gloves, and had pasted it into a scrapbook. It was the first of many such photos and articles that eventually filled the scrapbook she kept hidden in her closet.

When she was fourteen, she had asked her father why no ladies—that was the word she had used, ladies—were ever involved in gangland killings, either as victims or perpetrators. "Because," he had said in a patronizing tone, "the female gender is not endowed with evil impulses. It is a woman's nature to remain aloof from the kind of business that provokes such barbarity."

Now Margaret scanned the tables in the Empire Room, her gaze pausing here and there to scrutinize a face. What she wanted more than anything else at this moment, in this place, was to see a public enemy. She yearned to make eye contact with pure evil.

8

"*A*h, Mr. Sharansky, I am so pleased to see you. It has been too long since you honored us with your presence."

Fritz, the Empire Room's *maître d'*, shook Johnny's hand and accepted his hat, a light gray Stetson purchased that afternoon at Marshall Field's in the Loop. "I must tell you," Fritz added, "we are expecting big crowds for Victor Borge, very big—as you can appreciate, I'm sure. But I still have one very nice table for you and Mr. Bermann. Mr. Bermann will be joining you, yes?"

"Yeah, he'll be here, but not for another hour or so," Johnny said. "I'm running kind of early."

"And will there be ladies?"

"No, no ladies tonight. To my sorrow."

Fritz laughed sympathetically. "Ah, yes, it is always better with the ladies. Always more fun."

"Yeah, and always more expensive. Tell you what," he pulled a roll of bills from the right-hand pocket of his suit trousers, peeled off a fin, and slipped it into Fritz's free hand. "Hold the table for me and Joe. I'm going back to the bar for a while. I need a little time to analyze my case."

"Analyze. Very good, Mr. Sharansky. I will bring you

the claim check for your hat. At the bar."

The early show, a female vocalist backed by the George Hamilton Orchestra, started at 8:30. But Johnny was barely aware of it. His face frozen in a frown, he was staring intently into his second highball—"Canadian and water, make it light on the whiskey"—like one of the phony swamis on Maxwell Street staring into a crystal ball before spouting mystical claptrap about a sucker's future.

"Hey, Johnny."

It was a female voice. He raised his head and looked to his left. She was sitting alone, just beyond the turn in the bar. She was young, with shoulder-length blonde hair. He started to look over his shoulder, but stopped; she was definitely staring at him. He flashed an uncertain smile: "I'm sorry. Do I know you?"

"I don't think so."

"So who told you my name?"

"Nobody, it was a lucky stab. Did anyone ever tell you that you look a lot like Johnny Torrio? You know, the gangster."

"Please," he held up a hand, "you don't have to tell me who Johnny Torrio was. I used to drink at his place on South Wabash, for Christ's sake, excuse my language. But he hasn't been in Chicago for twenty years. Where'd you ever see Johnny Torrio?"

"OK, I only read about him. And I've seen photographs. You look like one of the photographs of him—that's what I should have said. And you're a lot younger, of course."

"Right, thanks. And don't forget the bullet wounds. I'm not perforated like he was."

She leaned forward. "How much do you know about that? The shooting."

"I make it a habit not to know about things like that." He paused and looked around at the empty bar. "So what's the deal—are we going to keep talking like this, long distance?" He wig-wagged his index finger, pointing to himself, then to the young dame at the end of the bar. "How about I move before the band starts up again?"

She made a halfhearted gesture toward the seat next to her. "Be my guest."

From a distance, he made her out to be a high-class *shiksa*, probably from one of the North Shore suburbs or Oak Park. He wondered if she was waiting for someone, a boyfriend or a husband. He put his drink on the bar next to hers, and did a quick, one-blink inventory while pulling the tall bar chair back to make room so he could sit. She was prettier up close, he thought, with great-looking gams, and a rock the size of Gibraltar on her left ring finger. He felt an urge to launch into his usual *shtik*—extolling her beauty, telling her she should be in movies—but stopped himself.

"Excuse me, sir, I believe that seat is taken." It was the bartender. "The lady is with someone this evening."

"I appreciate your vigilance," she told the barkeep, "but it's OK."

Johnny slid onto the bar chair to her right. "You know my name," he said. "You going to tell me yours, or you working undercover?"

"It's Margaret." She held out her hand, and they shook. "It's a pleasure to meet you, Johnny."

"Likewise, I'm sure. I guess you must be with someone, eh?"

She nodded. "Waiting for a friend—my fiancé, actually. He's always late."

"Is he a soldier?"

"My fiancé? Heavens, no." She laughed. "Bad knees. He's a lawyer in my father's firm."

Johnny shrugged. He had no problem with "F'ers." Joe, too, had avoided the draft back in 1917 and '18, though not because he had any physical problem—he was vice president of a family business supplying woolen goods to Uncle Sam. Johnny himself had avoided military service by never signing up for the draft.

"Maybe it's all for the better," Johnny said. "You see some of these young fellas who've been hurt over there ..." He shrugged again and shook his head, leaving the sentence hanging.

When Margaret slipped a cigarette out of the slender silver case resting in front of her on the bar, he reached over and retrieved the matching lighter. He held the flame under the end of her cigarette.

After inhaling, she tipped her head back and blew smoke toward one of the Empire Room's crystal light sconces, allowing Johnny to admire the smooth curve of her throat, before she turned on her barstool so she could face him. She studied his face.

"I envy those yummy blue eyes," she said. "Did Torrio have blue eyes, too"

"Dark eyes," he said, "brown maybe. But I can't remember for sure—that was a long time ago."

"So you actually saw him?"

"Lots of times."

"What about Capone?"

"We saw all those guys—Torrio, Capone, Charlie Fischetti, McGurn, Jake Guzik. All those guys. But it was no big deal. They weren't exactly shy, you know. Not in those days."

"Guzik. They say he's top dog in the Chicago outfit now."

Johnny looked surprised. His right hand came up to shield his mouth—a gesture learned in childhood from his Aunt Rose who had told him to contain the spit that flew whenever he spoke with excitement or agitation. "That's just newspaper talk," Johnny said impatiently. "All that stuff you read about Guzik, it's bullshit, pardon the expression. Guzik was always a green-eyeshade guy, a bean counter, and now they let him run a couple of gambling joints in the suburbs. But that's it. One way you can tell he's not the top guy—no bodyguards. Never carries a gun, either."

"Interesting," she said. "OK, if he's not the big man, who is?"

Johnny stared into her face. Most of the dames he spent time with, like Helen at the joy house on Erie, looked like they'd put on their makeup with a paper-hanger's brush. But with Margaret, the makeup was understated, just like the clothes and the jewelry. She's a natural, Johnny thought—she doesn't need any touching up. She is fucking gorgeous.

"Well?" Margaret leaned forward slightly.

Johnny shook his head slightly to clear the visual intoxication. "I thought everybody knew," he said. "After Nitti, it was always going to be the waiter, Ricca. He was next in line. And then after him was Accardo... ."

"I thought Ricca was in prison."

"He is. And everybody figured it was no big deal because he could run the outfit from the clink. Uh-uh. The warden down in Atlanta—he's got Ricca like this." Johnny placed the pad of his right thumb on the bar, raised his elbow, and pushed down hard. "Ricca can't wipe his ... he can't do anything without this guy's permission—that's what they say. So Accardo's making most of the decisions now. Tony Accardo. End of story."

"I don't think I've ever seen a picture of Accardo," she said. "Would you know him to look at him?" Her gaze shifted to the rapidly filling main room over Johnny's shoulder. "I heard that guys in the outfit sometimes come here with their wives or girlfriends."

Johnny had just taken a sip from his highball and almost choked. "Jesus, who told you that? Ten, fifteen years ago you might see a few good guys in downtown places like this, but that was when the city was more, you know, wide open. It's different now. Most of the good guys live out in the suburbs. Anyway, you don't want to see Accardo. Pretty, he's not."

Having survived for twenty-three years in the gray area between polite society and the city's criminal elements,

Johnny was pretty sure he recognized Margaret's type. Joe always called them "mob hounds"—law-abiding citizens who got their jollies being in close proximity to loan sharks, hired killers, and other shady types. It was harmless recreation most of the time, but it could have tragic consequences: An eye doctor was mowed down along with members of the Bugs Moran Gang on Valentine's Day in 1929; an assistant state's attorney came out of a Cicero gambling joint in April 1926 and walked right into an ambush intended for the mob gunmen with whom he'd just finished playing cards and drinking.

Hoods in the Empire Room—where do people come up with this shit?

She took another long draw on her cigarette. "Did you actually know any of the characters you mentioned—the ones in the outfit?"

"Sure we did. When I say we, I mean me and Joe—he's my best friend, the guy I'm waiting for right now. He's crazy about this piano player, what's his name...?"

"Victor Borge."

"Yeah, that's it. Anyway, me and Joe, we knew a few of the good guys. Hell, Joe knew Frank Nitti from the old neighborhood. Always called him by his Italian name, Francesco. Nitti used to cut his hair when he was still a barber. And they stayed friends. Joe even got a contract cancelled one time—he went to Nitti and saved a fella's life."

"I read somewhere his nickname was The Enforcer," she said. "I guess he must have been a pretty frightening character, eh?"

"Only if you knew who he was," Johnny said. "He wasn't scary to look at—little guy, maybe three, four inches shorter than me."

"Now you've got me really curious," she said. "You don't act like a hood. You don't dress like a cop. So what do you do?"

"You mean for a living?" He couldn't remember ever

being asked that question before. The people he encountered in his daily routines either knew the answer to the question already, or knew well enough not to ask it.

"Right," she said, "for a living."

He shrugged. "I gamble."

She cocked her head slightly to one side. Then she smiled. "I get it. You're a stock broker, or a trader."

"No, I gamble. You know, make bets on baseball games, prize fights, horses."

"Oh, my God, you're a professional gambler." She threw her head back and clapped her hands. "I never met a professional gambler before. You've got to tell me all about it. How long have you been a professional gambler?"

It had never occurred to Johnny that someone might be delighted to discover how he made a living. His family members had all professed to be ashamed. Women—the nice ones—couldn't get away from him fast enough when they found out. And now, this. He felt himself relax, joining Margaret's good-natured enthusiasm. "I guess I started back in '20 or '21. It was supposed to be a crazy fling—you know, like a vacation, except a vacation for a couple of years. But, hey, here I am, still pitchin'."

"That's amazing," she said. "You must be really good. Do you mean to tell me that in all those years, you never did anything else, never had a job?"

"Not since '21. But, believe me, that doesn't make me any smarter than the average gambler—just luckier."

He flashed a playful smile and lapsed into one of his theatrical personas. "Of course, every now and then I'd hit a bad losing streak, get low on scratch, be knocking at the poorhouse door." He pulled the lapels of his suit jacket together as if seeking refuge from a cold wind. "And you know what that would mean."

She shook her head. "I have no earthly idea. What would that mean?"

He held his hands at waist level and pointed his index fingers at her. "I'd have to go out and stick up a bank."

It was supposed to be a joke, but Margaret wasn't laughing. She reached out and clamped a vice grip on his forearm.

She hissed, "You pulled holdups?"

Johnny wanted to say no, no, no, he was just kidding, he'd never pulled a stickup in his life, never even thought about it. But the intensity of the dame's response made him hesitate. She was excited, and it was irresistible.

"Well, I don't really like to talk about those things. I'm sure you can understand ..."

"Did you work alone, or was your friend in on it?"

"Joe? Nah, he was never involved in anything like that. He's a very classy guy, Joe. I'm the bad apple. I always did the stupid things on my own."

He felt himself beginning to warm to his own story line. It was a pretty good story, worthy of embellishment. "Now, when I say I was on my own, I'm not counting the driver. See, on most heists you got to have a driver. You don't want to come out of some place with a bag full of cash and a gun and find a cop writing a parking ticket on your car. So you got to have a guy wait in the car. We used to call that guy the lammer. The inside guy, he was the yegg."

"Ah, Mr. Sharansky."

Johnny turned slightly to his left. It was Fritz. Johnny wondered how long he'd been standing there listening.

"I am so very sorry to interrupt, sir, but I thought you would want to know—Mr. Bermann is here. I have already taken him to your table."

"Thanks, I'll be with you in just a second." He turned back to Margaret. "I guess the show's about to start. You want to join us?"

"I'd love to, but my date is probably going to get here any moment now. And I'm pretty sure he's reserved a table for us."

Fritz, still standing just off Johnny's shoulder, snapped his heels and tipped his head slightly forward. "Yes, Mr.

Adams has reserved table No. 15."

Ever since talking with Joe on the phone that morning Johnny had been looking forward to reconnecting with his old friend, whom he hadn't seen in more than three weeks. But he was reluctant to walk away from Margaret. He had a hunch that if he left her sitting at the bar, he'd never see her again, yet he was reluctant to suggest another get-together or ask for a phone number, something he usually did without a second thought, even if he rarely had any intention of following up.

It was a potentially awkward situation. Not only was she young enough to be his daughter, or so he reckoned, she was also a society girl whose world was as alien to him as the inside of a church. To top it off, she was engaged.

And then, in an instant, it was over. She thanked him for being "such good company," and said she hoped he and his friend would get a kick out of Victor Borge. "They say he's absolutely the berries," she said, extending her right hand.

Johnny shook the offered hand and said, "Yeah, thanks, it was swell. See you around."

"See you around, Johnny." And then she smiled.

9

At the table, Joe got right down to cases: "I want to hear the whole story, my friend—how you got up off the canvas, got back in action. But before we get into all that, and if I'm not sticking my nose where it doesn't belong, who was the good-looking mouse at the bar? Didn't look like one of your working girls."

"Joe, please," Johnny recoiled at the suggestion. "This one's high class, strictly table grade. And get this—right out of the blue she starts talking to me because she thinks I look like Torrio."

"Johnny Torrio? Four Deuces—that Torrio?"

"Yup."

"That's *meshuge*. My sister Gertrude looks more like that mope than you do."

"Hey, I'm just telling you what she said. And here's the part for Ripley: I think I'm crazy about her."

Joe leaned back and studied his friend for a moment. "I'm trying to remember how many times I heard you say that before. What about the young lady? Was she making goo-goo eyes?"

"I don't know—hard to say. But there were a couple

times I got a feeling, you know—a feeling she might be interested."

"So what's the story—when are you going to see her again?"

Johnny put his right palm to his forehead as if he were checking for a fever and then looked up. "You thought the part about Torrio was *meshuge*—here's the real *meshugener*." He pointed to his own right temple. "I didn't get her number or anything. It was a Merkle play, Joe, but I just couldn't ask her. It was like I froze up or something. I don't know what happened."

"All is not lost. Maybe she's still here. Go find her and ask for the number."

"Forget it—she's with someone."

"A guy?"

"Yeah, the guy she's going to marry."

"This young lady you're so crazy about is engaged?"

Johnny nodded.

Joe held up both palms, making a stop sign. "Say no more, my friend. Consider the possibility, and I'm not making any judgments here, but consider the possibility you did yourself a very big favor when you didn't ask for a number. Like you're always saying, maybe it's all for the better."

"Yeah, yeah," Johnny said. "It was still a Merkle play."

George Hamilton, the band leader, had just started his introduction for Victor Borge. "Let's watch the show," Joe said. "We'll talk after."

Joe and Johnny stayed at the table for almost an hour after the show while Johnny spun an account, richly embroidered with profanity, of his humiliation at Frankie Aiello's handbook, his mistreatment at the hands of the rag picker, his winning parlay at Wrigley, and the all-or-nothing wager on Constant Aim.

"Now I know why you had to go clothes shopping this afternoon," Joe said. "Selling all those suits for pennies on the dollar—that took some testicles. What about your socks and underwear?"

"Still in the drawer," Johnny said. "I forgot. Missed a chance to get another two cents from that fucking bandit."

Joe took a sip from his highball. "I don't mean to be a nag," he said. "But you'd still have a closet full of nice clothes if you'd been smarter with your money."

"I know, I know," Johnny said. "I just ..."

"How is it I learned this game from you," Joe pressed on, "but I'm the only one who sticks to *your* rules? You go off halfcocked and bet your last C-note on some *cockamamie* race. Your last C-note!"

"That's what worries me, Joe. I mean it. I worry maybe I'm sick—you know, like sick in the head. We seen it a hundred times, you and me—guys who can't stop. They got families, kids, for Christ's sake, and they blow their paychecks on the horses. I'm not like that. Am I?"

Joe thought. "No," he said. "But you have your moments. *Oy,* do you have moments!"

They talked again about getting out of the gambling racket, agreeing that Johnny's brief plunge into penury might have been a warning. Johnny would be forty-four in August, Joe was forty-eight. They hadn't done a day's work in twenty-three years. Maybe the time had come to buy a little business and begin putting money away for old age.

With the economy revved up by war spending, Joe said, a neighborhood tavern might be just the ticket. Once the war was over and the G.I.'s came home, he said, the whole country would be in a mood to celebrate. "We could do a lot worse than sell booze at a big party like that."

If things ever got really desperate, Johnny suggested, maybe they could go back where they had started before Prohibition and ask for jobs in the Bermann family's business, which was now being run—or run into the ground, according to Joe—by Joe's brother Martin.

Martin was still jealous of Joe's first-born status in the family. Word had gotten back that he told customers or anyone else who would listen that Joe had forsaken the family, the business, and his own proud German-Jewish heritage to pursue a life of idleness.

"I don't know if I could be comfortable working for Martin," Joe said. "He's such a prick. Now my brother Benny would have been a different story. If he had lived, he'd probably be running the company right now. He was next in line after me and he had *seykhl*. Such a sweet kid. Jesus, what a waste ..."

"Do you know what Benny died from?" Johnny asked. "You never said."

"Cholera," Joe said. "Same as your mom. Except people weren't supposed to die of cholera by 1911, especially in my neighborhood. I never could understand it."

They sat in silence for a few moments.

"Nope," Joe said, "the family business would be a last resort."

"And that's not all," Johnny said. "We couldn't do anything legit unless we gave up gambling."

Joe nodded. "You're right—we'd have to swear off."

In the foyer just outside the entrance to the Empire Room, they stopped to claim their hats and kibitz with the hat-check girl, Carol. She told them she was nineteen and had come to Chicago that spring from Eagle River, Wisconsin, to be near her boyfriend, who was in training at the Great Lakes Naval Station. Joe told her he hoped the war ended before her boyfriend was put in harm's way.

"I hope so, too," Carol said.

"Ah, Mr. Sharansky." Fritz was gliding into the foyer from the hotel lobby. "I am so happy to catch you before you and Mr. Bermann leave us this evening. I was asked to give this to you after the show." He reached into the inside pocket of his tuxedo jacket and extracted a folded sheet of paper, which he offered to Johnny.

Johnny took the paper and glanced at Joe.

Joe leered. "I've got a five-dollar bill says I know who that's from."

Johnny thanked Fritz and gave him a dollar bill. After Joe and Johnny had walked into the lobby, Johnny stopped, turned away, unfolded the paper, a sheet of Palmer House stationery, and glanced down.

> *If you wouldn't be too bored, I'd love to hear your stories about prohibition, etc. Call Greenleaf 4693, but only between 1 and 3 weekdays. Margaret*

"Did I win the finski?" Joe said.

"There was no bet," Johnny said. He refolded the note and tucked it into a jacket pocket.

Joe chuckled: "I knew it was her."

"It's a North Shore number," Johnny said. "See? I told you she was high class."

They walked out onto Monroe Drive. "You want company? We could share a cab," Joe said.

"Thanks, Joe, you go ahead. I'll take the train. "I need to think about this."

"Looks to me like your luck has changed for the better—all the way around," Joe said. "But be careful. If she really thinks you look like Johnny Torrio, she might be a little, you know, *meshuge*."

"Hey, Joe, do you still have a gun?"

"No, got rid of it years ago. Why?"

"It's kind of a crazy idea, but I think I could use a gun."

10

*B*enedykt "Benny" Wojnarowski placed his palms on the wood counter in the small, cluttered locksmith shop. He leaned forward and shook his head deliberately, as if for emphasis. "You're asking for something I cannot do. If I get a phone call from the right people and they tell me it's OK, then we might do business. But get serious, Johnny. You can't just walk in here and order a thirty-eight revolver like you're going to Walgreen's for a chocolate malted."

For the past twenty-four years, Benny Wojnarowski, the proprietor of West Side Locksmith & Safe on Roosevelt Road, had enjoyed a substantially higher standard of living than the average locksmith because of his sideline: He was a supplier of explosives and untraceable firearms to Chicago's underworld. His services had assisted more than a hundred business-related hits and perhaps two-dozen bombings.

He also had been a third-party participant in a small piece of gangland irony: In 1929, when Capone's trusted contractor Jack McGurn was importing killers for a move against Bugs Moran, Wojnarowski supplied the two military-issue submachine guns and the 12-guage shotgun used to butcher Moran's gang on Valentine's Day; seven years later, after McGurn had become a high-profile embarrassment to the outfit, Wojnarowski subcontracted the three 9-mm pistols and hollow-point cartridges used to dispatch McGurn in a Milwaukee Avenue bowling alley.

Wojnarowski and Johnny had been high-school classmates—on days when Johnny wasn't majoring in truancy. The two of them had kept up with each other through mutual friends from the Nineteenth Ward, and had bumped into each other a handful of times in South Side cabarets during the '20s and '30s. Johnny knew that Benny was a hard-core jazz fan who did "favors" for the good guys. Benny knew that Johnny and his sidekick, Joe Bermann, were gamblers who had stayed out of trouble with the outfit's bookmakers for more than twenty years— a rare feat.

Of course, Benny now suspected that Johnny had finally gotten in over his head and needed a piece for protection. That suspicion was not dispelled by their conversation in the locksmith shop.

"For Christ's sake," Johnny said, "why make such a big deal out of this? I'm not asking you to jump off a fucking building, I just want a gun. You can sell it to me, you can loan it, I don't care. Jesus, you can wrap it and give it to me for my birthday. Nobody's ever going to know where it came from."

"You don't get it," Benny said. "Somebody always knows. Something bad happens, someone gets hurt, it comes right back to me. Maybe not right away, but sooner or later. I'm the one who has to answer for whatever happens."

Johnny was incensed. "Nothing's going to happen. Nothing! The fucking gun doesn't even have to be loaded. I'm not going to shoot it or anything like that, I'm just going to flash it."

"Flash it."

"Yeah, to impress someone. OK, a dame."

Benny's deadpan expression barely cracked, but his

shoulders betrayed the suppressed mirth. He looked away, savoring the absurdity of what was being proposed. "This broad better be dumber than a hydrant," he said. "You start waving an unloaded revolver around—anybody with half a brain can see there's no cartridges in the cylinder."

"Oh, so now I'm funny. Jesus, how am I supposed to know something like that? I don't know shit about guns."

"Obviously."

"Cut it out, Benny—help me here. Can't you see I'm desperate?"

Benny folded his arms across his chest and started shaking his head again. "I got a reputation to protect," he said. "I deal with a lot of serious people. What do you think's going to happen to my reputation when those people find out I'm handing out firearms to use as pussy bait? That's nuts."

Uttering an exasperated snort, Johnny snatched his hat off the counter and made a move toward the door—then turned. "It's not pussy, Benny, it's serious. You want to know how serious?" Still holding his hat in his left hand, he spread his arms. "Look at me. I'm seriously crazy about this dame. Forty-three years old, almost forty-four, and I've never felt like this before. Except maybe for Theda Bara when I was fifteen."

He dropped to one knee and clasped his hat to his chest with both hands, breaking into song with his best Bing Crosby impression. "*Can it be the trees that fill the breeze, with rare and magic perfume? Oh no, it isn't the trees, it's love in bloom.*"

Benny was still shaking his head, but he was smiling now.

"This isn't some floozy, Benny." Johnny got up off the floor and used his hat to swipe at the dust on his pant leg. "She's strictly high class—smart, educated. And I think she's interested in me. Me, for Christ's sake. But here's the rub. I don't think I can close the deal unless she thinks I'm a tough guy—you know, a guy who's got connections."

"One of those broads, eh?" Benny arched his eyebrows. "You better be careful, Johnny."

"Come on, Benny, have a heart."

Without unfolding his arms, Benny reached up with a forearm and scratched his chin. "Let me understand this. You just want a piece you can flash."

"Yeah, that's all."

"And you're just going to flash it around this one broad—nobody else."

"She's the only one, I swear."

"And it's not going to be loaded."

"Yeah, but you said she could ..."

"Forget what I said," Benny snapped. "I'm thinking out loud here. I'm thinking what you really need to flash is a forty-five automatic. Looks like a fucking cannon, but if the magazine is empty, it's harmless, and there's no way she can tell. So, here's the deal—because I'm a nice guy, or maybe because I'm stupider than I ever thought, I'll loan you mine. I'll get it from the house. A shoulder holster, too. You can come back after lunch today, or tomorrow, whenever. And since you're a nice guy, maybe you'll give me a little something for my trouble."

"You're a prince, Benny, a real prince," Johnny said. "I won't forget this, believe me."

There was a brief silence. Benny spoke first. "Theda Bara."

"What?"

"Before, when you were talking about this dame—you said something about Theda Bara, the movie star."

"Yeah, so what?"

"I still close my eyes and think of her sometimes—you know, when I'm with the missus. If you catch my drift."

Johnny reacted as though something unpleasant had just landed on the counter between them. "For Christ's sake, Benny, why do you tell me a thing like that?"

"Jesus, you don't have to get sore about it. You were the one who brought it up."

11

*W*ith her pale hands resting on the mahogany writing tray in her lap, she lounged in a chaise on the wide stone patio behind her parents' house, staring across the shaded lawn toward the lakefront beyond the yard's perimeter of trees. Out on the water, dozens of white triangles, some no bigger than specs against the blue, marked the positions of sailboats, most of them launched from Wilmette Harbor, just to the north.

A fountain pen and several sheets of onionskin stationery imprinted with her monogram lay on the tray, as if waiting for something to jog the listless inertia of summer. A glass tumbler of ice tea, as yet untouched, rested on the colored-tile surface of a small table next to her chaise, the tumbler giving up rivulets of condensation to the late afternoon heat. A shrill buzzing from the elms surrounding the yard announced the presence of cicadas.

Margaret removed the cap from the pen, turned the paper precisely thirty degrees counter-clockwise, and began to write:

Dear Gabrielle,

She stopped, crumpled the sheet and placed the ball on the table, taking care to avoid the puddle of water around base of the tea tumbler. Again:

Bien chère Gabrielle,

This is so frustrating. I have no way of knowing if my letters ever reach you, yet I must write, if only to give myself a feeling of staying connected to such a brave friend. Perhaps the letters will arrive in a bundle after this wretched war is ended, and you will be able to read all the news in one sitting. By then, of course, it will no longer be news. But it will still be news to you, won't it?

We hear reports that the Germans have been dislodged from your city, but only with great destruction and loss of life. I worry about you more than ever. If any harm were to befall you, I would never forgive myself for not making you stay in school and come here with me after graduation. It would have been grand fun, just the two of us misbehaving together. I'm still saving two enormous cigars for our next visit to the Michigan Shores Club.

I saw a movie about the French resistance at the Varsity. The movie was absolutely chilling because I couldn't stop thinking of you and how dangerous your situation must be. (It was a little hard to accept Maureen O'Hara as a French school teacher, however.)

And now the big news, the reason for this letter: Brantley finally proposed! He popped the question a month ago, and I know I should have written immediately, but things just seemed to speed up after that and time got away from me.

Naturally I accepted the proposal without hesitation—well, maybe with the tiniest bit. It's such a big step, so final. And Brant sounded so business-like. When he proposed, he said he might be made a partner sooner if we were married. Can you believe that?

I do think it is the right step for me. Brant is a decent man from a good family. I believe he will allow me the freedom I crave, the kind of freedom you and I used to talk about when we'd get stinko on cheap wine in Northampton. My mother didn't have that option, but the war seems to be changing everything. Anyway, I still have plenty of time to think it over. The wedding is set for next May 26, and I devoutly hope that you, my closest friend and faithful confidante, will be able to stand as my bridesmaid. Please, please, try to be here. I'm sure my parents will be happy to pay your passage— they think the world of you.

Oh, before I close, I must tell you about my little gambler friend.

The French door at the far end of the patio opened. A middle-age woman, smartly dressed with carefully coiffed auburn hair, peered around the corner of the door and smiled. "I'm home, dear. Goodness, aren't you burning up out here?" Her cultured British accent was still discernible after twenty-eight years in the states.

"No, thanks, I'm fine, Mom. How was your card game?"

"It was perfectly lovely—although I did hear the most dreadful rumor about our neighbors. People are saying the Heilmans could be German spies—can you believe such a thing?"

"Mother, please."

"You'd be surprised, dear. I'll tell you all about it at dinner. Will you be joining us or are you going into the city?"

"No, I'll be here."

"Very good, I'll remind Ulla to set three places. What are you doing out here anyway? You look so busy."

"Writing a letter to Gabby."

"Oh, wonderful—then you've heard something. How is she?"

"No. No news."

"What a shame. Such a lovely young girl. Well, carry on, dear."

Margaret looked down. After pausing to reread the last sentence, she resumed writing.

I met him earlier this week while I was waiting for Brantley at a snazzy club in the Loop (have I ever mentioned that Brant is never on time for anything—I'm sure he'll be late for the wedding). His name is Johnny, and he really is a professional gambler. At least that's what he says, and I believe him. He's older, but kind of cute in a dapper sort of way. And here's the best part: I suspect he must have connections in the underworld (you know how that grabbed my attention). He called earlier this afternoon, so maybe I'll find out more when I see him tomorrow. Yes, I slipped him my number—though not directly, of course. While Brant was in the euphemism, I used the maître d' as an intermediary. Give me a couple of Manhattans and I am such a wicked girl! But I don't want to give you the wrong idea. I'm not going to do anything foolish

She tilted her head back and let the pen slip from her right hand. It rolled towards her, making a soft clack as it came to a stop against the raised edge of the writing tray. A smile slowly illuminated her face.

Her peal of giddy laughter rose briefly over the buzzing of the cicadas.

12

Seated across from Johnny in a booth at Ashkenaz Restaurant & Delicatessen on the city's far North Side, Joe frowned. "What the hell is that thing?" he said, pointing at a narrow leather strap, visible between the lapels of Johnny's suit jacket.

Johnny glanced furtively at the early lunchtime crowd. "I'll show you—get a load of this." He opened his right lapel just far enough to allow a glimpse.

"For cripe's sake, Johnny!" Joe, too, looked around to make sure no one was watching them, then spoke in a strident whisper. "When you told me you wanted a gun, what did I say? I said don't do anything stupid. This is what I was talking about—this is stupid!"

"Joe, calm down. It's not even loaded."

"Not loaded."

"Yeah, it's just for show. I'm thinking—if I'm packing heat, maybe this dame will think I'm one of the good guys."

"What dame? Not the mouse from the Empire Room, the one with the fiancé?"

Johnny's smile was apprehensive: "Yeah, Margaret. That's her name. I'm going to see her in a little while."

"*Oy, vei.*" Joe clapped both hands on the top of his head and sagged forward. After several seconds, he looked up at Johnny. "Let's go outside."

"What about lunch?"

"Forget lunch. I need to understand what's going on."

Joe slid out of the booth, snatched his hat off the chrome rack, and walked from the restaurant section, through the front deli, and out onto Morse Avenue with Johnny behind him. On the sidewalk, Joe walked quickly to the curb and turned to face Johnny, who had stopped just outside the entrance to the delicatessen.

Johnny approached cautiously, extending his right hand, palm up. "Joe, what the hell—I never seen you look like this."

"Well, that makes two of us because I've never seen you carry a gun before. What are you trying to do, get yourself killed already?"

"I told you, Joe, nothing's going to happen. It's not loaded. If you don't believe me you can check it yourself." He started to reach inside his suit jacket, but Joe took a step forward, reached out and grabbed Johnny's wrist.

"Jesus, don't pull that thing out on the street," Joe said, teeth clenched. "This is exactly what I'm talking about. What if a cop sees you do that? Does he know it's not loaded? No, all he sees is some fella waving a gun around in public."

"Joe, it's not a big deal. I know what I'm doing."

"Are you kidding? This broad's got you goofy. You're going to flash a gun in her face and she falls madly in love with you? Is that how it works? Spare me. And what happens if this dame's fiancé comes looking for you? You going to wear a sign around your neck that says, 'Don't shoot me, my gun isn't loaded'?"

Now Johnny's face was flushed. "Knock it off." He spat the words without shielding his mouth, and poked his index finger into Joe's chest. "Don't ever talk to me like my fucking father."

"You're right, you're right." Joe held up his arms in a gesture of surrender. "I'm just trying to make a point here."

"So what's your goddamned point then?"

Joe looked to his left and noticed that most of the people in the delicatessen had come to the front plate glass window to observe what probably looked like a pantomime drama that was about to break into a fist fight on the sidewalk outside.

"We're giving too much entertainment for nix," Joe said. "Let's get away from here—go for a walk."

They walked in silence around the corner, heading north for a block, then turning toward the lake. "Take your jacket off," Joe snapped as they passed into the shade of the underpass beneath the "L" tracks. "You've got that goddamned thing on backwards. You don't want this dame thinking you're a complete idiot." Joe helped Johnny rearrange the shoulder holster with the strap in back, the pistol now under his left armpit instead of his right, and the walk resumed.

As they neared their starting point, Joe again broke the silence. "I don't suppose there's any way to stop you from doing this, so I'm just going to say one thing: Be careful."

"I told you, don't worry," Johnny said. He glanced as his wristwatch. "I got to run—I'm supposed to meet her in fifteen minutes."

Joe held up an index finger: "One more thing, my friend. This dame—is she Jewish?"

"Jesus, you sound like my father again." This time Johnny said it with a smile. "What's the difference?"

"Big difference," Joe said. "Believe me, I can tell stories."

"Maybe some other time." Johnny dug into his pants pocket. "I almost forgot—I need to put a couple of hundred on the Cubs. You going to be near handbook before one o'clock?"

"Keep your cash," Joe said, holding up a hand. "I'll get

a bet down—if you're sure. The Pirates have won six in a row, you know."

"Yeah, but Chipman's going for the Cubs," Johnny said. "He's won his last four. Plus which, if he doesn't beat the Giants in the first game of that twin bill last Sunday, I'm tapped out. I'd probably be working in a fucking factory right now."

"I understand perfectly," Joe said. "Don't give me your cash. In honor of Bob Chipman, your savior, I'll get bets down for both of us. Just give me a call later. I'll probably be at home. Have a good time."

Joe slid into the driver's side of the Ford convertible he had parked on Morse Avenue, and spent a minute staring through the windshield.

Like Johnny, Joe had sold his car when the government announced gasoline rationing. In June, though, Joe hit a big night playing poker at the Rock Garden Club, a mob joint in Cicero. One of the pots he won included a stack of gas coupons and a green "B" sticker, supposedly reserved for essential drivers.

So he went out and bought the Ford, a used '39.

Now Joe remembered that on the same day he bought the car, he and Johnny had lost eleven hundred dollars on the horses. It was the start of the epic losing streak.

Joe reached out and patted the dashboard. "You're not a jinx, are you," he said softly. "Nope, it's all a matter of probabilities."

After shaking his head, as if trying to restore order to his own thoughts, he glanced at his watch and spoke out loud again.

"Jesus, I better get those bets down."

13

Margaret had put the kibosh on Johnny's suggestions that they meet in the Loop. Same with Evanston. Too much chance of running into someone she knew.

So they had agreed to meet at the "L" station on Howard Street, a commercial thoroughfare that for much of its length served as the boundary between Chicago and Evanston. Because Evanston had been dry for ten years, the clubs, restaurants and package stores along the Chicago side of Howard Street were among the closest places where the suburb's thirsty residents could purchase legal alcohol.

After downing two fingers of her father's scotch to calm her nerves, Margaret took a taxi to the station. Feeling slightly lightheaded now, she stood inside the station, near the newsstand, listening to the rumble of trains overhead while keeping an eye on the wide stairway connecting the ground level to the elevated platforms.

The thought of being recognized by someone she knew made her stomach do flip-flops—that was part of the reason for the scotch. As a precaution, she wore sunglasses and had a dark Hermés scarf covering her hair. It was 12:20 when she spotted him in a knot of people coming down the stairway. He came through one of the turnstiles and walked quickly in her direction, but seemed to be scanning the area beyond her. When she realized he was going to walk right past her, she took a step forward and spoke.

"Hey, fella, you going my way?"

"Jesus," Johnny did a double-take and snatched his hat off his head, "I didn't recognize you. I mean, with the dark glasses and all, I thought maybe it was Lana Turner standing there."

She laughed. "Oh, sure, Lana Turner. Isn't she a brunette these days?"

"Who can keep up with these things? You're better looking than she is, anyway."

"Hey, no jokes about the way I look, OK?"

"I was kidding on the square, honest. So how you doing?"

They stood in the station's concourse while they made small talk. He complimented her on her outfit—a simple white blouse, silk, with puff shoulders and a calf-length beige skirt. She said he looked sharp in gray. With a weak smile, he asked if she recognized the suit—it was the same one he'd worn to the Empire Room. She lied and said no. She asked if he had enjoyed Borge's show. He lied and said yes, but added, "I didn't understand some of the Hitler stuff—I mean, what's so funny about Hitler?"

"His Charlie Chaplin moustache?" she suggested.

He asked if her fiancé had shown up in time for the show. She said yes, but explained that he was always busy with work and was often late for their dates.

"Well," she said after a couple of minutes, "it's been great seeing you. I hope we can do this again sometime."

He looked stunned, then laughed. "You're right, let's get out of here. You want to get a drink somewhere?"

She looked away. "I already had a drink."

"OK, let's take a walk. Down to the lake maybe. It's just a couple of blocks."

When they reached the lakefront, Johnny pointed to one of the east-facing benches on the narrow sward between the beach and Lakeview Terrace. "We got lucky," he said. "We can sit in the shade."

He took the monogrammed handkerchief from his breast pocket, made a few quick swipes over the bench's worn wooden slats, then bowed slightly and motioned for her to sit. She curtsied and sat.

Margaret asked if Johnny had family living in Chicago.

"My older sister," he said. "But she's down on the South Side. We don't see each other that much—just holidays."

"How about your parents?"

"Both dead," he said. "Yours?"

"Still around. Which one of yours gave you the blue eyes?"

"My mother," Johnny said. "She was a real looker. That's what everybody said. I don't have any memory of her. She died when I was just a baby."

"I'm sorry," Margaret said. "What did she die from?"

"It was the collar," Johnny said, "supposedly."

"What do you mean, supposedly?"

"My Aunt Rose—that was the aunt who raised us, me and my sister—she said it had something to do with me being born, and she said my father always blamed me. Which I could believe because he always treated me like shit, pardon the expression. And he was always nice to my sister. "

"Did you and your father ever make peace?"

Johnny shook his head. "Never got off my back."

"Sounds like we might have something in common," she said.

His eyebrows shot upward as his head swiveled to look at her. "What are you saying—you hate your father?"

"Hate's a little strong," Margaret said. "Resent is more like it. I resent the way he treats me."

"You mean he knocks you around?"

"No, he doesn't hit me," she said. "He'd never do that. But it seems like nothing I do or say is ever good enough for him, or ladylike enough, or smart enough."

"Right, never good enough," he said, folding his arms and scowling, "sounds real familiar. What about your mom? Is she like your old man?"

"No, nicer," she said, staring out at the lake, "but you'd never in a million years describe her as the mothering type." Margaret lapsed into a caricature of an upper-class English accent. "She's British Empire you know. Was sent over here during the Great War. Old money—attitudes to match. Jolly good, stiff upper, and all that."

Johnny frowned. "Old money?"

"Family money," Margaret said, "going way back. Enough to keep us living quite comfortably, thank you—even after father's law business went down with the Crash. Also enough to pay for nannies. They raised me until I was civilized enough to mingle with adults."

"A dandy little game," Johnny said. "So you got all civilized and everything. Now what?"

"I don't like to think about that part," she said. Changing the subject, she asked what the city had been like during Prohibition.

He thought a moment, slowly unfolding his arms and looking for words or images that would explain the Noble Experiment to someone who hadn't been in the middle of it.

"It was crazy," he said, "like a huge New Year's Eve party. Bands playing, people dancing and eating. Gambling. Lots of gambling, most of it illegal. And drinking, of course—everybody was drinking. And almost every day somebody would get shot, killed. Sometimes a lot of guys would get killed. But you'd hardly notice. People just kept dancing and drinking. It went like that for thirteen years ... well, except when Dever was mayor. Then the action moved out to the suburbs."

"Is that when you started rubbing elbows with wise guys? During Prohibition?"

He gave her a funny look. "You mean Weiss guys?" he said. "No, me and Joe never spent time around those guys. We were more like Capone guys. We figured we'd live longer if we stayed away from jamokes who had connections with O'Banion and Weiss."

"Let's go gambling," she said.

He was slow to react to another abrupt change in subject.

"Take me gambling," she said.

"Well, sure, but where do you want to go?"

"You're the gambler—you tell me."

Johnny cleared his throat. "It depends on what kind of action you want," he said, adopting an authoritative tone. "You want to get some money down on a race or a ballgame, or do you want to do the casino thing."

"Casino—I've never been in one before. Is there one around here?"

He shook his head. "We'd have to go out on Irving Park, just over the city line. The place is a dump, but they got roulette and all those crazy games."

"What are we waiting for? Let's go."

Johnny stood. "Wait, I got a better idea," he said, delighted by his own brainstorm. "How much time you got?"

She said she was free for the afternoon and early evening, then had a commitment—dinner with her parents and a friend, but it wouldn't matter if she arrived a few minutes late.

He assumed the friend was her fiancé, and knew she'd be more than a few minutes late, but what the hell. "I'm going to show you a place—and don't get the wrong idea here—it's still a dump like the place on Irving Park, except this joint used to have the biggest handle in the county. Not the biggest in the city," his hand came up to shield his mouth as his words flew, "I said the biggest handle in the whole fucking country. Excuse my French."

She put her hand on his forearm again. "It's going to make me very uncomfortable if you keep apologizing for your language. I'm a grown woman—I can handle it. Now, where is this dump?"

Johnny smiled and drew himself up, as if to make an official announcement: "My lovely, we are going out to beautiful Cicero."

In the back seat of the Yellow Cab, Margaret put her dark glasses in the small clutch bag she was carrying. She undid the loosely knotted scarf under her chin, pulled the scarf off her head and shook her hair free. "Jesus, you look great," Johnny said. "And I'm not kidding around."

"Thanks," she said. "You're looking pretty suave yourself."

Johnny asked the driver to check WGN to see who was winning the Cubs-Pirates game at Wrigley.

"Sorry, bub, no radio," the driver said.

Margaret looked out the window on her side of the cab. "Are you a baseball fan?"

"Yeah, but I don't pay much attention unless I've got a bet on a game. This wartime ball is strictly from hunger. Too many players in the service, so you got all these old guys and gimps in the majors—F'ers. It's like a freak show."

She looked back at Johnny. "Are you married?"

Johnny shot a surprised look at Margaret and laughed nervously. "What does that have to do with baseball?"

"Nothing, I'm curious, that's all."

Johnny said he wasn't married, never had been. And he added his usual *shtik* line: "Forty-three years without a bride and people wonder why my life is so sad and lonely."

Margaret gave him a dubious look. "Lonely. I'll bet. How about a lady friend? Anyone special?"

Johnny shrugged. "Not recently," he said. "I don't have time."

They rode in silence for a while.

Johnny glanced out. They were on Western Avenue now, heading south. He figured the driver planned to take a right on Ogden Avenue, which angled to the southwest toward Cicero and the other western suburbs.

Margaret broke the silence. "That guy you mentioned, Weiss—he was murdered, wasn't he?"

"Yup, they got him, Capone's people did. Right on Clark Street. In front of a church already. You were probably a little school girl."

"What did he do to get in trouble?"

"It was business," Johnny said. "He got greedy."

"I hope you don't take this question the wrong way," Margaret said after another silence, "but are you attracted to men or women?"

Johnny's head swiveled to face her, eyes wide, mouth agape. "There's a right way to take that question? I mean, what kind of goddamned question is that?"

"Jesus, don't get so defensive," Margaret said. "Look at it from a woman's point of view. Here's a nice-looking guy, sharp dresser, never been married, doesn't date, and when I see him out for a night on the town, he's meeting another guy—Joe, right?"

"Yeah, Joe," Johnny said, shielding his mouth. "But you read it all wrong. Look at me, I'm a fucking gambler. That's why I'm not married. Women don't waste time on guys like me and Joe. But believe me, we're not pansy boys."

"So how did the two of you get together? Were you friends when you were kids?"

Johnny shook his head. "Uh-uh, we both grew up in the Nineteenth Ward—but different neighborhoods. And Joe was older, so we were never in school together. I was never in school anyway, but that's another story. Me and Joe, we didn't meet until I was fifteen—at a Sox game. Right out of the blue, he walks up and starts asking questions. He wants to know why Joe Jackson waved to me from the field. Then he accuses me of playing hooky from school, and I accuse him of ducking out on his job. We been friends ever since."

While he was talking, she reached across and pulled his hand onto her lap. When Johnny finished, she said: "It wouldn't have made a big difference to me, you know," patting the back of his hand, "whether you and this Joe were friends or ... well, you know. But I think I'm a little more comfortable with you this way."

While Johnny leaned in through the passenger side window to settle with the cabbie, Margaret stood on the sidewalk and studied the front of 2131 Cicero Avenue, a drab two-story building next to the "L" station two blocks beyond the Chicago city limits. The cabbie pulled away from the curb. Johnny turned and stepped next to Margaret.

"If this is the place," she said, "you were right. It looks like a dump."

"And, believe me, the outside hasn't changed," he said. "It was just like this in the '20s, back when I was a cute-looking kid, except right up there," he pointed to a spot under the tall, second-story windows, "right up there was a little sign, looked like it was painted by a school kid, said The Ship. That's what it was called, The Ship. Torrio had it, then Capone, then Nitti. There was so much action here, it was like State and Madison. Most nights, you could hardly get in here. Now it's the Rock Garden—one of the joints Accardo lets your boy Guzik run."

She kept her eyes on the front of the building, but slipped her left hand under Johnny's right arm and pulled herself closer. "This is kind of exciting—maybe we'll see some interesting people here."

"Yeah, interesting, if you think bums like me are interesting."

"Will you stop it?" she said. "Let's go."

The first-floor dance hall was dark except for slivers of sunlight slicing through the heavy drapes that covered the front windows. At the long bar along the back of the ballroom, a lone bartender moved listlessly through setup for the evening drinkers.

"The action's upstairs," Johnny said, steering Margaret toward the elevator. "You want the elevator or the stairs?"

Before she could answer a bouncer the size of a bungalow heaved himself up off a folding chair in a dark recess next to the staircase and approached them. "You going upstairs?"

"Yeah," said Johnny, "we're just looking for a little action."

"Not with that, pal." The bouncer pointed to the left side of Johnny's suit jacket. "You leave that down here."

"Sorry, forgot." Johnny removed the unloaded .45 ACP from its shoulder holster and offered it to the bouncer, who cursed softly as he deflected the muzzle with his left hand before lifting the pistol from Johnny's grip.

"Next time," the bouncer said, "keep the business end pointed in the other direction, OK?" He hefted the automatic a couple of times, gave Johnny a quizzical look, then gestured the two of them toward the stairs. "Elevator operator don't get here until seven," he said.

As they reached the first landing on the staircase, Margaret grabbed Johnny's arm. "What in the name of God are you carrying a gun for? What's going on?"

"It's nothing," Johnny said. "You know how these things go—sometimes you need a gun. You know, in case of trouble."

"No, I don't know how these things go," she hissed, her voice threatening to break through the agitated whisper. "What kind of trouble are you in?" Her grip tightened on his right arm. "Tell me, damn it."

Johnny shook his head. "Can't." His mind raced. The gun had produced the desired reaction, but now he had no plausible explanation for carrying the thing. Why hadn't he thought this through beforehand?

"What I mean is," he tried to keep his voice down to a

whisper, "I can't talk about it here—too many nosy people. I'll tell you later."

"You promise?" She glanced around at the empty stairwell.

"Yeah, I promise. Now lighten up on the arm a little, you're putting creases in my sleeve."

"Oops, sorry."

"Forget it, let's go upstairs and win some milk money for the kids."

14

The second-floor casino had the tired, worn-down look of a middle-age prostitute who'd long since gone to seed and whose few Johns no longer cared. And it was so quiet you could hear ice cubes tinkling in glasses on the far side of the room.

"Jesus," Johnny said looking around, "this joint's deader than Kelsey's nuts."

The room was dimly illuminated by two dozen ceiling fixtures, each of which seemed to have as many missing or burned-out bulbs as lighted ones. Gaming tables were positioned in orderly rows, one under each light fixture, except a number of the tables, no longer in use, were now covered by dingy sheets. All the tables rested on oriental rugs, frayed at the edges, marred by cigarette burns, and worn down to the backing in places.

Heavy drapes, similar to those in the downstairs dance hall, covered all windows twenty-four hours a day—as if Cicero police and the state's attorney were oblivious to what had been going on in the big upstairs room at the Rock Garden for the past twenty-five years.

Along the wall to the right of the elevator, toward the

front of the building, was a bar with about fifteen stools. To the left, or rear, were the cashiers' windows and a heavy locked door leading to the counting room and office. An office door led to a small rear staircase used to remove proceeds from the premises in advance of police raids that were almost always known beforehand.

Johnny bought a hundred dollars' worth of five-dollar chips and gave them to Margaret. "Go ahead, knock your brains out," he said.

"But I don't know what to do."

Johnny scanned the room. A long row of chrome-plated slot machines—the chrome now dulled by time, smoke, and haphazard maintenance—occupied the windowless wall farthest from the elevator and stairwell. Roulette and craps tables were grouped near the windows on the street side of the room, with "21" and baccarat in the middle, and various kinds of poker on the alley side.

Johnny suggested "21": "It's pretty easy to play, and the house doesn't have that big an edge. The only thing you got to worry about are players sitting to your right," Johnny said. "If one of those mopes keeps making sucker plays, you might not get the cards you need."

"So that means the people on my left really need to worry," she said.

"Not really," he said. "If you keep going over twenty-one, somebody who's on a cold streak might get pissed. But a guy who's winning won't say a word. It works both ways."

"I don't think I know what you're saying," she confessed.

"Hey, just stick with me—I'll keep you out of trouble."

In midafternoon, "21" was being played at only one of the four tables that would be used that evening. There were two empty chairs, one to the left of the dealer and one at about four o'clock on the semi-circle. Johnny walked to the latter, pulled the chair slightly away from the table, and gestured to Margaret to have a seat. He positioned himself behind her, just over her right shoulder.

Margaret played cautiously, risking one five-dollar chip on each deal. After thirteen deals, she was down twenty dollars and hadn't yet pissed off any of the three players sitting to her left. On the fourteenth deal, she carefully peeled the front edges of her two cards off the felt surface, lifting them just enough to show Johnny.

"Jesus," he said, "turn 'em over."

Margaret had an ace and a jack, both spades. The dealer quickly counted five ten-dollar chips and slid them across the table—a ten-to-one payoff. Margaret clapped her hands, even though she didn't understand why her twenty-one was worth more than the two others she had seen on earlier deals.

After four more rounds, all losers, Margaret tipped her head to one side and motioned to Johnny to lean down close to her shoulder. "I hate to say this," she whispered, "but I don't think I have the patience to do this for very long."

"Then let's try something else," he said.

After picking up her chips and excusing herself from the "21" table, she asked Johnny, "Are you disappointed?"

"Are you kidding? I'm the same way. Some of these people can sit here for hours. Joe's like that—he can play cards all night, for Christ's sake. But me, I'd rather jump off the Michigan Avenue Bridge."

"Maybe Joe should get together with my mother," Margaret said.

"Your mother's a card player?"

"Canasta—constantly and forever."

Johnny shrugged. "It could happen to anyone."

She flashed a tentative smile and searched his face, waiting to see if his comment had been serious or a wisecrack.

In fact, the comment was one of three endlessly repeated aphorisms Johnny had picked up as a child from his Aunt Rose, the other two being, "Maybe it's all for the better," and "You never know the next person's business." Johnny's sister still repeated them, too, but used them as humorous punctuations. To Johnny, the three represented the encapsulated wisdom of the ages. No events or situations in life escaped being distilled into one of those truisms. So when he used one of them, he was never trying to be humorous.

They wandered over to one of the roulette tables. Margaret watched the croupier and the five players while Johnny offered a commentary on the betting options.

"I used to play this game a lot," he said. "It's a great way to blow a lot of scratch in a hurry. But you can also win a lot, and you already hit the biggest payoff they got in '21', so maybe this is your lucky day."

Margaret took one of the ten-dollar chips from the "21" table and played it on twenty-four.

"Why twenty-four?" Johnny asked. "Why not one of these bets over here with shorter odds?"

"Just a feeling."

"Good," he said. "The odd-even stuff is OK if you're just killing time. But it's like playing cards—you could sit here all day and come out a few bucks either side of even. Waste of time."

The croupier started the wheel in one direction, the ball in the other. Moments later the ball danced briefly on the wheel before clattering into one of the slots. "Six red," the croupier announced, adding Margaret's chip to the house winnings.

Seeing Margaret place two ten-dollar chips on fourteen, Johnny reached in and retrieved one of the chips. "Don't start raising your bets," he said.

"But I might win twice as much."

"Humor me on this," he said. "You're making a sucker play. I'll explain it later."

The fourteen was a loser. Another ten-dollar chip went to the house's take.

Margaret put her index finger to her lips as she studied

the numbers. "Play your age," Johnny suggested, hoping to find out, without asking, how old she was.

"No," she said, "I want to play the high number, thirty-six red."

Johnny flashed a pained smile. "I don't have a real good feeling about that number. But it's your play."

She put a ten-dollar chip on thirty-six.

The ball danced, then fell into thirty-six red. Margaret screamed and started bouncing on her toes. She gave Johnny a hug. The croupier, who seemed almost as delighted as Margaret, pushed three hundred fifty dollars in chips across the table. Watching Margaret grasp at the chips, Johnny shook his head. "Jesus, what are the odds on that?" he said, talking more to himself than to Margaret. "Baby, where were you when I needed you two weeks ago?"

Still tasting the nectar of gambler's euphoria, Margaret gave Johnny a coy look. "I suppose you'd advise me against putting all these chips on another number."

"Hey, the way you're going today, you might hit back-to-back numbers. Anything can happen. But you're pretty smart, so you already know what the smart play is."

"Humm—take the money and walk away?"

"You're a natural. Let's get a drink."

Margaret gave Johnny an exaggerated pout before gathering up the chips. Johnny told her to leave a chip for the croupier—"it looks cheap if you hit a big score and don't leave a little something for the guy"—then took a stool at the far left end of the empty bar and waited while Margaret exchanged the remaining chips for four hundred and ten dollars in cash.

"Here," she said when she joined Johnny at the bar, "this actually belongs to you."

He waved it off. "Hey, you won it fair and square—keep it."

"That doesn't feel right to me," she said. "Here, at least take the original hundred. And another fifty—we'll call it a retainer."

"I get it," Johnny chuckled humorlessly. "A fee for sharing my vast knowledge. Maybe I should hang out a shingle. Anybody who wants to throw away fifteen or twenty years, I'm the fella to see."

Margaret shrugged. "Call it a fee if you want. I prefer the retainer idea."

They exchanged a prolonged glance, interrupted by the bartender, who had been out on the floor serving a round a drinks to six men at one of the poker tables. "Get you folks something?"

Johnny ordered a Canadian and water, with a light pour on the whiskey. Margaret said she'd have the same.

"Is that how you feel about being a gambler?" she asked. "It was a waste of time?"

"Yeah, sometimes," he said. "We missed out on a lot of things, me and Joe. Like having our own families—that kind of thing. We always figured we'd have plenty of time for all that after our luck ran out, because nobody beats this racket forever. You can duck and duck and duck, but sooner or later you're going to get clipped. Except me and Joe—we're still ducking."

"You talk like an old man," she said. "But you're still young. Kind of. So why did you ask me to bet one chip when I tried to bet two? Is that a personal rule of yours?"

"Yeah, it is. See, you bet ten dollars on your first number, so that's where you stay. Ten dollars. Win or lose. I've seen hundreds of guys, when they start losing, they start upping the ante. They think they're going to win back the lost money. We call that looking for evens. Only suckers go looking for evens."

"But if you keep betting larger and larger amounts," Margaret said, "sooner or later you're bound to win it all back."

"That's what every sucker thinks," Johnny countered. "But it doesn't work. Believe me, if you want to go broke in a hurry, just go looking for evens. I can say this from experience. To my sorrow."

"That reminds me," Margaret said, "what happened two weeks ago? At the roulette table you said something about two weeks ago."

"Eh, it was nothing." Johnny looked away.

"It doesn't have anything to do with the gun, does it?"

Johnny took a deep breath and exhaled. He stared at the top of the bar in front of him. "Yeah, sort of," he said. "But it's not what you're thinking, not that kind of trouble. I was in the shitter for a month, worst losing streak I ever had. Started looking for evens—what I just told you not to do. And, bingo, I went bust. That's what happened two weeks ago."

"You went against your own rule?"

"Gambling can make you goofy," he said, taking a long slug from his highball.

"Did your friend help you get back on your feet?"

"No, I would never ask him to do that. And he wouldn't ask me. No, I hocked all my belongings—clothes, the whole shebang. Got lucky. The night you saw me in the Empire Room—that was right after my first big score in a month."

"But you weren't carrying a gun that night, were you?"

"No. "

"I still don't understand."

Johnny cleared his throat. "Well, it's ... I'm still pretty jammed up, even with that big score." He kept his face tilted down toward the bar but shifted his eyes to the right, observing Margaret out of the corner of his eye. "See, I need to pay off some debts. So I'm thinking," he cleared his throat again, "and this is just between me and you—I'm thinking I need to pull a heist."

"Oh, my God," she whispered, leaning in close. "You mean this place? Today?"

"Jesus, no—not this place. Uh, what I mean is it could have been this place but it wouldn't have been a smart play. Too many people know who I am. And I'd be wearing cement shoes by Sunday morning, if you catch my drift."

"I read the papers. I know what happens to people."

"Right, so you understand why I don't want to add to the list of stupid things I've done in my life. These jobs ... you know, they take time. I'm still looking for the right situation. It has to be right."

"How long does it take?"

"Probably a week. Maybe longer."

"Will you tell me when it's going to happen?" She reached over and put her hand on top of his.

"Yeah, I'll tell you."

Johnny knew he really hadn't explained why he packed a .45 into a joint run by the outfit. He'd merely created a diversion. But for now, that was enough. Besides, it was an interesting diversion. The diversion had potential.

It was close to 5:30 when they went outside to wait for the cab that would take Margaret back to her dinner engagement in Evanston.

"When can we do this again?" Johnny asked.

"Call me," she said. "You remember the routine, right?"

"Yeah, weekdays only, between 1 and 3. I keep your note right here in my jacket, next to my heart." He tapped his left lapel with his right hand.

"That's really sweet."

"Hey, it's the same suit, remember."

Margaret laughed as a Checker cab pulled to the curb and stopped. She leaned forward and kissed Johnny on the mouth. Before he could slip an arm around her waist, the kiss was over.

"Gotta run," she said.

15

"She's doing the tango," Joe said. "She's dancing between her safe little world and your world."

They were sitting on a bench at the lakefront end of Howard Street—though not the same bench Johnny and Margaret had occupied—watching the Saturday-morning crowd of mothers and children at the beach. It would have been easier to meet at the Morse Avenue Beach, closer to Joe's apartment, but they had agreed long ago that the mommies in the Howard Street neighborhood were, on average, younger and easier on the eyes than the dames around Morse Avenue.

The two of them had their hats in their laps, the better to catch the morning sun. Joe had given Johnny three hundred and twenty dollars, the winnings on Friday's Cubs-Pirates game.

"So what's the harm?" Johnny said. "I'm nuts about her. She's having fun, and I think she really likes me."

"She likes what you represent," Joe said, tilting his head back and closing his eyes to absorb the sun's warmth. With his high forehead, aquiline face, and large, half-lidded eyes, Joe was the more traditionally handsome of the two.

Johnny was often described as cute, a word that didn't apply to Joe. He was suave.

"No, it's more than that," Johnny said. "She knows I'm a gambler—she doesn't care. She knows me and you have been doing this for over twenty years. She's impressed that we've lasted as long as we have, which when you think about it is a pretty fucking impressive thing. And, get this—she thought maybe you and me were fairies."

Joe, his head still tipped back, smiled.

Johnny went on: "What I'm saying is, me and her—we're attracted to each other. No playacting, Joe. I think it's for real."

"Doesn't matter," Joe said without changing position. "Even if you're right—and I'm not saying you are, I'm just saying *if* you are—it's not going to work out, not with a nice little society dame from the North Shore. From the looks of her, she's probably young enough to be your daughter. And I'll bet you a hundred bucks she's not Jewish."

"Joe, why make a big deal? Hell, Jolson must have been my age when he married that dancer. And she was Catholic, for Christ's sake."

"Jolson was a huge international star," Joe interjected. "You're a gambler. And you've got the wrong last name." He tipped his head forward, took his hat off his lap, and placed it on the bench next to him. He looked out at the lake. "When a Jewish guy starts running around with a *shiksa*, people get upset. Especially when it's a high-society *shiksa*. It's like a big scandal. Believe me, I know."

Johnny gave Joe a quizzical stare. "What do you mean?"

Heaving a sigh, Joe gave Johnny a condensed version of his love affair with high-school classmate Rosalie Merlo during the summer between their junior and senior years; how the families—*both* families—had been horrified when they found out, how his father and her Uncle Mike had ended the relationship by sending Rosalie to a Catholic boarding school in Iowa for her senior year.

"I didn't know it, but my letters never got to her, and her letters to me never got mailed," Joe said.

"Jesus," Johnny said with genuine surprise, "you never told me. Is that when things went sour between you and your father?"

"Never forgave him," Joe said.

"How did you find out about the letters?"

"Francesco told me," Joe said. "That's when he was still a barber—you remember, in that little shop on Centre ..."

"Never went there. We didn't have money for haircuts, remember? First time I ever went to a fucking barber shop was after you got me a job in your family's business. Before then, Aunt Rose always cut my hair."

"Right." Joe nodded without expression. "Where was I? Oh, Nitti had big-time connections, even then. He found out Rosalie's uncle made sure the nuns intercepted all the letters. I don't know how many she wrote. I probably wrote a dozen."

"Her uncle—that wasn't the same guy ..."

"Yup, *that* Mike Merlo."

"Jesus, Joe, you were messing with powerful people."

"Except Merlo wasn't a big shot yet. He didn't get hooked up with the Torrio gang until years later."

"So what happened to the girl?"

Joe stared out at the lake. "Never saw her again," he said. "She got married right after graduation. A Catholic guy, natch. But that's not the point—you understand why I told you the story, right?"

"Sure. Except my father can't stick his nose where it doesn't belong anymore."

"I'm thinking about *her* father," Joe said. "If he's still around, I don't think he and the missus are going to be too pleased about you seeing their daughter. And I think she knows it. That's what I'm trying to tell you. Times haven't changed that much, my friend."

They sat in silence, then Johnny spoke. "Let me ask you one thing, Joe. Even after all the *tsores* and the tumult in your family, and … even knowing all the things you know now, would you give up that summer?"

Now they were looking at each other. A smile slowly creased Joe's face. "Probably not," he said. "Hell, I'm still carrying a torch."

"So you understand."

Joe nodded slightly. He took a deep breath and exhaled with an audible sigh. "I guess I do."

Johnny took his hat off his lap and stood up. "Thanks for getting that bet down. You want to go to the ballgame tomorrow?"

"Aren't you going to see your ..."

"Can't call her until Monday. No weekend calls."

Joe shook his head. "She's hiding you—this is not good. I'm betting on a fast ride and a hard fall, my friend. Enjoy it."

16

"There's no risk, it's easy money," Johnny explained. "I walk in, I walk out—and bingo-bango, you're fifty bucks to the good."

Johnny was standing in the rear stockroom of Marty O'Hallahan's Army-Navy Store, 4719 North Broadway. Marty, his feet propped up on a World War I Army desk, folded his hands over his round belly and frowned.

"Surely you've got to be nuts," he said. "I can think of a thousand things that can go wrong—and that's not even counting the fact it's a loony idea to begin with."

Marty, a rumpled bear, was a devout Catholic with six kids, five of them now grown, and a gambling habit. He had started gambling during Prohibition, swearing off for good—or so he said—when the habit almost got him killed in the summer of 1938.

"But can't you see?" Johnny argued. "If anything goes wrong, it lands on me. Nothing happens to you. You're in the clear."

"Look at me, you damn fool—I'm already in the clear. Why should I invite trouble into my life? Which is exactly what you're asking me to do. What the hell have you been smoking, Johnny?"

"Jesus, Marty, if there's one guy in this world I figured I could count on it's you. Whatever happened to gratitude? I mean, here you are, still walking around. The way I see it, you owe me one."

Marty swung his feet off the desk and stood up, shaking his finger at Johnny. "Oh, no you don't," he said, his voice rising in volume. "You don't pull that blarney on me. You know damn well it was Joe that talked to Nitti. You didn't have a thing to do with it. Not one thing. If I owe anybody, it's Joe, bless him. But Joe's too much of a gentleman. He would never come in here looking for a favor. And he sure as hell wouldn't come in here with a shit-for-brains idea like staging a phony holdup."

Johnny took his hat off and ran his fingers through his hair. While he was trying to think of what to say next, a high-pitched bell tinkled in the main part of the store. "Somebody's up front," Marty said. "I got to go see what they want."

He returned to the storeroom a few minutes later. "Another tire-kicker," he said. "Everybody wants to look, nobody wants to buy." He turned his attention to Johnny. "OK, out with you."

"In a minute," Johnny said. "I'm trying to appeal to your better nature here. The favor I'm asking, I know it's big. But I'm seeing this dame—a nice girl. Educated. Good family. A real looker. And it's hard to explain, but this favor ... it would really put me in like Flynn."

"Oh, so now it's a love story, is it?" Affecting a dreamy look, Marty put both hands over his heart and batted his lashes before turning serious again. "Look, Johnny, times are tough. I mean, who needs surplus goods? Half the country's out there wearing brand new Government Issue. Lord knows, I could use the fifty. But even if I were Cupid himself, there is no way I could go along with something like this."

"How about a hundred bucks?"

"Interesting, but no. Good luck to you and your lady friend."

"Make it two hundred."

"That's a lot of money, Johnny. Are you sure? Two hundred?"

"That's what I'm offering," Johnny said. "Is it a deal?"

"Not yet. I need more information first—like exactly how you see this playing out."

Johnny hadn't put together a detailed plan, or even a rough plan for that matter. He preferred to do life without a plan. At the same time, he didn't want to give Marty an excuse to back out. He began improvising, sketching the outlines of a holdup that would be pure theater—except it would look real to someone outside the store, say, someone sitting at the wheel of a getaway car.

"When is this going to happen?" Marty asked. "What day? And what time of day?"

"That's where I need your help," Johnny said. "It has to be a slow time on a slow day."

"They're all slow," Marty said. "But it's a retail business—you can't predict when the store's going to be empty. And in case you hadn't noticed, that intersection up the street from here, that's Broadway and Lawrence. You want me to tell you when there's a slow time at Broadway and Lawrence? That time doesn't exist. I don't know, Johnny, this whole thing sounds half-baked to me."

"There's a couple of rough spots maybe, but you and me, we can fill in the details, no problem," Johnny said. "It'll go off like eggs in coffee. Bingo-bango. So do we have a deal?"

"For two hundred, I'm tempted," Marty said, scratching the stubble around his chin. "I'd be lying if I said otherwise. That's four months' rent at my place. But it just feels too loosey-goosey, Johnny. I can't do it."

"Christ, Marty, you really got me over a barrel here. I need your help on this. Tell you what, I'll throw in another C-note. That makes it three hundred bucks."

Marty's ample eyebrows registered surprise. "Three hundred," he said. "Jesus, Mary and Joseph, you're totally serious about this crazy stunt, aren't you?"

17

She waited for a green light at Sheridan Road and Wilson Avenue, then turned right onto Wilson, easing the big Packard convertible to the curb when she saw him waiting on the sidewalk fifty feet from the corner.

"Nice ride," Johnny said as he slid onto the leather seat beside her. "Yours or somebody else's?"

"Nice suit," she said, looking him up and down.

"How about a little kiss," he said.

Without removing her hands from the wood steering wheel, Margaret leaned to the right. They kissed, lips slightly parted. To Johnny, it seemed maybe a fraction of a second longer than their parting kiss on Friday.

"Hey," she said as she straightened back up in the driver's seat, "don't you know you're supposed to keep your eyes closed when you kiss someone?"

"You mean there's rules for kissing?" he said.

"No rules, just conventions," she said. "Next time, try it. See if it's not better with your eyes closed. Now where'd you get the suit?"

"I asked about the car first," he said. "Is it yours?"

"Indirectly," she said. "It's one of my family's cars—the one my father drives to his weekend golf games."

Her father, M. Charles Turner, had put her through something that felt like a cross examination when she asked if she could use the Packard. He asked where she was going, what she planned to do, how long it was likely to take, and whether she was meeting anyone.

Seemingly as an afterthought—although she suspected it was the real point of her father's lawyerly questions—he also asked where she'd been Friday afternoon, when she returned home forty minutes after the agreed-on starting time for a dinner to which she herself had invited Brantley. She lied on all counts, saying she'd been looking at bridal gowns on Friday, let the time get away from her, and then had trouble getting a cab.

That's why she wanted to use the car, she explained, so she wouldn't be at the mercy of the cabbies after she finished her wedding errands on Tuesday afternoon.

"All right," Charles Turner said. "I'm pretty sure there's gas in the tank. But if you need gas, the ration stamps are in the little table in the foyer. Just be careful. And don't take the car into the city."

"Why not? That's where the good stores are."

"The stores here in Evanston are perfectly adequate. Do not—I repeat, do not—take my Packard into the city."

"OK, if that's what you want."

"Yes, that is exactly what I want."

"What is this," Johnny asked, running his hand over the mahogany trim on the dashboard, "a '38? I never saw a convertible like this one, you know, with four doors."

"It's a '39," she said. "My father's. It's the only one of its kind, supposedly. Now tell me about the suit. You look sharp in blue—sets off your eyes."

"Thanks. I went to the Loop on Saturday—started rebuilding the wardrobe. It's just a start."

She reached out with her right hand and touched the front of his pin-striped jacket. "You carrying that roscoe again?"

"No, but I can get it. And where did such a nice girl learn a word like that?"

"I read it someplace—maybe in the *Saturday Evening Post*. So what are we doing this afternoon? Gambling again? Which reminds me, what about that right situation you were talking about on Friday? Found anything yet?"

He nodded, gesturing that she should pull away from the curb and continue west on Wilson Avenue. At Wilson and Broadway, he motioned for a right turn. The eight-cylinder Packard rumbled under the "L" tracks where they angled across Broadway and approached the light at Leland. "OK," he said, "stay on Broadway, but keep to the right and slow down—it's in the middle of this next block."

As they cruised by 4719, Johnny jerked his thumb to the right, being careful to keep his hand low. "That's the place right there," he said.

"The Army-Navy Store? Are you sure?" She seemed perplexed. "It doesn't look very promising."

"That's the beauty of it," Johnny said. "It's an easy score. In and out, real fast. Bingo-bango."

"Look," she said as they approached the light at Broadway and Lawrence Avenue, "here's the Uptown Bank. Wouldn't this be a better situation?"

"Are you kidding? Look around, for Christ's sake—this is one of the busiest intersections on the North Side. And a bank has guards, with guns. Any fucking thing could happen here. Too dangerous, too complicated."

"It was just an idea," she said, feeling defensive. "Where to now?"

"Let's get a drink. I got something I want to ask you."

"Is there a decent place around here—some place where I don't have to parallel park this barge?"

"There's the Green Mill right here on the left," he said.

"But what say we put on the dog. How about one of the bars at the Edgewater Beach? They got a garage there."

With its lakefront location on the North Side, the Edgewater Beach Hotel had been one of the city's prime venues for charity galas, debutante balls, and society weddings through the 1920s. Even now, after fifteen years of hard economic times, the hotel ranked high on the list of majestic destinations for visiting dignitaries and movie stars in Chicago. The property was showing early signs of age and deferred maintenance, but the decline, noticeable only to the most discriminating, was sure to be reversed once the war was over. It was a dearly loved institution— by swells and celebrities alike

The lounge on the lake side of the hotel was still a sanctuary of refined tranquility, decorated in creamy whites and brightened at this hour of the day by daylight filtering in through the massive French doors and small-pane windows that looked out on the marble veranda or "Beach Walk," as it was called. Potted ferns, small palms, and fig trees accented the décor.

Johnny wanted to sit at the bar, but Margaret held out for a table in the deserted lounge. She selected a table surrounded by three low armchairs and a loveseat, sidling onto the loveseat and placing her handbag on the table in front of her. When Johnny started to ease himself into the armchair on the other side of the table, she patted the cushion next to her on the loveseat. "Over here," she said. "I won't bite."

When the bartender came to the table, Johnny ordered his usual Canadian and water.

Margaret was about to follow suit, but hesitated. "Bring me a Manhattan," she said. "Straight up."

Johnny squirmed in the loveseat. "The guy you mentioned in the Empire Room," he said, looking at the floor, "the one you're going to marry—is he OK with this?" He pointed at her, then at himself. "He's not worried about you running around with a two-bit gambler?"

"I don't tell him everything," she said. "We're not married yet. Even if we were, I'd still get to pick my own friends. And I wish you'd stop making disparaging comments about yourself. What are you trying to do—convince me to stop being your friend?"

As the drinks arrived at the table, she reached for her handbag and extracted the sterling cigarette case. Johnny fished a Zippo lighter out of his jacket pocket and held it under the end of her cigarette. She held his wrist, gently, as if to guide the flame to its target. Johnny noticed for the first time that the engagement ring was missing from her left hand.

"When's the wedding," he asked, "you got a date yet?"

"Not until next May," she said, turning her head away to exhale a cloud of smoke. "Is this what you wanted to ask me about, my fiancé?"

"No," he cleared his throat. "I'm just making conversation." He took a long pull from his highball, then held the glass toward Margaret. "Hey, here's looking at you."

They clinked glasses gently, and Margaret took two sips from her Manhattan. "OK," she said, "I'll go first. I'm curious about when you started gambling."

"Ninth grade," he said with a visible sigh, "to my sorrow."

"So this was before you met Joe?"

"Way before," he said, his eyes going blank. "The problem was, I hated school, couldn't see the point. Gambling was a way to kill time and stay out of sight when I was cutting classes. I was a smart-mouth little kid, shooting craps with the coloreds, betting on ball games."

"Skipping school like that, didn't you ever get in trouble?"

"Got caught once," Johnny said. "I gave fifty cents to a news vendor, an old Russian guy with a big beard, to pretend he was my father at the discipline hearing. My old man never did find out. Now, Joe he never did stuff like that—he was a good boy. He learned all the bad stuff from me."

"You're a good teacher," she said, one eyebrow cocked. "Joe must be a very bad boy by now."

They laughed, Margaret enjoying her little witticism, Johnny amused by the thought that Joe could ever be bad.

"OK," she said, "it's your turn. What were you going to ask me?"

"What I wanted to ask you was," he paused and looked away for a moment, "I ... I'm not sure how to say this—I mean, I never said anything like this to a dame before. And if you say no, that's OK. But here it is: When I hit that place on Broadway, would you consider being my driver?"

Holding the Manhattan away from her body to avoid spilling on herself, she leaned against him and put her head on his shoulder. "Jesus, I thought you'd *never* ask," she said. "Of course I'll do it. I can't wait. When is it going to happen?"

"Later this week, or maybe next week. I haven't decided."

"You'll have to tell me exactly what to do."

"Don't worry, we'll go over the whole routine. The only important thing is to have an easy getaway. That way, we're gone before anyone knows what happened. We can go over there right now and I'll show you the route."

"No, not now," she said. "Let's get a room."

Johnny almost jumped out of his skin. "Here? At the hotel?"

"Uh-huh."

They spent the rest of the afternoon on the tenth floor of the Edgewater Beach.

She made him kiss her with his eyes closed.

"In the car," he said, "if you knew my eyes were open, you must have had your eyes open too."

"Somebody has to enforce the rules," she purred.

The second time they made love, she put her hand on his ass and whispered, "Slow down, gambler man."

He did. Slower was better.

When they were spent, lying next to each other, she said: "I went to the library and looked up that baseball guy you mentioned, Jackson. He was a big star. Why *did* he wave to you?"

Johnny turned and propped himself up on one elbow. "I used to light Joe Jackson's cigarettes, for Christ's sake," he said. "I'd read the sports page to him. All the Sox players, they'd hang out in a couple of saloons on the South Side. I'd run errands, do favors—you know, for tips. That's how I got the money for gambling."

Margaret smiled, nodding. "I'm impressed," she said.

They each cleaned up in the bathroom and started to dress, but a glance and a smile passed between them and they returned to the rumpled bed. This time he shifted his body and put his head between her legs—something, until that moment, she'd only heard Gabrielle and other girlfriends talk about.

As for Johnny, he wasn't even sure how to do it. He just knew he wanted to please her. She helped, holding his head, guiding him, and hissing the word "yes" when he was on target.

After a thunderous orgasm, she told Johnny she wanted to return the favor.

He smiled nervously: "I don't think I can, ah, you know... "

"I'll bet you can," she purred, "if you tell me what to do."

And she was right.

18

Margaret heard the faint chiming of ice cubes jostling in a highball glass, a sure sign that her father was home from the office and coming down the hallway outside her room.

She had been lying on the bed, her head propped up by two pillows, reading a Lillian Smith novel, *Strange Fruit*.

"Hello there, kitten," he stopped in her doorway. "I was remiss in not asking you yesterday—did you have a successful shopping foray?"

"It was OK," she said, lowering the book onto her chest. "I didn't see any gowns I really liked."

"Really. Where did you look?"

"Oh, you know, the usual places. Field's here in Evanston, the little bridal shop ... a couple of other places."

Charles Turner took a sip of his scotch. "You didn't take the Packard into the city, did you?"

She shook her head. "I said I wouldn't. Remember?"

"Yes, I remember very well." He took another sip and stood there looking at her. "Your mother says dinner's going to be on in about ten minutes."

19

On Thursday, with mid-summer showers sliding across northern Illinois, Margaret drove the Packard into the city, having deliberately ignored the ritual of asking for her father's permission.

With windshield wipers flapping in frantic cadence, Johnny and Margaret cruised the Army-Navy Store again, this time approaching from the east on Leland and turning onto Broadway less than a hundred yards from the store entrance.

Johnny explained how they could avoid the traffic light at Broadway and Lawrence, thus ensuring a clean getaway, by turning onto Clifton Avenue, a short stub of a street that angled behind the Uptown National Bank building, intersecting Lawrence a half block east of the light.

He said they would be on Lawrence only long enough to travel under the "L" tracks. Once they were on the east side of the tracks, he instructed, they would take a hard right into the alley paralleling the tracks, following the alley all the way back to Leland. They'd turn left on Leland— traveling slow and easy to avoid drawing attention—and go east to Sheridan Road, where they'd take another left.

Johnny would leave the car at the first stoplight on Sheridan. Margaret would continue north to Evanston.

They drove the route once, then again. After the third repetition, Johnny said he'd decided to pull the heist at about 2 o'clock Tuesday afternoon. "Are you in?"

She nodded.

"OK, pick me up at Kenmore and Wilson," he said. "Northeast corner. About one?"

Again she nodded.

"That covers it then," he said. "Bingo-bango!" He asked if she'd like to get out of the rain, go someplace nice for a late lunch.

"Too excited," she said. "I think I must be running on adrenalin right now. Come to think of it, maybe you could help me burn off a little of this excess energy. We could go someplace like ... oh, let me think. The Edgewater Beach?"

"Oh, baby," Johnny laughed. "You know me—I'm just a boy who can't say no."

"Is that the way it is with all the girls?" She was being playful.

"Only you. Have I mentioned that I'm nuts about you?"

"I like you, too, Johnny."

"So what do you like best about me," he asked, grinning, "my good looks or my riches."

"You already know what I like," she said, glancing toward him and cocking her left eyebrow. Her mind was reeling from all the talk about the holdup, but she was still cool enough to be calculating a special plan—one that was already making her pants wet.

As soon as the door closed behind them in the tenth-floor room at the Edgewater Beach, they kissed and began undressing each other. They were naked, standing, when Margaret pulled away from Johnny's embrace and went to her purse, which had been flung onto the bed as they entered the room.

"I'd been saving these for next Tuesday," she said,

reaching into the purse, "but I want you to have them now."

She handed Johnny a pair of gray silk gloves. He looked up at Margaret, unsure what to say.

"Don't ask," she said. "Just put them on—now. And then come around behind me and touch me all over—but especially here," she brushed her hand over her breasts, "and down here."

She knew Johnny would go along with it. And she knew it would be almost unbearably exciting.

Afterwards, they lay next to each other, limp with pleasurable exhaustion, on the bed.

"Hey." She turned and propped herself up on one elbow. "Do you ... I mean, do men like to do it—how can I say this? Do most men want to put it in ... you know, the behind?"

"Huh?" He looked surprised. "Are you talking about taking it in the keister?"

She giggled. "I never heard it put that way, but yes."

"If that's what you want," he said, "I'll do my best. Anything for you, Baby. But I got to be honest here—the idea kind of gives me the heebie-jeebies."

"You don't like to do that?"

"No."

"Good, I'm glad."

He frowned. "So why did you ask about it?"

"Oh, just curious. This is all pretty new to me."

It was close to 9 o'clock when Joe came to the Chelsea and knocked on the door of Johnny's room. He leaned in close to the door. "Johnny, it's me, Joe."

Seconds later, the door opened "Joe, come on in. What's up?"

Joe walked in, spun his hat onto the Murphy bed, and sat down in the one overstuffed chair in the apartment. "I really didn't think I'd find you here at this hour," Joe said, "but I thought I'd give it a shot. Hell, I haven't seen you since Saturday, my friend."

"It's been a crazy week, Joe, a crazy week."

"You have my undivided attention. But why don't you tell me all about it over at the Green Mill? You need to hear the singer over there. Italian guy. Absolutely sensational."

The Green Mill, once a favored Capone jazz hangout, was a long, narrow club with a bar running down one side of the room, booths down the other, and a few tables near the bandstand in the open area beyond the turn in the bar. Except for the long mirror behind the bar, the walls were decorated with bucolic murals—the primary color being green.

After the first set ended at 10:30, Joe leaned across the small table. "OK, what's been going on? I know you haven't spent all week in your apartment."

"Joe, I never thought I'd hear myself say these words— never in a million years. But ... hey, you're right, by the way. This guy, the singer, he's terrific. But why isn't he in the Army?"

"He's 4-F," Joe said, "but it's not legit. Accardo arranged it. Long story."

Johnny glanced over his shoulder, as if someone might be eavesdropping, then looked wide-eyed at Joe. "What I was about to say was, I'm having a—what's the word?—a romance. Me, a romance. Can you believe it?"

"Of course I can. Are you saying you're in love?"

"I must be, Joe. I never felt like this before—and don't roll your eyes at me. I really mean it this time. I can't get her out of my mind, Joe. I can't wait to see her. When she's not around, I don't feel right. When she's with me, I feel like a million bucks."

"It does sound like a bad case of love, my friend. So why aren't you with her right now, tonight?"

"It doesn't work," Johnny said. "She can't see me at night. We're doing the matinee cha-cha. Weekdays only."

"Matinees, eh? I guess this means she hasn't invited you to dinner with Mom and Dad."

"Enough with the sarcasm, Joe. It could happen. Someday."

"Yeah, anything is possible. But don't hold your breath. Not that I wish you any bad luck. I think it's great you feel this way. But I worry, as you already know."

"Joe, don't worry about me."

"Hey, somebody has to," Joe said. "Your mom's gone, so whether you like it or not, I'm your substitute worrier." Joe fished the olive out of the bottom of the martini glass in front of him and placed it in his mouth, chewing deliberately. "Besides the things I normally worry about, what else is going on—anything interesting?"

Johnny looked away. "Nope. Just the romance."

20

*J*ohnny had just finished shaving when someone rapped on his apartment door. Rubbing his face with a towel, he walked to the door, glancing first at the clock on the nightstand. A couple of minutes past 9:30 in the morning.

"Joe, is that you?" he said through the closed door.

"Sharansky?" The muffled voice on the other side of the door wasn't familiar to him.

"Who wants to see him?"

"There's someone downstairs wants to talk to Sharansky."

"He's busy."

"I think you'd better come downstairs. Now."

The implied threat brought Johnny up short. He tried to remember if there were any bookies he might have stiffed during his losing streak, any shady characters he might have hit for a loan when his judgment was clouded by too much Canadian Club. "I'll be down in a minute," he said.

"I'll wait here."

The voice on the other side of the door belonged to a long drink of water—at least a head taller than Johnny—

wearing a cheap-looking brown sports jacket, a plaid shirt, dress slacks that probably hadn't been pressed since the day they were purchased, and thick-soled brown shoes. Johnny made the guy out to be an off-duty cop or a private dick. They rode down in the elevator without speaking a word. On the ground floor, the tall guy motioned Johnny toward the entrance to the Chelsea Grill.

An immaculately dressed man, seated with his legs crossed at a small table near the lobby entrance, looked up and smiled. "Ah, Mr. Sharansky, I presume. Do sit down and join me."

"If it's all right with you, I'll stand."

The tall man, looming behind Johnny, clamped his hand on Johnny's right shoulder. "Be polite and do like the gentleman says—sit."

"OK, OK, I can take a hint." His heart rate beginning to accelerate, Johnny slid into the seat across the table from his early-morning caller. Johnny figured the dark pinstripe suit had to be custom tailored; threads like that didn't come off a rack, even at Rothschild's or Capper & Capper. And the black wing-tips looked as though they'd just been polished.

The caller lifted a spoon and stirred his tea. "Would you care for anything, Mr. Sharansky—some coffee, if they have it, or a cup of tea?"

"No, thanks. But since you already know who I am, I'd kind of like to know who the hell you are."

"You're right, I should have introduced myself. My name is Charles Turner, and of course you've already made the acquaintance of my associate here, Mr. Shockey. Mr. Shockey is a private investigator who does a good deal of work for my law firm. I believe you've also made the acquaintance of my daughter, Margaret. Would I be correct about that?"

"Yeah. So what's up?" Johnny fidgeted in his chair. This was not the way he had imagined meeting Margaret's father.

"We'll come to the purpose of my visit in a minute. But first, I must say you are not an easy man to find, Mr. Sharansky."

"I prefer it that way—an old habit," Johnny said. He glanced up at Shockey, still standing about four feet from the table, hands gripping each other at crotch level.

"If you didn't want to be found," Charles Turner said, again stirring his tea, "perhaps you should have been a little more circumspect when you signed in at the Edgewater Beach Hotel yesterday, especially considering the thoroughly reprehensible purpose of your visit there."

Johnny could feel the hot flush in his cheeks.

"And another thing," Charles Turner continued. "Your name—I don't believe I've ever encountered that name before. What kind of name is it? Where does it come from?"

Johnny said his father had come from Russia. "What does that have to do with anything?"

"So you're a Jew."

Johnny wrinkled his nose and shook his head. He said he really wasn't religious at all, hadn't set foot in a temple or a church of any kind since he was twelve or thirteen.

"No," Charles Turner corrected, "I mean you're of the Jewish race. Whether or not you go to a synagogue is of no concern to me. What does concern me, as I'm sure you are already beginning to suspect, is your relationship with my daughter. Simply put, Mr. Sharansky, I want it to end."

"What?" Johnny felt a rush. "Jesus, why come to me? Why don't you talk to her? Or has she already told you to go to hell? She likes me, you know—likes spending time with me."

"Margaret will come to her senses eventually, I can promise you that, Mr. Sharansky. Especially when she learns about your background. But she is a willful young woman, as I'm sure you've noticed. If I approached her now, it would just cause strife in the family. And it might jeopardize her engagement to a very fine young man.

Better to handle things quietly, outside the family circle, if you know what I mean."

"This is crazy," Johnny said, eyes now blazing. "You can't tell me what to do—or what not to do. Or maybe you should give me your address so I can come over sometime and tell you how to run *your* fucking life, eh? For your information, I'm crazy about your daughter. And I'm not going stop seeing her just because you tell me to."

Charles Turner's doughy face hardened. "I wouldn't be too sure about that if I were you, Mr. Sharansky. I can be very persuasive. If you cannot be persuaded, of course, it would be relatively easy for me to create problems for someone like you. Serious problems. But I prefer not to use my lawyerly skills in that way."

"Hey," Johnny said, veins beginning to bulge on his neck and face, "don't do me any favors, OK?"

Charles Turner raised a cautionary hand. "Please, let me finish. I'm a reasonable man, Mr. Sharansky. I want you to consider what I've asked you to do. Keep in mind that I have the means to make it worth your while. Or to put it a little more crudely, I can pay you a substantial sum of money to go away. Without getting into details, that's the outline of my offer. I suggest that you think it over."

Johnny moved his hand to his crotch. "And you can think about this," he snarled. The quick move caused Shockey to unclasp his hands and take a step closer to the table.

Charles Turner glanced at Shockey and gestured emphatically, the way one might signal a dog to sit or lie down. He placed a dollar bill on the table and stood. "Your coarseness is quite repellant, Mr. Sharansky. For the life of me, I can't imagine what my daughter sees in you. Mr. Shockey and I will be in touch again soon—after you've had a chance to think about what I propose to do for you. Then we can talk hard numbers. Good day to you, sir."

"Yeah, see you around." Johnny was breathing hard.

His face felt flushed. He had an urge to yell something—what was the word?—ah, yes, something coarse, but before he could frame the thought, Turner and his hired dolt had exited onto Wilson Avenue.

"Yeah, go fuck yourself," he said under his breath.

He bolted out of the restaurant through the lobby entrance and went back to his room. As his heartbeat returned to normal, the unpleasant conversation in the Chelsea Grill began to play back in his memory. The implications hit him like a hod full of bricks. M. Charles Turner knew everything that was going on. He and his gumshoe had messed up everything. Because of them, Johnny would have to rethink the bogus holdup. He might even have to tell Margaret the plan was off.

Or would he?

Johnny walked into the cramped tile bathroom, rested both hands on the edges of the sink and leaned forward to look at himself in the medicine cabinet mirror.

"Who does he think he's dealing with?" he said to his own reflection. "I'm not his goddamned flunky."

This was one of those times when he really needed to talk to Joe. He knew damn well he was running hot, needle way up in the red. But he couldn't tell Joe—too complicated, too much to explain, too much to fuel Joe's worry machine.

21

She wheeled the big convertible off Wilson and onto Kenmore Avenue, rolling to a stop just past the corner. Johnny, wearing his gray suit and brandishing a screwdriver, opened the door and entered the front seat.

"What's that for?" she said. "Did you decide to screw them out of money?"

"Funny," he said without smiling. He instructed her to go to the next corner, double back to Wilson Avenue, and then drive west, which would take them away from the scene of the intended heist.

"What's going on?" she asked. "This isn't anything like what we went over last week."

"Just a little added precaution," he said. "I want to be sure everything goes like we planned."

They spent the next fifteen minutes cruising various North Side alleys and streets, including the narrow curved roadways meandering through Graceland Cemetery. Johnny looked over his shoulder a couple of times, finally directing Margaret to retrace their route back to Wilson and Kenmore, where he pointed her into an alley about a half block north on Kenmore. "Let's put the top down," he said after she had stopped. "It's not going to rain."

While Margaret lowered the convertible top, Johnny went to the front and rear of the Packard and used the screwdriver to remove the car's registration plates. He tossed the plates onto the floor of the rear seat. Still standing in the alley, he pulled a handkerchief out of his inside pocket, folded it into a large triangle and then looped it around his neck, tying a small knot with the corners of the triangle. "OK, let's go," he said. "Remember—it's going to be a can of corn."

She looked at him and frowned.

"Baseball lingo," he snapped. "Forget it. Let's go."

She drove north to Leland, turned left, and approached the light at Leland and Broadway. "Unless somebody comes up behind you, wait here until you see me go inside," he said as he got out of the car. "Then pull around to the front of the store."

"What happens if somebody comes up behind me?"

"Hey, you're the driver. You'll think of something." He walked briskly north on Broadway to the front of the Army-Navy Store. Looking back, he gave a small wave to Margaret, and then entered the store, setting off the tinkling bell that announced all comings and goings.

He had come to the store earlier, a little before noon, to give Marty a brown paper bag containing the cash. "There's six hundred bucks in here," he had said. "Half of it's yours, like we agreed on. The other half is what you give me when I come back. Just leave it in the bag."

Marty was incredulous. "This isn't a bloody bank," he said. "No one's going to believe this place keeps three hundred dollars in the register."

"She'll believe it, trust me," Johnny said. "Besides, it's not going to work if I waltz out of here with twenty-five or thirty bucks. It has to look like a big score."

"I knew I shouldn't have let you talk me into this," Marty said.

Now, two hours later, Johnny looked toward the rear of the store and saw Marty standing near the cash register. The brown bag was on the counter next to the register. Marty formed a circle with his right thumb and index finger, giving Johnny a silent OK sign. He waved his arm to indicate there was no one else in the store.

Johnny strode to the counter, pulling the handkerchief up to cover the lower half of his face. He reached inside his suit jacket with his right hand and extracted the .45 automatic.

"Holy mother," Marty exclaimed, "where'd you get that thing?"

"It's a loaner," Johnny said looking at the piece in his hand. "Borrowed it from a guy with connections, a guy I know on the South Side."

"You never said anything about a gun."

"Hey, it's a fucking holdup," Johnny snapped, "remember?"

"Not any more, it isn't," Marty said, grabbing the bag and putting it under the counter. "I'm out, and this is over. You can come back and get the cash later."

"We made an agreement, Marty."

"The agreement's off," Marty said.

"No, it isn't." Johnny raised the .45 and pointed at Marty's chest. "Now give me that goddamned bag."

Without taking his eyes off the muzzle of the automatic, Marty bent at the knees, lowering himself slowly until he could reach out and grasp the bag. Still moving slowly, he straightened up and held out the bag.

Johnny snatched it with his left hand and began backing toward the door, still pointing the pistol at Marty.

"You're a crazy bastard—you know that?" Marty yelled. "Totally nuts. You're going to get us all killed."

"Shut up," Johnny yelled back. "Nobody's going to get hurt. This thing isn't even loaded."

Marty's shoulders slumped, as his head tipped forward.

He muttered under his breath.

Johnny laughed. Reaching the door, he confirmed that the Packard was parked at the curb out front. He looked to the right and left, then yanked open the door, again setting off the bell, and walked into the daylight, the handkerchief still covering half his face, the .45 still in his right hand.

Approaching the car, he heard the electric starter begin to crank.

Just as his hand touched the handle on the passenger side door, he heard a man's voice. "Stop, stop right where you are!"

He looked in the direction of the sound and saw an overweight Chicago patrolman lumbering toward the car from the other side of Broadway, struggling to unholster his sidearm as he ran. The cop was still about sixty yards away, but the distance was closing quickly.

He opened the door, tossing the paper bag onto the floor of the rear seat with the license plates. "Go," he yelled, yanking the handkerchief down and jumping into the seat next to Margaret. "We got to get out of here."

After one more laborious crank of the starter motor, the Packard's 282-cubic-inch straight eight roared to life. Margaret shifted into first gear and popped the clutch. The car lurched away from the curb.

"Police ... stop, stop or I'll shoot."

There was a gunshot. Then another.

"Jesus fucking Christ," Margaret screamed, "don't just sit there. Shoot!"

"I can't," Johnny yelled back, "no bullets."

"It's not loaded?" She was incredulous, shrieking. "Are you some kind of idiot?" She angrily jammed the shift level into second gear, steering to the right to put the car on Clifton Avenue, on the backside of the Uptown National Bank building.

There was a third shot. And a fourth.

Margaret cried out. A bullet hole surrounded by a nimbus of crazed glass appeared in the lower left corner of the windshield, just above the dashboard, on the driver's side. Johnny was startled to see blood on the windshield and dashboard—a few flecks on his suit pants and left sleeve, too. He leaned forward to get a better look at Margaret and saw the bloody mess near her left shoulder.

She kept on shrieking, "I've been shot, god damn it!" She kept screaming and cursing, trying to use her right hand to haul the steering wheel to the right at Clifton and Lawrence. They weren't going to make it—Johnny could see they were headed directly toward the row of concrete and steel stanchions down the center of the underpass.

He quickly shifted the .45 to his left hand and reached across the front seat with his right hand, grabbing the top of the steering wheel and pulling hard, increasing the angle of the Packard's turn. Seconds later they were around the corner, rolling past the stanchions under the "L" tracks— at least momentarily out of the line of fire.

Margaret turned the nose of the Packard into the alley on the east side of the tracks and slammed on the brakes with the car blocking the sidewalk.

Johnny glanced back toward the underpass. "Why are you stopping?"

"Out," she screamed. "Out, out, out!" Her face was red. He could see the veins in her neck and forehead. The left sleeve of her blouse was red with blood.

"This wasn't part of the ..."

"I said out! Get the fuck out of my car, you idiot. Now!"

He opened the door and stepped onto the pavement, still holding the pistol in his left hand. The rear wheels chirped as Margaret gunned the big Packard down the narrow alley toward Leland.

Johnny watched the car bounce down the potholed alley.

"Hey, stop right there, asshole." The voice was faint.

Johnny looked to his right and saw the cop—or was it a different cop?—approaching the other side of the underpass, pointing a revolver in his direction.

His thoughts still spinning crazily, Johnny wheeled and sprinted across Lawrence, heedless of traffic, and ran north into the alley between the "L" tracks and the Aragon Theater. About halfway up the alley, he ducked into a narrow gangway. He kept running until he broke into the open at Winthrop Avenue, then slowed to a walk until he had crossed Winthrop and entered another gangway, this one between an apartment building and a three-flat.

When he reached the next alley, he stopped and untied the handkerchief from around his neck. He used it to wipe the .45 clean, then wrapped it around the pistol. After looking both directions to be sure there was no one else in the alley, he stooped down and nestled the bundle into a small stand of weeds and prairie grass behind a lineup of battered trash cans, noting the numbers 4813 crudely painted on one of the metal containers.

He stood and looked around again—no one in sight.

Now starting to calculate what to do about the blood spatters on his suit, he walked east between two apartment buildings that fronted on Kenmore Avenue, but stopped at the opening of the gangway and stepped back between the buildings to let a southbound car creep by on Kenmore.

When the slow-moving Plymouth sedan was directly in front of the gangway, Johnny could see the driver through the open window on the passenger side. It was Shockey. Their eyes met, and the Plymouth dove to a stop.

"Jesus fuck." Johnny wheeled and ran back to the alley. He sprinted north into the next block before turning east, checking first to see if Shockey was anywhere in sight. As he crossed Kenmore , he thought he could hear the whine of an automobile engine coming from the alley he'd just vacated.

Panting and sweating, he worked his way south and east, warily searching for any glimpse of the gray Plymouth. He stuck mainly to alleys and gangways, once entering the rear door of a drug store and walking through the store to reach Sheridan Road.

Eventually he reached the end of an alley next to the Windsor-Wilson Hotel, directly across the avenue from the Chelsea. He entered the Windsor-Wilson through an alley door and walked to the front of the building. After snatching a two-day-old copy of the Tribune off a table in the tiny lobby, he took a seat in an armchair near one of the front windows, where he could watch the entrance to the Chelsea.

After an hour, he shuffled through the newspaper in his lap, pulled out the classifieds, and began reading. He took the section with him to a pay phone in a hall leading back to the service entrance, made a call, then returned to the armchair.

At nightfall, he crossed the street to the Chelsea and went to his room. He undressed, putting his clothes in a pile on the bed. After taking a five-minute shower, he changed into the blue suit, the one Margaret had liked, selecting a white dress shirt and a red and blue striped tie. He gathered up the clothes from the bed, walked down to the end of the fourth-floor hallway, and stuffed the bundle into the trash chute.

Returning to his room, he yanked a large suitcase from the closet behind the Murphy bed. With the case lying open on the bed, he packed all of the remaining shoes and clothing in the room, then closed the case and moved it to the floor. After gathering up the cash hidden in the hatbox in the closet, he took time to arrange the bills—low denominations on top, big bills on the bottom, all bills facing the same direction—then folded the stack once and slid it into the left front pocket of his trousers.

Hefting the suitcase, he walked to the rear stairway and descended to the first floor, leaving through an alley door on the rear of the building.

An hour later he rang the buzzer on the resident-manager's apartment at the Beyla Hotel, one block from the Howard Street "L" station on the city's far North Side.

"I'm John Turner, the guy who called about the vacancy," he said. He paid the manager a month's rent, $42.50, in cash, and moved into a third-floor room overlooking Paulina Street.

He was on the lam.

22

Chicago Tribune, Wednesday, July 26, 1944

Man Dies, Socialite Wounded In Kidnapping and Robber

By Wendell Darby

A Chicago man was killed and the daughter of a prominent attorney was wounded as police and an armed bandit exchanged fire following a kidnapping and holdup Tuesday afternoon on the city's North Side.

Police identified the dead man as Stanley R. Brzeczek, 56, of 4526 N. Hoyne ave., who was not involved in the holdup. Brzeczek, a custodian in the Uptown National Bank building at N. Broadway st. and W. Lawrence ave., was killed by a single shot to the neck when he apparently came out a rear entrance of the building where he worked after hearing gunfire, police said.

The wounded woman, Margaret Turner, 26, of Evanston, was hit in the left shoulder as she was forced to drive a getaway car from the scene of a holdup at Martin's army-navy store, 4719 N. Broadway, according to police reports. She later showed up at Evanston hospital, where she was still being treated at press time.

According to official reports and witnesses at the scene, shooting broke out after a foot patrolman spotted a holdup man brandishing a pistol and carrying a paper bag that was believed to contain cash taken from the army-navy store. The patrolman, Richard Sullivan, 52, assigned to the 23rd district, opened fire with his service revolver after the bandit ignored orders to halt and began firing his weapon from the getaway car driven by Miss Turner, police said.

Miss Turner's father, Loop tax attorney M. Charles Turner, said his daughter had driven one of the family's cars into the city to shop for her wedding trousseau. He said she was kidnapped and forced at gunpoint to participate in the robbery, escaping only when the gunman stepped out of the automobile for a moment near the intersection of Lawrence and Winthrop aves. a few minutes after the robbery.

"She reacted with great bravery when she saw her chance to get away," Mr. Turner said. "She knew her life was in grave danger."

Turner, whose LaSalle st. law partnership includes alderman Colin R. Moran (D-11), added that his daughter was planning to give full cooperation to police investigators once she was sufficiently recovered from her wound.

The office of Mayor Edward J. Kelly issued a statement describing the deadly shootout as an "unacceptable reminder of the lawlessness that plagued Chicago in the days of Prohibition."

The mayor said he had asked police superintendent Thomas M. Cavanaugh to launch a citywide search, stressing the "importance of identifying, arresting and prosecuting the person or persons responsible for this brazen crime."

Police investigators said they had not determined whether Brzeczek and Miss Turner were hit by shots fired by Officer Sullivan or the bandit. They were hoping to recover the weapon used in the holdup to make a positive determination.

Martin O'Hallahan, 49, proprietor of the store that was robbed, told police the gunman, who wore a bandana to conceal his face, entered the store shortly after 2 p.m. Tuesday and demanded all the money in the cash register. O'Hallahan said he placed the cash, which he estimated at less than $40, in a paper bag and handed it to the bandit, who then exited.

Police said neither the bag nor the stolen cash had been recovered.

According to police, O'Hallahan described the bandit as about 5 feet 10 inches tall with blue eyes and brown hair, wearing a gray suit.

A spokesman for Evanston hospital said Miss Turner was in stable condition late Monday and was expected to remain in the hospital for at least 24 hours.

Bill McCulloch

23

Margaret Turner, her left shoulder heavily bandaged, her left arm in a sling, opened her eyes, her gaze meeting her father's as he sat in a chair pulled close to the hospital bed.

As usual, Charles Turner's face betrayed no emotion. "Feeling better?" he asked.

She nodded. "A little."

"Good—because we need to talk. You did the right thing yesterday—calling me from the emergency room. That was good, very good. Now we need to plan for what's next. But first, some rules."

Margaret, slightly groggy with sedatives, frowned. "Rules? What kind of rules?"

"Just a few guidelines to help us get through the days ahead as smoothly as possible," he said, brushing a lint speck off his trouser leg. "This is a huge mess you've created, my dear. I daresay it is going to require all of your father's skills and connections to make this nasty bit of business disappear. But I believe it can be done—if, as I say, we follow a few simple guidelines."

Charles Turner stood and walked to the window.

"I'm sorry, daddy, I really am—especially about the car.

143

I know I shouldn't ..."

"You should be sorry," he said without turning away from the window. "But you're a lucky young lady. You could be sitting in a holding cell right now. You could even have been killed—like that poor fellow on the sidewalk."

"Oh, my God!"

"Sorry, I thought maybe you knew. Just some janitor—a foreigner, I believe."

He turned and came back to sit in the chair. She began to speak, but he quickly held up his right hand in a wordless stop sign. "Before you say another word," he said, "let me state rule number one: I do not want to know your version of what happened yesterday. It just muddies the legal waters. We have a story that will keep you in the clear, and we're going to stick to it."

Charles Turner crossed his legs at the knee and tipped his head back until he was looking at the ceiling over her head. "Rule number two: You are not to say anything to the police or the newspapers, ever. If the police want to question you, I will be present and I will do the talking. I've already given a statement to the *Tribune*. If they call again, refer them to me."

Now he leaned forward and looked her in the eyes. "Rule number three: You are never again to spend so much as a single second with your little partner in crime, although I can't imagine you'd have any interest in seeing him—not after what's happened."

"I'm not a little girl anymore," she said, abruptly shaking off her grogginess, "I think I can pick my own company, thank you."

"Not any more, my dear. You may be fully grown, but you have demonstrated what we lawyers call diminished capacity when it comes to picking your companions. Until you come to your senses, you are grounded. Confined to the house, period. You can see your true love Brantley as often as you like at home. I'm sure he'll be quite solicitous in view of the terrible trauma you've been through.

"You may accompany me to church on Sundays, if you like. But the rest of the time, you will stay out of sight and, need I say, out of trouble."

She took a deep breath, wiping the back of her hand under one eye to catch a welling tear and looking away from her father. "I know I did a very stupid thing," she said. "And I ... I can only imagine what you must be thinking, but you have to try to understand—it never occurred to me things would turn out the way they did. I never imagined anyone ..."

"Stop it," he snapped. "I told you I do not want to know your version of what happened. That includes any facts or assumptions, and especially any remorse you may now feel. Just keep all of that to yourself."

There was a long silence. He stared at her. She continued to look away. "He's really not a bad person," she sniffled. "His name is Johnny, and he's just a guy I met at the Empire Room when Brantley and I went to see ..."

"Have you not listened to a word I've said?" He was visibly cross now. "These are things I do not want to hear—no lawyer does. Please understand: I have created a defense that will keep you out of trouble. For that, I expect your compliance. Even your gratitude, if that's not asking too much."

She looked down at the back of her right hand, which was resting on the sheet covering her lap. "If it makes you feel any better," she said without expression, "he and I were just casual friends."

Charles Turner sighed softly. "Don't ever try to play games with your father, dear. Next you'll be wanting me to believe that you and this *casual friend* of yours spent last Thursday afternoon playing canasta at the Edgewater Beach."

Margaret's eyes flashed. "You bastard." She blinked away another tear.

"I think I've made myself clear," he said. "Once you've had a little time to reflect, you'll agree the sooner you put this chapter behind you, the better." Charles Turner's brow knit as a thought flashed into his mind. "Of course, even though you won't be trying to contact your casual friend, he might try to contact you, in which case you are to be nice, find out where he is, and call me at once."

"He wasn't arrested?"

"Not according to the papers."

"Do the police know who he is?"

"They do not," he said with a discernable note of satisfaction, "although they are trying to find out. They may or may not succeed, but it doesn't matter. For the time being, I think it's best we let his identity be our little secret. Yours and mine."

"Then you know who he is?"

Ignoring the question, Charles Turner uncrossed his legs, and stood. "I've got some out-of-town business," he said. "St. Louis again. Bad timing, but I'll be back in two days, or maybe three. Just remember, talk to no one, absolutely no one, while I'm gone. I'm leaving a copy of this morning's *Trib* on the nightstand, and I suggest you read the story carefully before they send you home. As far as your mother is concerned, that's the way it happened, and we are not going to disabuse her of that notion. There's no need to upset her. The same goes for Brantley. I think you'll agree that he should be spared the lurid details of your, ah, casual friendship."

He walked to the door of the private room, turning back to his daughter before opening the door. "Incidentally," he said with just a trace of a smirk, "unless I miss my guess, the police are the last of that little sheeny's worries."

Margaret looked up: "Johnny's a Jew?"

24

Benny Wojnarowski was freeing up the tumblers in a balky combination lock, selecting tools from an oilskin case that lay unrolled on the counter in front of him, when the door of West Side Locksmith & Safe opened and two men entered from Roosevelt Road. He recognized both of them. "Mike, Tony," he said, feeling the beginnings of edginess, "haven't seen you guys in a long time."

"Yeah, long time," said Mike Greenberg. "How've you been, Benny?" Greenberg, just under six feet tall, wiry build, and even more homely than the last time Benny had seen him, was a cleaner and general troubleshooter for the outfit. Greenberg's short, squat companion, Tony "Home Run" Capezio, was a driver and collector, known for his use of a baseball bat on collection calls and other enforcement errands.

"Everything's good," Benny said. "Kind of early for you guys to be out, isn't it? What you got there?" He pointed toward what looked like a shoebox tucked under Greenberg's arm.

Greenberg placed the box on the counter, carefully moving the oilskin case to clear a space. "It's a little puzzle we're trying to solve," he said. "We figured if anybody can help us, you're the guy."

"Yeah, you're the guy," Capezio said.

Greenberg used both hands to lift the top of the box. "Ever seen this before?"

Benny was almost positive he was looking down at his own pistol, but he couldn't imagine how or why it had fallen into the hands of these two hoods, or why they were now in his shop asking him about it. He wondered if something had happened to Johnny, or if Johnny had done something to get both of them in trouble.

"Forty-five A-C-P," Benny said leaning down to look in the box. "I've seen a few of 'em. What's the deal?"

"We don't care how many you've seen," Greenberg said. "We just want to know if you've seen this one."

Even though Benny was already on guard, the coldness of Greenberg's response startled him.

"Do you mind if I take it out of the box?" Benny said.

"Go ahead," Greenberg said.

"Please, be our guest," Capezio chimed in with chilly courtliness.

Benny lifted the pistol and turned it over in his hands. The little nicks on the grip eliminated all doubt; it was definitely his pistol. He released the magazine from the grip; it was empty. He pulled back on the mechanism and closely inspected the chamber, then raised the pistol to his face and sniffed. "Model nineteen-eleven," he said. "Probably issued before the big war. I used to have one like this. It was, eh ... it was stolen."

"Recently?"

"A long time ago," Benny said, fully aware this small lie was only going to make things worse if Mike and Tony already knew it was his pistol and were just playing a sadistic game, a possibility that couldn't be ruled out. "It was that time when somebody broke into my house. You heard about that, right?"

"No, we didn't hear about that," Greenberg said. "So is

this it? Is this the, eh, stolen piece?"

"Jeez, Mike, there's a lot of these in circulation," Benny whined. "They all look pretty much alike."

"Cut the crap, Benny," Mike snapped. "If it was your piece, you'd know it. The fucking serial number hasn't even been messed with. What do you think, we're stupid or something?"

"No, no—nothing like that," Benny said. "I'm just saying my memory ain't what it used to be. But now that I get a close look, I can tell it isn't mine. I never saw this particular forty-five auto before. But I don't get it, what's the big deal with this one?"

"Somebody ditched it up on the North Side," Greenberg said. "A couple of kids found it, tried to pawn it. We think the piece might have been used in a heist that's causing a little uproar."

"Holy shit." Benny reacted as though the automatic had developed a fever, quickly sliding it back into the shoe box. "You mean this forty-five was part of that shoot-'em-up on North Broadway?"

"It's possible," Greenberg said.

"Very possible," Capezio echoed.

Benny felt a wave of cautious relief. "I got some news for you," Benny said. "This couldn't be the piece from that holdup."

"How come?" Capezio said.

"It hasn't even been fired."

"You sure about that?" Greenberg pressed.

"Check it out yourself," Benny said. "It's clean as a virgin's pussy. Hasn't been fired in weeks, maybe months. I'd swear to it in a court of law. Somebody sent you guys on one of those goose chases."

Greenberg and Capezio exchanged a glance.

"You're the expert," Greenberg said with noticeable insincerity. He slipped the lid onto the box, and cradled the box in his left forearm. "But you won't mind if we get a second opinion, right?"

"Hell, no," Benny said. "Anybody with an educated nose will tell the same thing. You'll see."

"One other thing," Greenberg said. "The initials J-A-S; they ring any bells with you?"

Benny looked off to one side, repeating the letters aloud twice. He shook his head. "Boy, you guys really do have a puzzle," he said. "Where'd you get the initials?"

"Handkerchief," Greenberg said. "Probably not important." He turned and walked slowly toward the door to the street.

Capezio lingered at the counter. "If there's anything you think we ought to know, anything at all, now's the time," he said.

"Wish I could help," Benny said, trying to look earnest. "If I hear anything, believe me, you guys'll be the first to know."

Capezio studied Benny's face. "That thing you said about your memory," he said, "how it's not so good anymore. That's a real shame." A subtle smile animated his chubby face, then flickered out. He wheeled and joined Greenberg near the door.

"See you around," Greenberg said.

25

Mike Greenberg, carrying the shoe box, and Tony Capezio exited Martin's Army-Navy Store on North Broadway and walked to the black Buick four-door parked at the curb, Capezio circling around to enter from the driver's side.

"Somebody's fucking with us," Greenberg said once they were inside.

"Most definitely," Capezio agreed.

"Right up there," Greenberg said, pointing in the direction of the Uptown Bank building, "some poor *shmuck* got shot dead. The lady in the car took a slug in the shoulder. The cops said there was so much shooting it's a miracle nobody else got hurt. But the gun we got hasn't been fired since Christ wore sandals—we got the polak and one other guy who swear to that. On the other hand, this paddy says the gun looks a lot like the one that was pointed at him. And the gun was ditched just three, four blocks from here. So nothing adds up. Yet. All we know is the paddy lied to the cops about how much money got taken. So he probably lied to us, too."

Greenberg made an unpleasant face. "Jesus, Tony, did you just fart?"

"Can't help it," Capezio said.

"A little consideration would be—eh, fuck it. Let's go back in and find out what kind of business this mick's running here."

"Yeah, maybe he's running a bank," Capezio said.

"Or he's got his own little numbers operation," Greenberg said, turning to look at the front of the store, "in which case he needs a reminder of how things work in this town. Let's go."

When Marty O'Hallahan looked up and saw the two hoods reenter the store, he felt a sudden loosening in his bowels. "Hey, now, I don't want any trouble, fellas," he said. "I already told you everything I know."

"Not quite," Greenberg said, walking deliberately to the table where Marty had just begun straightening a pile of pea coats. "You didn't tell us about the money, Marty. We know how much money that guy took out of here. It ain't even close to what you told the cops."

"Look, I can explain that business," Marty stammered. "What I told the police, that was just for the insurance. You know how these things work, right?"

"Tell me something, Tony," Greenberg said without looking at Capezio. "Do I look like a *putz* to you?"

"A what?"

"A dope."

"No, Mike, you don't look like no dope," Capezio said, even though he and Greenberg were looking straight at Marty.

"That's funny, because I must look pretty fucking stupid to our friend here. You better get the bat out of the car."

Marty was almost sure he was going to shit his pants. "Wait, wait, wait—I can help you guys, OK? I don't want any trouble. I can tell you who pulled the stickup. I know the guy."

"Forget it," Greenberg said. "We already know who it

was. We want to know where to find the sonofabitch."

"He lives right here in the neighborhood," Marty blurted. "Over by the lake, the Chelsea, I think."

"Already been there," Greenberg said. "Not there anymore. Where's he holed up?"

"As God is my witness, I don't know," Marty said. Tears were beginning to well in his eyes.

"All right, then tell us about the scratch."

"It wasn't even my money," Marty said. "Honest. He brought it to me, Johnny did. And the gun he had, it wasn't loaded. That's what he said."

Greenberg and Capezio exchanged a glance.

"Let me understand," Greenberg said. "Some amateur points an unloaded piece at your kisser, and you hand over three hundred clams."

"That's what I'm trying to tell you," Marty said, the tears now running down his cheeks and into the stubble on his jaw. "It wasn't a robbery. The whole thing was a put-up job. It was his own money. *All of it.* He was—how to say it—like playacting. It was supposed to impress the lady, the one in the car."

"You're saying the lady was there because she wanted to be there?" Greenberg's tone was incredulous.

"I can't swear to it," Marty said. "I never spoke to the young lady, never even laid eyes on her. But he told me he was nuts about her. He thought it would put him in like Flynn—as God is my witness, those were the very words he used, in like Flynn—if he pulled a stunt like this and she believed it was a real stickup. That's what he said."

Greenberg shook his head. "You realize, of course, if you're jacking us around, you're a dead man. You also need to realize it doesn't really matter anymore. Somebody got killed. A big-shot's daughter got hurt. And you're right in the middle. What about the gun? Did he say anything about the gun?"

"He said it wasn't loaded, that's all," Marty said. "But let me think, there was something else. He said—he said he got it from a guy he knows. Something like that. No, wait, he said he borrowed it from a guy on the South Side. And the guy was connected. That's what he said."

Again, Greenberg and Capezio looked at each other.

"I knew that polak was blowing smoke at us," Greenberg said.

"Me, too," said Capezio. "Tough break."

26

"Joe, I need help—I'm in big trouble."

"No shit," Joe snapped. "I almost croaked when I read the paper."

Johnny, speaking in a ragged whisper, was calling from a wall-mounted pay phone in a drug store on the ground floor of the Beyla Hotel building. For five days he had been living on soft drinks and canned goods—vegetables mostly because he lacked ration stamps for meat—purchased at a sundry shop across Paulina Street from the drug store, never venturing more than half a block from the Beyla.

"The paper's part of the trouble, Joe—they got it all messed up, for Christ's sake. I don't know what to do."

"Where the hell are you? The kid working the desk at your place on Wilson said he heard you scrammed."

"Yeah, I had to move. Did he say anything else?"

"Yeah, he said a couple of palookas were in there asking about you—cops maybe."

"Jesus, I really got to see you."

At Johnny's suggestion, they agreed to meet at Howard Street Beach. Johnny bought a pair of dark glasses before leaving the drug store, and walked toward the lake on a residential street, avoiding the congested business district on Howard Street. In the middle of one block, he left the sidewalk, entering an alley on his right, and darting into a gangway between an apartment building and a yellow brick three-flat. He stopped and peered around the corner of the three-flat, looking back toward the street. After listening to the throb of his pulse pounding in his ears, he returned to the street and continued toward the lake.

As usual on a summer Sunday afternoon, the lakefront was teeming with mothers and children, older couples, teen-agers, a few guys in uniform with their wives or girlfriends. With the sun riding low in the western sky, it was a good time of day to stroll, eat sandwiches, or lie on blankets, napping or necking while a cooling breeze came in off the lake.

He saw Joe, hat in his lap, back to the afternoon sun, already seated on one of the benches.

"I got a bad feeling, Joe," he said as he sat down on Joe's left, tossing his hat onto the bench next to him. "I think the good guys are looking for me."

"I don't want to talk about it," Joe said without looking at Johnny. "I don't want to talk about anything yet."

They sat in silence, watching their own shadows grow longer, stretching onto the beach and then fading out as the sun slipped behind the apartments on the west side of Eastlake Terrace.

"It wasn't a kidnapping," Johnny finally blurted.

Joe, staring at the lake, tipped his head back slightly and rolled his eyes. "Yeah, that part didn't exactly sound like your M-O," he said.

"And it wasn't a real robbery."

"Give me a little credit here—I didn't think you'd be stupid enough to hold up a place owned by someone you knew."

"So you're pissed at me, Joe?"

"I was." Joe took a deep breath and exhaled. "But now I just feel sad."

"Sad—you mean sad about what a stupid fucking thing I did?"

"That's part of it," Joe said. "What's really sad is you kept it secret. That night at the Green Mill, you must have known what you were going to do. Right?"

Johnny nodded.

"But you couldn't tell me—me, the guy who was always like a big brother to you," Joe said. "Then you go and drag Marty O'Hallahan into your *mishegas*—I mean, what'd he ever do to deserve that? And now I'm sad because the cops think you're some kind of desperate criminal, and it's hard to see a way out."

"I know I should have told you, Joe." Johnny leaned forward, resting his elbows on his knees and holding his head with both hands, staring at the ground between his polished wingtips. "I just couldn't. I knew you'd try to talk me out of it, just like you tried to talk me out of packing that goddamned gun. And I ... it was like I didn't want to be talked out of it."

Again they sat in silence, Joe staring out at the lake, Johnny slumped over.

"What makes you think the outfit's on your case?" Joe asked.

"Those two guys who were asking questions at my old place, I don't think they were cops," Johnny said. "It was probably Greenberg and that dago with the baseball bat— the same guys who were down on the South Side talking to Benny."

"Benny who? Not Benny the jazz hound?"

"Yeah, that Benny. I talked to him on the phone the day before yesterday."

"Benny's dead."

"What?" Johnny sat upright and stared at Joe, his eyes wide.

"He's dead," Joe repeated. "They got him yesterday."

"Jesus, how'd you hear?"

"The usual," Joe said. "Some guys were talking about it

at a handbook last night. They said he'd been grabbed off the street on his way to work. But what's Benny got to do with all this?"

"He's the guy that gave me the gun," Johnny stammered.

"I don't get it," Joe said. "How can you be so sure this has something to do with that gun? Maybe it's another beef altogether."

"No, it's the gun. Greenberg had it when he talked to Benny. He was asking questions about it."

"What?" Now it was Joe's turn to be incredulous. "How the hell did the piece get from you to Greenberg?"

"I don't know. I ditched the gun—somebody must've found it."

"But you never fired the piece." Joe gave Johnny a hard look. "Or did you?"

"No, honest. It was never loaded."

Joe rubbed his chin. "It doesn't add up. You're telling me Benny was capped because he gave you a gun. But the gun wasn't used for anything except grandstanding. It's not just the gun—there's something else going on. There has to be."

"It doesn't matter," Johnny said. "What matters is, Benny told me everything's under control, and it's not. If those two mopes were poking around my old place on Wilson, then they knew more than they let on to Benny. That means Benny was fucked the second they walked into his shop and started asking questions. And now I'm fucked. Margaret, too—I've got to get word to her somehow. She's up to her neck, same as me.

"I wouldn't worry about the lady," Joe said. "She's got her big-shot father running interference. She's a kidnap victim, remember? You should be so lucky."

"Jesus, Joe, what about you? Isn't there somebody you can talk to? You got connections. Somebody must owe you a favor."

"Not anymore," Joe said. "Francesco was my only solid

connection. Accardo and the other new guys don't know me from Dizzy Dean. And they sure wouldn't do me any favors. In fact, Greenberg is going to come looking for me pretty soon. He'll figure I know where you are. I don't want to know, so don't tell me."

Joe looked at his watch. "This is making me tired," he said. "I'm going home."

"Before you go, let me ask this one thing," Johnny said. "Let's say I hole up—you know, go on the lam. Nobody sees me for a month or two months or something. Nobody hears my name. Do you think this thing'll blow over?"

"I wish," Joe said, standing up and putting on his hat. "The police might get off your case once they get the facts. But things don't blow over with the outfit. You know that as well as I do. The good guys never forget. Good night, my friend."

27

$\mathcal{A}$t 1 o'clock Monday afternoon Johnny emerged from the Beyla Hotel and entered the drug store on the Paulina Street side of the building, walking back toward the prescription counter. He had already spent several minutes peering out windows in the Beyla's front stairwell, checking to see if any of the parked cars on Jonquil Terrace were occupied.

Now he was moving cautiously across the back of the store, checking each aisle, even though he suspected the exercise was pointless. If Greenberg and the fat dago had gotten onto his trail, they wouldn't be reading copies of *Popular Mechanics* in a drugstore, they'd be up in his room at the Beyla beating the daylights out of him—or worse.

But he'd never been on the lam before. He had no way of knowing what was too cautious and what was too cavalier. Caught between those extremes, he preferred looking foolish to being dead.

His eye fell on the store's display of razors, lathers, and lotions, and his mind flipped back more than twenty years to a neighborhood pharmacy, similar to this one, on the South Side, where he had gone to buy a styptic pencil. He had made a pass at a good-looking young girl who turned out to be with her mother. The mother was easy on the eyes, too, so he had flirted with her, and she had invited him over to their flat. He was a cute kid who wore expensive suits.

"Can I help you find something?"

The pharmacist's question almost caused Johnny to fly out of his own skin.

"Uh, yeah. I'm looking for a phone booth?"

"There's a pay phone on that wall right over there, sir. Don't I remember you making a call there—yesterday maybe?"

"No, wasn't me. Never been in here before. Never even been in this neighborhood. You got a nice phone, but I'm looking for one in a booth. You know—for privacy."

The pharmacist said he thought there might be one near the restrooms in the bar two doors from the drug store in the direction of the "L" station. "Not the little bar right next door," he said. "It's two or three doors after that, the one with a package store on one side."

Johnny stood in the drug store entranceway for a moment. After studying the figures walking on Paulina Street, he pulled his hat down over his face, thrust his hands into his pants pockets, and walked the sixty yards to the combination bar and package store.

Seated in the booth, Johnny closed the bi-fold doors, fed a nickel to the phone, and dialed the Evanston number. He felt his heart began to accelerate. Realizing he didn't have any idea what he was going to say, he quickly returned the receiver to its cradle, and heard the nickel drop into the coin return. He sat there breathing hard, then fished the coin out of the opening at the bottom of the phone and started over again.

Margaret answered the phone. "Turner residence."

"It's me."

"You bastard," she hissed, lowering her voice. "You've got some nerve calling me! You almost got me killed.

162

Jesus, what nerve."

Margaret uttered a stifled snarl that was cut off in mid snarl as she hung up. A moment after the line went dead, Johnny's nickel clanked into the phone's coin box.

He slumped slowly forward, his forehead gently coming to rest against the phone box folding the felt front of his hat brim down to the bridge of his nose. He had a momentary urge to say fuck it and return to his dingy little room at the Beyla, or maybe go up front to the bar and tie one on. Instead, he fished another nickel out of his pocket and redialed.

Again she answered: "Hello."

"Margaret, baby, I really need ..."

"You can't call me here," she blurted. "Understand? If the police find out, they'll know my story isn't true. Where, uh ... never mind. Just stop calling me."

"But how could the cops...?" He was talking to no one. He kept the phone receiver pressed to his ear, listening to the dead line. After a while he returned the receiver to its chrome-plated cradle and just sat there.

"Hey, pal." The muffled voice beyond the closed door of the booth belonged to a beer truck driver with bushy sideburns, matching eyebrows, and an impressive gut. "I got to use the phone. You making a call or taking a dump in there?"

28

*J*oe walked to a shaded spot near the sea lion exhibit in Lincoln Park Zoo and dropped a copy of that morning's *Tribune* on one end of the green-painted bench. He removed his suit jacket, folded it and placed it at the other end, then sat in the middle, effectively claiming the bench.

The lakefront zoo's wide walkways were already filling with people seeking relief from the heat of the city streets west of Lincoln Park. It being a weekday morning, the relief seekers were mostly mothers with young children, day campers, and older couples. Able-bodied men were at work or at war.

Joe smiled and doffed his hat to a dark-haired woman pushing a stroller. She smiled back and continued walking, glancing over her shoulder once. Joe smiled again and wiggled his fingers in an "I caught you peeking" wave. She quickly looked away.

Joe continued holding the hat in his hand a moment, then placed it on top of the newspaper to his left, resting the hat on its crown to avoid ruining the rakish flare of the brim.

He had been sitting on the bench about ten minutes

when he spied Mike Greenberg and Tony Capezio walking toward him from the direction of the sea lions. Capezio was dripping with sweat. Greenberg was scowling. As they neared, Joe moved the suit jacket to his lap and motioned for Greenberg to sit down.

Without speaking, Greenberg removed a folded handkerchief from his jacket pocket, dabbed the bench seat with it, and then took a look at the white cloth. Seeing it was clean, he unbuttoned his jacket and sat. Capezio sidled to the end of the bench next to Greenberg and remained standing, like a corpulent bookend.

"Where's your friend?" Greenberg said.

"Yeah, where is he?" Capezio added.

Joe turned to look at Greenberg. "Mike, where are your manners? Whatever happened to hi, Joe, how're you doing, haven't seen you in a long time, and all that?"

Greenberg took a deep breath and exhaled, closing his eyes for a moment before restarting. "Yeah, it's been a while, Joe. Couple, three years maybe. Good to see you. And thanks for letting our people know where we could find you. Saved us a trip up to your place. Very considerate."

"I figured you were going to come looking for me sooner or later," Joe said. "So I thought to myself, What could be lovelier than a little get-together in the park? And now here we are, just the three of us. Nice."

"OK, cut the crap," Greenberg said. "You know who we're trying to find. And you know where he is."

"I'll level with you, Mike—if I knew, I'd do just about anything to keep it secret. But I don't have to keep it secret. I made a point of saying to him, 'Don't tell me where you're staying—I don't want to know.'"

"So you talked to him."

"Talked to him, saw him. He called me yesterday, and we met at the lakefront."

"Where on the lakefront?"

Joe held up a forefinger. "I'll tell you in a minute, Mike.

But first, I think you owe me an explanation. We're talking about my best friend here. Day after day I keep trying to figure out why the outfit's looking for him, and it doesn't add up. Did he leave some bad markers out there, or what?"

"Come on, Joe, you weren't born yesterday," Greenberg said. "I mean, kidnapping, armed robbery, one guy shot dead, half the city in a fucking uproar—we can't have freelancers dumping all over our territory like this."

"I still don't buy it," Joe said. "You guys know as well as I do the gun wasn't loaded, probably wasn't even fired, which means it was the police that killed that poor mook. Either that or he shot himself. And the dame wasn't kidnapped, she was in on the whole thing, which wasn't even a real thing—it was all bogus."

"Yeah, yeah, we know it was phony. But the young lady—I'm not so sure. We hear two stories. One guy says she was, you know, like an accomplice. But our people tell us she didn't want to be there, hardly knew your friend."

"What?" Joe's voice rose with disbelief. "Are you fucking kidding me? Who says that?"

"Hey, don't get agitated," Greenberg made a damping-down motion with his left hand as he look around at the women and children on the walkway. "It's the only story that makes sense. Face facts, Joe, this broad was way out of your friend's league."

"Wrong," Joe shot back. "Johnny and her were in love. They were spending kip time together in the afternoons, for God's sake."

Greenberg looked up at Capezio and raised his eyebrows.

"That's some crazy shit right there," Capezio said.

"It's not crazy," Joe said, his voice again on the rise. "It's true. But, hey, just for the sake of argument, let's say it's not true. There's still no call for you guys going after Johnny. The police, maybe. But the outfit? Uh-uh, the eagle does not hunt flies."

"Look, Joe," Greenberg said, adopting the tone of a weary school teacher explaining something obvious, "we don't really care what was going on. We're like soldiers, see? When we get orders from our people, we don't ask why, we don't want to know the life story. We just carry out the assignment. That's all we're trying to do here. Now—where on the lakefront?"

Joe groaned. "Howard Street," he said. "But it doesn't necessarily mean he's in that neighborhood. We meet there a lot, been doing it for years."

"It's a start," Greenberg said. "We'll be seeing you around."

29

With nothing to do except be careful, Johnny stayed close to the Beyla, leaving his room only to buy food or call Joe. Whenever he went out, he carried all his cash so he'd have money to live on if he had to make a run for it.

By the end of the second week in August, he knew he would have to move; the sooner the safer. Clerks at the corner food market across from the Beyla now greeted him as a regular customer—though they still didn't know his real name—and the two bartenders at the combination bar and package store where he made his phone calls were openly trying to guess his occupation.

"I got it figured," one of the bartenders said as Johnny walked to the street entrance after a call to Joe. "You're working for a bookie, right? Phoning in bets."

"I'm calling my sick mother in the hospital," Johnny shot back.

"Sure you are."

Johnny had called Joe at home twice, but they knew the calls were risky. Calls could be traced; Joe's line would be an obvious target for anyone trying to find Johnny. So they worked out a system. At 10 a.m. on Mondays and Fridays, Johnny used the phone booth near the men's room in the back of the lounge to call a pay phone in the Morse Avenue "L" station. If the phone rang more than once, Johnny would hang up—placing a second call at 10:10. If there was still no pickup after one ring, the call was off for that day.

Even on the lam, Johnny continued to gamble, using Joe as a go-between. Joe took Johnny's picks over the phone, and used his own money to place the bets, keeping a written record of wins and losses.

On the morning of the third Friday in August, Joe answered on the first ring and spoke what had become his usual greeting: "Hey, Johnny, you still hanging in there?"

"It's not easy, Joe." Johnny sounded distressed. "My room at the—Jesus, I almost said the name. I got to be more careful, I could have put you in a bad spot. Anyway the place where I'm holed up—it's making me crazy. I mean, how can people live in these dumps, for Christ's sake? Now I know how Ricca must feel down in Atlanta. Except he's got better laundry service. Anyway, I got to get out of here pretty soon—the neighborhood's getting too cozy."

"Maybe I can cheer you up," Joe said. "Have you seen a sports section today?"

"Just bought a paper—haven't looked at it yet."

"The Pirates won both games. That's ten in a row. Nice little streak you're on, my friend. I wish you could be here to see all the money you're winning."

Johnny told Joe to place bets on two games that afternoon—fifty on the Pirates, again, and fifty on Cleveland.

Joe repeated both bets back to Johnny, then changed the subject: "Whatever happened to that dame you're so crazy about? You been in touch?"

"I tried to call," Johnny said. "But she was still pretty steamed about everything. Didn't want to talk."

"Can you blame her?"

"I guess not," Johnny said. "Maybe it's all for the better."

"So what are you saying, it's a closed chapter?"

"Maybe."

After the call, Johnny entered the dimly lit lounge and headed toward the front entrance, waiting for the bartender to make another wise-ass crack about his phone calls.

"Don't you dare walk past me, you creep."

The female voice was barely audible and was so cold it sent a shiver through his body. Startled, he turned to his left and peered into the dim light. She was alone in a booth, wearing the same scarf and dark glasses she had worn the afternoon they went gambling in Cicero.

Seeing her sitting there, he experienced the same surge of schoolboy giddiness he had felt when she accosted him in the Howard Street "L" station that day. The pleasurable glow was almost instantly eclipsed by panic.

He slid into the booth so he was facing her across the plastic-top table, sticky with dried beer, placing his hat on the seat next to him. He wasn't smiling. "What are you doing here, for Christ's sake?"

"Looking for you, dummy, what do you think?"

He leaned forward, speaking in an agitated whisper. "No, I mean what are you doing *here*? How the hell did you find this place?"

"The phone company," she said with a shrug. "They keep a record of calls to the house—for my father's business. But that's not important right now ..."

"Not important? For Christ's sake, if you can find this place, so can other people. Like your old man—he could walk through that door any second. And that doesn't bother you?" Johnny glanced back over his left shoulder.

"Do you seriously think I'd be here if there was any way he could find out? I'm not even supposed to be out of

171

the house, for pete's sake—I'm grounded, under house arrest. Probably forever, thanks to you. And if you must know, my father's out of town. He's not going to find me."

Johnny sat back in the booth and stared, trying to figure what was going on behind the dark glasses. He leaned forward again. "I don't get it," he said. "I thought you were pissed at me."

"That's putting it mildly," Margaret said. "But I got tired of sitting around feeling screwed over. So I decided to get some goddamned answers."

"Answers from me?"

Margaret scanned the empty bar to her right. "Yeah, you—unless there's somebody else in here who called my house from that phone back there"

"Jesus, I need a drink." He slid to his left, and got out of the booth, tossing his hat back on the seat.

"Get me one, too," Margaret said without expression. "Whatever you're having."

The clock over the pinball machine at the back of the room read 10:51—bar time probably—when Johnny walked back to the end of the empty bar where the bartender was working a newspaper crossword puzzle. "Give me a Canadian and water," he said. "Same for the lady."

The bartender put down his pencil. He took two highball glasses off the back bar and held both in his left hand while he used a metal scoop to shovel ice from the metal bin near the wash and rinse tanks. Still holding the glasses by their bottoms, he snatched a bottle of Canadian Club from the back bar and eyeballed a generous ounce into each glass. He went to the center of the bar, briefly pressed each glass into the cradle that activated the water spigot, and then put the glasses on the bar in front of Johnny. "Seventy cents," he said.

Johnny took a single off the outside of the roll he carried in his left pocket and flipped it on the bar. "Keep it," he said.

The bartender reached for the dollar bill, but kept leaning forward until he was stretched across the bar, his face coming closer to Johnny's. He smiled and tilted his head toward the booth. "Glad to see your mother's up and around," he said in a low voice.

"Real funny," Johnny said without returning the smile. "Maybe you should pay more attention to your own business."

The bartender stood upright. "No offense, bud—just trying to bring a little humor into your drab and dreary day."

Johnny took a slug off the drink in his right hand and returned to the booth. He put the drinks on the table and slid into the booth.

"Before you start in," he said, "there's ..."

"No," she cut him off, "I go first." She took a sip from the highball and leaned back in the booth. "I still can't understand why you pulled that job with no way to protect us." She spoke in a level cadence—and so quietly, almost a whisper, Johnny had to strain forward to be sure he could hear the words. "I know I messed up when I turned the ignition off. That was stupid—I don't know what I was thinking. But even with that, we'd have gotten away clean if you'd had a loaded gun."

She glanced to her right again, then back at Johnny, although it was hard for Johnny to tell what she was looking at because of the oversized sun glasses. "You didn't have to shoot anybody, just fire a couple of shots and send that cop looking for a place to hide, that's all. But no, he kept coming after us, kept shooting. He shot me, for God's sake—and he accidentally killed somebody. And all because we were totally defenseless out there. I mean, I know you're not dumb, so why would you do something like that? Were you *trying* to get us killed? Or do you get a bigger thrill when you take stupid chances? Is that how you lost all your money?"

Johnny took a deep breath. "OK, this is on the level,"

he said, emphasizing the point with a sideways chopping motion.

"You mean," she interrupted, "as opposed to all the B-S you've been dishing out before now?"

He nodded, stung by her sarcasm. "Yeah, I guess you could say that. See, the stickup was going to be quick and easy. I didn't need a loaded gun because there wasn't going to be any trouble."

"That's my whole point," Margaret said, now losing patience, but still trying to speak in a whisper. "There *was* trouble. You weren't prepared for it."

"You don't understand—there wasn't going to be trouble because it wasn't a real stickup."

There was a momentary silence. Margaret leaned forward. "What?"

"It was a setup—like playacting. I know the guy that owns the store. I paid him to let me rob the place."

She exploded, snatching the dark glasses off her face and glaring, "I almost got my arm blown off in a fucking charade? Is that what you're saying?"

Johnny looked down to the break the eye contact. "It was ... it was a Merkle play," he said quietly.

"A *what*?"

"A mistake—you know, but like a World Series mistake."

"No, no, this goes way beyond a mistake," Margaret snapped. "This was huge. Some innocent man is dead. I was wounded. Now I'm grounded, for God's sake! And you're telling me the whole thing was a sham?"

"I know, I know. But I can explain."

Margaret snatched her purse off the seat, slid to the right, and stood up, replacing the dark glasses on the bridge of her nose. She looked down at Johnny, still sitting there. With one quick motion, she reached down with her right hand, picked up her highball, and, with a cry of "Damn you!" flung it at Johnny.

Johnny reflexively raised his hands to protect himself,

but the glass caught him near the center of his forehead, ricocheting to the wall where it shattered, ice cubes and pieces of glass flying like shrapnel.

Margaret was striding toward the front of the bar when Johnny grabbed his hat and followed her, pleading, "No, you got to hear this."

"Not interested," she yelled, without turning her head. At the front of the lounge, she shifted her purse from right hand to left, and used her right to give a shove to the worn brass plate on the doorframe. The heavy door began to swing open, except Johnny had already reached around Margaret's left side and grabbed the metal push bar across the door's painted plate glass center. He violently jerked the door closed, knocking Margaret backwards and almost off her feet.

"Shit, we've been had," he said, looking through the unpainted rectangle in the center of the door.

"Stop this," Margaret commanded. "Don't fuck with me."

"Stay away from the door," he commanded. "It's your old man's P.I."

"What? What are you talking about?"

"The tall guy, on the other side of the street."

Johnny grabbed Margaret's left arm and began pulling her toward the back of the lounge. "Hey, pal," he shouted, "is there a back way out of this place?"

"Yeah, but it's locked."

"Stop," Margaret commanded, "that's the arm, you idiot. You're hurting me."

"Unlock it, for Christ's sake," Johnny shouted, "we got to get out of here. I'll give you a finski, but you got to step on it."

The bartender came out from behind the bar, fumbling in his pocket, and led them back past the men's room and the phone booth. He opened the door to the storage room and flicked a wall switch, lighting two naked bulbs about twenty feet apart down the center of the room. They walked past the stacked cases to the rear door. Margaret, now rubbing her wounded left shoulder, no longer resisted.

Johnny slipped a five off the roll of bills he was carrying and offered it to the bartender once the rear door was unlocked and open. As the bartender reached for the bill, Johnny grabbed his hand and held it. "If a tall guy with a bad suit comes in asking questions, you don't know anything—got it?"

"Hey, if this guy's a cop—I don't want any trouble."

"No, he's a private dick. Gets his jelly beans taking dirty pictures, if you know what I mean."

"Oh, gotcha." The bartender looked at Margaret, then back at Johnny. "You better scram."

Standing next to Margaret in the alley, Johnny pulled his hat brim down close to his eyes, wincing when the sweatband made contact with the welt rising on his forehead. He looked north toward Jonquil Terrace, then south. The alley was bordered on one side by the drab backsides of the bars and other businesses that fronted on Paulina Street and on the other by a concrete retaining wall, roughly eight feet high, that marked the boundary of the Howard Street railyard where "L" trains sat when they weren't in service. The cracked, crumbling pavement in the alley was strewn with the usual urban detritus—broken glass, empty bottles, newspapers decomposing to pulp, shards of wood from pallets and crates.

"How'd you get here?" Johnny asked. He kept looking up and down the alley. "You drive?"

"No, I took a cab." She was rubbing her shoulder. "Why? What the hell's going on?"

"It can't be coincidence," Johnny said, more to himself than to Margaret. He stood in the alley scratching his jaw, staring into the distance while he considered the situation. "I mean, what are the odds on that? It must have been the thing with the phone."

"What on earth are you talking about?" Margaret demanded. "Why are we standing in this godforsaken alley?"

"You want to get out of here, walk that direction," he ignored her irritation and pointed south. "The alley takes a left turn down there. Just follow it to the left and you'll come out on Paulina, real close to Howard. There's a cab stand around the corner. Be sure that P.I. doesn't see you."

He turned and headed in the opposite direction, toward Jonquil.

"I'm coming with you."

He stopped and wheeled. "For Christ's sake, a minute ago you couldn't get away from me fast enough."

"You're not leaving my sight until I find out what the hell is going on," she said, jabbing an index finger at Johnny. "Not until you tell me about this business with my father?"

"I told you—that shamus works for him. Now I got things to do. I got to get out of this fucking neighborhood."

He thrust his hands into his pants pockets and walked rapidly north, Margaret, behind him, breaking into a jog every few steps to keep pace. When he reached the Beyla Hotel building at the end of the alley, he studied the service entrance, but there was no way to open it from the outside. He continued to the alley's outlet on Jonquil. Noticing that Margaret was shadowing him, he shot an imploring look at the heavens, then gestured that Margaret should stay behind him and also as close as possible to the side of the building.

Standing next to the Beyla's west wall, he removed his hat and slipped a glance around the corner. "OK, let's go," he said. He stepped onto the sidewalk and sprinted the seventy-five feet to the entrance of the hotel. He held the door so Margaret, also running, could enter the vestibule, then used his room key to open the inside door.

As soon as the door closed behind them in the room, Johnny set the deadbolt lock, then placed his hat on the nightstand, and went to the room's only window. Still breathing hard from the short sprint, he peered around the corner of the drawn shade at Paulina Street, three floors below.

Margaret, also panting, remained just inside the door, her arms wrapped around herself, as if she were cold, or perhaps reluctant to come in contact with anything in the cramped, fusty-smelling room.

"There's his fucking car," Johnny muttered. "Right across from the bar. I'd pay good money to know what that nosey piece of shit thinks he's doing down there."

He came away from the window, pulled a suitcase out from under the bed and laid it open on the bed. He yanked open a top drawer in the small dresser, removed two handfuls of underwear and socks, and tossed them into the open suitcase on the bed. "Hey, sit down, for Christ's sake." He pointed to the straight-back wood chair next to the dresser. "Please. You're making me nervous standing there."

"How do you know this man," she asked, "the one you saw? And what does he have to do with my father? Tell me, damn it."

Johnny opened another drawer and pulled out a stack of folded dress shirts. "I already told you, the guy's a shamus—and he works for your father," he said, pushing the underwear and socks to one side in the suitcase and placing the shirts next to them.

"Yes, but how do you know anything at all about my father?"

"I don't," he said. "All I know is what I read in the paper. And I also know he wears expensive suits and he's an asshole—acts like he's real used to getting his way."

Margaret stiffened: "Please tell me that was a lucky guess."

"No, I met him."

"Oh, my God." She stepped past Johnny and slumped into the chair next to the dresser. "When was this?"

"Weeks ago. Came to see me at my place on Wilson. Had that big guy with him—the gumshoe. Told me to stop seeing you, and said he'd make it worth my while."

"I can't believe this is happening," Margaret said, her head now buried in her hands. "He offered you money to stop seeing me? What did you tell him?"

"I told him to go fuck himself."

Margaret choked. Her head snapped up to look at Johnny. "You what?"

"OK, that's what I should've said, but I didn't," Johnny said. "I just told him to butt out, you know, mind his own business. He didn't want to hear that. He said he'd get back to me."

She shook her head, then looked up at the ceiling. "Let me be sure I've got this: My father was aware, all along, of what was going on with us?"

"Right, that's where the P.I. comes in."

"Shit, of course that's how he knew." She groaned, head now bent forward. "We were being followed."

She paused, then looked up. Johnny could almost see the flash of awareness. "Wait," she said, becoming agitated again, "we were being followed, and you knew it. But you still went ahead with your idiotic stunt. How could you? You fed me a line of B-S, made me think I could trust you, and then you put me in harm's way. And the whole time, we were in a goddamned fish bowl. Maybe I'm the idiot here. I thought you actually cared about me."

Johnny was standing directly in front of her now. "I *did* care," he said, tears welling in his eyes. Now the words came in a torrent. "This is what I wanted to explain. I was mad about you, crazy about you. I thought maybe, you know—I thought I was in love with you. I still do. But I figured there was no way you'd ever fall for a mope like me unless you thought I was a tough guy. So that's what I was trying to do. I was trying to be like one of the good guys—

179

trying to cook up something that was, you know, exciting..."

"Exciting?" she interrupted, her voice rising in pitch. "That stunt of yours wasn't exciting, it was terrifying, fucking horrible. I'm almost having a heart attack right now just thinking about it."

"Jesus, baby, I don't blame you," he said, "I got to admit, I was scared too. As soon as I heard those shots I knew it was the stupidest thing I ever did in my life. But I thought I had to make like a tough guy, because it was the only way you'd give me the time of day."

There was a long silence in the room. Johnny could hear his own breathing. But Margaret seemed to have turned a switch, going from livid to composed.

She slowly removed her dark glasses and placed them on the dresser top next to her. She looked back at Johnny's face. "Time of day? Is that your cute little phrase for what I was putting out at the Edgewater Beach?"

"Jesus," Johnny protested, "I wasn't talking about that—I wasn't even thinking about it. I mean, sure, I think about it every day. But not just now."

Margaret pulled the knot under her chin and removed the scarf, placing it next to the dark glasses as she shook her hair to free. "Well, I am."

"You're what?"

"Thinking about it." Unsmiling, she looked him square in the eyes. "That was the exciting part, you dummy."

He searched her face for some flicker of expression that might signal where this was going. His stomach felt queasy, a feeling that seemed to intensify the longer their eyes remained locked. "It was great," he blurted at last, "like nothing that ever happened in my life before. Honest. But we can't be thinking about that right now. We got to be thinking about getting out of here, for Christ's sake. Seeing you in that bar was like a signal—in big red letters." He drew his hand from left to right to create an air marquee. "It said, Get out now, before it's too late. And then the P.I. showed up—that was the clincher."

Margaret flashed a skeptical look. "I don't get it," she said. "If that man really does work for my father, why is he looking for you?"

"It could be anything, for Christ's sake," Johnny said. "Maybe he's trying to find out if I'm with you. Or maybe he's working for somebody besides your old man. Believe me, whatever he's up to, it's N.G. These gumshoes—I'm not saying all of them, but ninety percent of them—they must take an oath to play both ends against the middle. They never ... Baby, what are you doing?"

She had reached up and unfastened the button at the collar of her blouse. Her hand moved slowly down and undid the next button. "I hadn't really planned to be here, but I'm thinking, maybe we can make the best of the situation—carpe diem, as they say. You want to see my wound?

30

*E*ven though their intercourse seemed different—more detached somehow—Johnny had trouble keeping his mind on it. He knew Charles Turner's P.I. was somewhere on the street, probably in the bar with the pay phone, flashing money and asking questions. And the gumshoe wasn't necessarily working for Turner; he could be working for anybody.

"What are you thinking?" Margaret, lying on her stomach and propped on her elbows, stared into Johnny's face.

"I'm thinking about that bartender." Johnny lay on his back staring at the peeling paint on the plastered ceiling, a wrinkled sheet covering his midsection.

"I don't think he'll say anything," she said. "You heard him—he doesn't want any trouble with the police."

Johnny snorted. "You think I'm staying in a dump like this to duck the cops? Trust me, the cops are the last thing I'm worried about right now."

Margaret felt a jolt of surprise—or was it apprehension? "Then what are you worried about? Not that private eye?"

"No, you're the one who needs to worry about him," Johnny said. "Me, I'm worried about the outfit. They've had a couple of hoods looking for me all over the city."

Margaret waited, looking for a sign Johnny was playing games with her. "Come on," she said, "are you serious?"

"You want serious?" Johnny lifted his head off the pillow and met her gaze. "I'll give you serious: I'm pretty sure there's a contract on me. And it has something to do with that goddamned stickup."

"That's awful." She thought a second. "But it doesn't make any sense."

"Yeah, Joe says the same thing. But with the outfit it doesn't have to make sense. They got their own rules."

"What makes you think it has something to do with the holdup?" Her face was creased by a wry smile. "Does the outfit have a rule against idiotic charades?"

Ignoring the gibe, he told her about Benny and the pistol—how Benny disappeared the day after Greenberg and Capezio had come around asking questions about the .45. "That's why I called you at home, even though I knew you were sore at me. I was worried they might be looking for you, too—except now I think it's just me."

She slid closer to him, coiling her right arm around his waist and resting her head on his chest. "They're stalking you," she said in a half whisper, "like an animal. You can never relax, can you? Not for a minute. I think we'd better hurry."

"Baby, that's what I was trying to say before." He looked down at the back of her head and the blonde hair cascading across his chest, waiting for her to lift herself off him. "I got to move out of this dump right now."

"I don't mean that," she said coldly.

The arm that had been around his waist tightened for an instant to arrest any thought of escape, then uncoiled, the right hand sliding down his belly and underneath the sheet to its surprised target. "Humm," she purred, "I hear some people like it doggie style. You want to try?"

"Your bathroom is disgusting," she said after she started dressing.

He made no response, his mind busy calculating the chances that both of them could get out of the neighborhood without being seen by Turner's P.I.—or anyone else. He returned the suitcase to the top of the bed, then went to the bathroom and fetched his shaving paraphernalia and toiletries, all of which he dumped into one side of the open suitcase.

She stopped dressing and studied him. "Johnny."

He looked up.

"Are you a Jew?"

"Huh? What the hell does that have to do with price of argyles at Wieboldt's?"

"My father says you're a Jew."

"Yeah, he asked me the same question," Johnny sighed. "What difference does it make?

"I don't know—maybe none." She studied him, knowing the time had come to say what had been on her mind since they'd uncoupled and collapsed on the sagging mattress. "We can't see each other anymore," she said. "Not for a while anyway."

One corner of Johnny's mouth curled into a smirk. "Yeah, if we were doing the Lindy on Rush Street it'd kind of blow your kidnap story."

"So you understand."

He nodded again. "I don't like it, but there's nothing I can do. Not while I'm on the lam." He walked to the window and looked down at the street again. "Still there. Hey," he turned back toward the room, "come here and look at this."

Margaret, her brow knit, reached the window in three strides.

Johnny stepped aside so Margaret could peek around the corner of the drawn shade. "He's talking to some guy on the street—right next to the gray ..."

"*Oh, my God.*" She backed away from the window, her hand to her mouth.

"What, what?"

She smoothed the front of her skirt and brushed her hair away from her face. "Nothing," she said. "For a second I ... I thought it was someone I know, or knew, but it wasn't—I was just being paranoid."

"Who did you think it was?"

"Not important," she said. "But I think I'd better go. Is there some way to get out of here without being seen?"

After she'd retied her scarf and donned the dark glasses, he walked her from the room to an unlighted stairway at the end of the hall, away from the front of the building. He said the stairway would take her to an alley door—the one he hadn't been able to open. She could unlatch it from the inside, and once she was in the alley, all she had to do was walk south in the direction of Howard Street. She'd be in a cab headed for home in less than five minutes.

They exchanged a passionless kiss.

"So I guess our ... uh, this afternoon means you're not sore at me anymore," he said.

Her face hardened. "No, I wouldn't say that. I'm still angry. I decided to see what angry sex was like."

Dropping the subject, she opened her handbag and removed her wallet. "Do you need money? I don't have a lot, but ..."

"Jesus, that reminds me—what happened to the money from the army-navy store?"

"I never saw it," she said. "I guess my father found it—probably turned it over to the police."

"Yeah, what are the odds on that?" Johnny said. "If the cops had seen what was in that bag, they'd still be asking questions. I'm betting your old man didn't want that much attention."

"How much was it?"

"Three hundred. And it's yours—if you can get it from your old man."

"We'll see," she said. "So what's the answer—do you need money?" She started to open the wallet.

"No, I still got plenty—I'm on a hot streak."

She flashed a bemused smile. "You're still gambling?"

"Why not? That's what I do."

"Well, keep your head down, gamblin' man. Oh, you might want to put some ice on your forehead—that's a nasty bump you've got there." She turned, descending into the darkness of the stairwell.

31

A few minutes before midnight, Johnny took one last glance in the dresser mirror to be sure his hat was straight, then hefted the suitcase and slipped out of his room at the Beyla, leaving the room key on the dresser. As the door latched shut, he froze in his tracks, sensing he was not alone in the hallway.

He waited, mind racing, wondering if there would be any warning before ...

"Hey, Jew boy, remember me?"

Still frozen in place, Johnny turned his head toward the husky voice, making the turn as deliberately as possible. Any sudden movement might be misinterpreted. A tall figure, feet spread wide, stood under a ceiling bulb about 25 feet away. At that distance, the speaker's facial figures were indistinguishable under the brim of his hat, but there could be no mistaking the oafish build and the ill-fitting clothes.

"Yeah, I remember you," Johnny said cautiously. "What's going on?" He took a quick look over his shoulder. A red-lighted exit sign at the end of the hall marked the entrance to the back stairway.

"There's a guy wants to see you."

"Again?"

"Uh-uh, different guy," Shockey said, ambling toward Johnny. "What are you trying to do, leave town?"

"No, just taking my shirts to the Chinese laundry. Who wants to see me?"

Shockey's crooked grin revealed a row of uneven, discolored teeth, a single gold tooth directly below the left eye. "It's your girlfriend's fiancé."

Johnny's eyes widened. Joe's long-ago warning about a confrontation with Margaret's suitor had been hypothetical, not to mention sarcastic. But this was real. Johnny figured the odds were at least seventy-to-one against a pleasant encounter.

"Maybe some other time," he said, glancing again at the red exit sign behind him. "I'm a little busy right now." Leading with a shoulder, he angled to his own left to brush past Shockey in the hallway—except that Shockey stepped to the right, keeping himself in front of Johnny.

"I think you better see the gentleman," Shockey said. "He's got a proposition—you'll want to hear it."

"Yeah, what kind of proposition?"

"You'll see. Come on, let's go."

"Wait—where are we going?"

"Just up the street," Shockey said, jerking a thumb in no particular direction. "He's expecting you."

At the end of the hall, Shockey held up a hand and stopped. "One thing," he growled. "The gentleman knows you was seeing his lady, but he doesn't know you was the guy who pulled that caper on Broadway. All he knows is what was in the papers. So don't spoil things, if you know what's good for you."

Johnny drew his head back and frowned. "I don't like games," he said. "You know the real story. Her old man probably knows, too. So why keep the fiancé in the dark? He's bound to find out."

Shockey looked at Johnny with contempt. "What are you, stupid?"

Johnny searched Shockey's pockmarked face. "Oh, I get it," Johnny said slowly. "The old man doesn't want his future son-in-law to know he's getting damaged goods. Or maybe it's not the old man—maybe it's you. Playing your own dandy little game. Am I getting warm here?"

"You really expect me to answer that?" Shockey snorted.

"OK, answer this one: How'd you find me?"

"You're a nosy little kike, aren't you," Shockey said. "Let's just say it's what I do. Which reminds me." He reached into an inside pocket. "Here, you might need this someday."

Johnny looked at the small white rectangle. "What the hell do I need your card for?"

"You never know," Shockey said, his eyes narrowing as he pushed his faced down closer to Johnny's. "I heard there's *other* people looking for you. So maybe I can be of service, you know, making sure word doesn't get around about where you are."

"Gee, that's swell," Johnny said. "But then I'd have to trust you. Not interested." He flipped the business card over his shoulder.

Shockey started to turn, stopped, and turned to face Johnny again. "That took some balls—signing into this flea trap under the name Turner. Your idea of a joke, I suppose."

"I did it out of respect."

Johnny saw the eyes flash, but barely had time to turn his head away from the blow. The heavy fist landed, like a wooden club, between his left eye and his left ear, sending his hat flying across the hall and knocking him to the floor. He landed hard on his right shoulder, ears buzzing from the force of the blow.

"I been wanting to do that since I first laid eyes on you," Shockey said, rubbing the knuckles of his right hand. "Now get your sorry ass off the floor and let's go."

32

*T*hey turned the corner and walked south on Paulina, teeming with the usual Friday night crowd of couples, servicemen, barflies, punks, hustlers, and derelicts. As they neared Howard Street, Shockey stopped in front of a recessed door painted black with yellow lettering that read "Boda's Billiard Parlor."

The door led to a narrow flight of stairs. Johnny, a bluish knot rising on the left side of his face, stopped at the foot of the staircase. "It was her father's thing with the phone company, wasn't it?" he said.

Shockey, who already had taken the first riser and had his foot on the rubber-covered tread of the second one, paused and turned to scowl at Johnny. "Huh? What the hell are you talking about?"

"How you found me," Johnny said. "It was the calls to the house, right?"

"Jesus, don't you ever quit? Let's go." Shockey waved Johnny past him on the stairs.

In the dingy second-floor parlor, Johnny glanced around and guessed it contained between eight and ten tables. Even if all the tables had been in use, it would have been easy to spot Margaret's fiancé—a downtown lawyer in a working stiff's pool hall. At this hour, though, he was the only guy in the joint except for the attendant, a grizzled old guy snoring in a chair at the back of the pool room, his jowls flapping with each exhalation.

Johnny recognized the boyfriend as the guy he'd seen talking to Shockey. *No wonder Margaret went bughouse.*

With his suit jacket draped over the back of a chair, Margaret's fiancé was playing at a table next to the far wall. He was dressed in a white shirt and a dark blue-and-green-stripe tie fastened to his shirt front by a small diamond stick pin. His trousers were held up by dark blue suspenders. Both shirtsleeves had been rolled to his elbows, and he walked around the table like someone who knew what he was doing, tapping the cue in gentle rhythm on the raised side. He stopped and leaned forward, spreading the fingers of his left hand on the cushion and steadying the cue with a curled index finger.

Shockey reached out to stop Johnny's advance toward the table until after the shot. The stick drove into the cue ball with a sharp crack, detonating a rapid series of clicks as balls caromed around the table, glancing off each other, ricocheting off the rubber side cushions and finally coming to rest.

"Here's your boy," Shockey said. "I'll wait by the stairs."

Johnny shifted the suitcase from his right hand to his left, and stared at Margaret's fiancé. The two stood motionless maybe eight feet apart, sizing each other up. It was Johnny who broke the ice. "Am I supposed to know you?"

"Don't play dumb—you know who I am," Brantley snapped. He grabbed one of the small blue cubes off the cushion and chalked the end of his cue stick, then smiled. "What happened to your face?"

"I fell out of bed," Johnny said. He heard Shockey snort.

Johnny took a quick glance around the pool hall, looking for another way out in case, well, just in case. "So I'm here," he said. "What do you want?"

Brantley stopped chalking and glared at Johnny. "Did you hear what I just said? I said don't play dumb. You know what I want. I want you to stay away from Margaret Turner." He returned his attention to the table.

Johnny sucked on his gums. "That's it? That's the proposition?"

"There's more." Brantley leaned forward from the waist, leveling the cue stick into position, drawing it slowly back before thrusting forward to launch another shot.

Johnny cursed softly. He placed the suitcase on the floor, and leaned his backside against an adjoining table. After removing his hat and placing it, crown down, on the table next to him, he crossed his arms. "OK, let's hear it."

Brantley leaned forward over the table, appearing to study his next shot, then straightened up and began chalking the end of the stick again. He spoke without looking at Johnny. "Margaret hasn't been herself since that ordeal last month—I'm sure you're aware of what happened."

Johnny studied Brantley, looking for a sign he knew more than he was letting on. "Yeah, I read about it in the paper. Must have been, eh ..."

"It should be obvious," Brantley continued, still looking past Johnny and disregarding the response, "that none of that would have happened—none of it!—if Margaret hadn't been driving into the city alone. She knew she wasn't supposed to—even tried to keep it a secret. And now I know why. She was consorting with riffraff—someone far below her station."

"You talking about me?"

Brantley's eyes flashed. "God damn it, I said ..."

"Right, right, right." Johnny uncrossed one arm and held up his hand to signal he'd heard enough.

After a slow exhale, Brantley bent at the waist, leveled

the stick, and again sent balls into clacking geometric caroms. "I have no idea what prompted you to start calling the Turner residence," he said.

Johnny, nodding almost imperceptibly, glanced in Shockey's direction.

"Nor do I have the slightest clue why Margaret was spending time with you. Frankly, I don't really want to know. All I know is this—it's done, finished. Starting right now, you are to stay away from that woman."

Johnny was beginning to fidget. "What gives you the right to pick her friends? Last time I checked it was a free country."

Brantley's head jerked to look Johnny in the eye. "Not anymore!" he barked. "Not for the likes of you."

Johnny brought his right hand up from his folded arms and clamped it over his mouth. He could feel the heat rising from his neck into his face. "So, what are you going to do," he said, "throw money at me and hope I'll go away?"

"Not my style," Brantley said. "My daddy told me never do business with Jews. No, the only thing I'm going to throw at you is a chance to stay out of jail."

Johnny flashed another look in Shockey's direction.

Brantley laid the cue stick on the table. He placed both hands on the cushion and leaned forward, his face transformed into a mask of macabre shadows by the light suspended above. "This city is crawling with human garbage like you," he snarled. "Men who think they can ignore all the laws and social norms. But they all go to jail eventually, and that's where you're going, too, you little shit, if you even think about defying me."

Johnny was sure he had it figured now. "Don't bet on it," he said. "Nobody's going to lock me up for some penny-ante stunt, no matter what you try to make of it. I didn't kill anybody, for Christ's sake. That fat cop ..."

Shockey bolted up out of his chair. "Hey," he yelled, pointing at Johnny and then jerking his open hand across his throat.

With a fleeting expression of puzzlement, Brantley motioned for Shockey to sit down. "Easy, Lloyd, I've got this," he said—then turned back to Johnny and smirked. "Penny-ante, eh? Tell that to the U.S. attorney. He'll laugh in your face. The feds can hardly wait to get their hands on tax evaders like you, especially now with the war. They love to make examples of deadbeats."

"Fuck that," Johnny interjected, adopting an indignant tone. "If I don't pay taxes—and that's all I'm saying, *if* I don't—it's because I don't have to. I don't have a job, for Christ's sake. Haven't had one in years."

"Ah, yes, I forgot. Mr. Shockey tells me you're a gambler—you and some friend of yours." Brantley looked away, affecting a dramatic pause. "And since none of your gambling income is traceable, or so you think, you just assume you don't have to pay Uncle Sam a penny."

"Hey, I barely got a pot to piss in," Johnny said. "Check it out if you want."

"Oh, Mr. Shockey already has," Brantley said with a slightly triumphant tone. "We know more about you than you might think."

Johnny blew out his breath, picked up his hat and fiddled aimlessly with the brim. "You're bluffing," he said finally. "You don't know my business."

"Don't be so sure," Brantley said. "I think Internal Revenue would be interested to hear about a fellow like you—a fellow with no job and no reportable income who walked in and paid cash for a '38 LaSalle coupe. Brand new. And he'd be fascinated by the story of a certain unpaid bill at Michael Reese Hospita ..."

"Hold it right there, mister, that's family business," Johnny snapped, jabbing an index finger at Brantley. "Keep your nose out of my family business."

"But why would you want to keep it a secret?" Brantley said, feigning surprise. "It's such a heartwarming story— little brother comes to the rescue of big sister. Again, paid in cash."

"I had a couple of lucky days at the track," Johnny shot back. "Big deal."

Brantley chalked the end of his cue stick. "I seem to recall that one of our Chicago gangsters used that same defense."

"Yeah, yeah, Frank Nitti," Johnny said. "What's your point?"

Brantley exhaled and hung his head. "Mr. Nitti is no longer with us," he said, shifting into the patronizing tone that never failed to irk Margaret. "He killed himself. No, I'm referring to Paul Ricca. You've heard of him, I assume. He tried to tell the government he had no taxable income. All of his cash and property came from gambling. Guess what? The feds didn't care where the money came from, they just wanted the back taxes and penalties."

"Yeah, I saw it in the paper last year," Johnny said. "Before he went to the clink. What does this have to do with me?"

Brantley glared. "Here's what," he said. "Mr. Ricca is in very deep trouble. But not because of his taxes. And why? Because he got himself a top-notch lawyer. A specialist. My future father-in-law, as it happens. You, on the other hand, will not be able to afford that kind of representation. And where Mister Ricca was able to settle for a small fraction of what the feds were demanding," here Brantley held a closely spaced thumb and forefinger in front of his face to illustrate the fraction, "you will be ordered to pay back taxes and penalties in full, and if you don't—off to the penitentiary. That's the way the system works, my friend."

"I'm not your friend," Johnny said coldly.

"Finally, something we can agree on," Brantley said. "But I digress. My point is no jury's going to believe you've been living in the poorhouse—especially when you're walking around in a two-hundred-dollar suit ..."

"Two seventy-seven," Johnny shot back.

Brantley smiled, pushing himself away from the table and into a standing position. Moving deliberately around the table, advancing closer to Johnny, standing as straight as possible to emphasize the height difference between them, he rolled his sleeves down, fishing small diamond studs from the shirt pocket and fastening the French cuffs. "I rest my case," he said.

"OK, big shot," Johnny said, his chin jutting forward, "if you're so fucking sure of yourself, why go through all this grandstanding? Why don't you just turn me in right now?"

"Because I may not have to," Brantley said, still smiling. "Mr. Shockey tells me you've angered some powerful people in this town—the human garbage I spoke of earlier. I'm assuming those people are going to handle my little Jew problem for me. But just in case they don't, I've still got something that'll settle your hash for a long time."

Then the smile vanished and he leveled an index finger at Johnny. "So listen up. Stay away from Margaret Turner. Far away. Our marriage is a birthright, if you have the slightest idea what that means, and I'll be damned if I'm going to let you screw things up." Brantley stopped and looked Johnny up and down. "God, you disgust me. Starting right now, just stay with your own kind. If you crawl out from under your rock again, I promise I will put you in more trouble than you ever thought possible."

Brantley retrieved his suit jacket from the chair back and slipped it on.

"I didn't know you were such an asshole," Johnny said.

"And I expected you to be taller," Brantley said, shooting one shirt cuff then the other. "What a disappointment for both of us."

Johnny clapped his hat on his head, wincing again when the sweatband hit the lump on his forehead, and snatched the suitcase off the floor. "I've heard enough of this crap," he said, glancing over at Shockey, who was sitting in a chair near the staircase.

"Does the suitcase mean you're moving to another city," Brantley said, "or is that wishful thinking?"

"Just taking a little vacation," Johnny said, looking toward the stairway to the street. "Taking the wife and kids up to the Dells."

"Don't hurry back. And don't forget to do something about those nasty looking bruises on your face."

"Yeah, fuck you, too."

Brantley brayed loudly.

Near the top of the stairway, Johnny stopped and looked at Shockey. "Who the fuck are you working for?"

Shockey rose slowly from the chair, and looked down at Johnny. "Do you really think that's any of your business? Get out of here before I put another knot on your head."

Johnny was in the act of pushing open the street door when Brantley shouted from the top of the staircase: "Don't cross me, you little shit. You'll be sorry."

Johnny looked over his shoulder, shouted, "You're a four-flusher, a nothing guy," then turned and stepped out onto Paulina Street.

33

*J*ohnny used two taxis and the "L" to trace a zig-zag route across the North Side before arriving near the intersection of Lincoln and Belmont.

It was 2:45 in the morning when he roused the clerk sleeping behind a caged-in front desk at the Umber Hotel in the 1600 block of West Belmont. "I called yesterday," he said. "Name's Greenberg. You still got a room near the fire escape?"

Yawning, the clerk scanned the lineup of keys hanging from numbered hooks on the wall behind the desk. "Third floor, rear" he said. "Got a better room on the second floor. Not close to the fire escape, though."

"I got a thing about fire," Johnny said.

Johnny had assumed no room could be shabbier or more claustrophobic than the one at the Beyla. But this room was serious competition. Cigarette burns on the dresser and nightstand, a bed that sagged like a hammock, handles missing from most of the drawers. Worst of all, the room was hot and smelled like a wet dog.

On the plus side, Johnny noted, the room's only window led directly out to the rear fire escape—handy for making a getaway. On the minus side, the only access to the fire escape for all other residents on the third floor was through Johnny's room.

"It's crazy," he told Joe during their first Monday phone conversation after the move. "One of the panels in the door to my room is glass."

"Jesus, you mean people can just look in?"

"No, no. The glass is painted. Same color as the rest of the door. But get this—there's a big fucking sign on the door that says, In case of fire break glass. So you break the glass, reach in and unlock the door, and that's how you get to the fire escape."

"I never heard of anything like that."

"Well, now you have. Hey, here's one for Ripley, I had a run-in with Margaret's boyfriend."

"Jesus, the fiancé?"

"Yeah, that one."

Joe whistled. "I'll bet that was pleasant. How the hell did that happen?"

"The son of a bitch found me, found where I was staying—just as I was leaving, too. If I'd gotten out five minutes earlier, I'd have ducked the bastard. Oh, and Margaret found me, too."

"Holy cripes, you're lucky Greenberg didn't find you," Joe said. "But I don't get it—if the lady is going along with her old man's kidnapping story, why'd she come looking for you?"

"Hard to tell," Johnny said. "The way it started out, I think she wanted to tell me how pissed off she was, which she did—and then I told her the robbery was a setup and she got even more pissed off. Like scary pissed off. She beaned me with a highball glass, for Christ's sake. But we ended up on friendly terms."

"Friendly terms," Joe repeated. "Interesting. And the boyfriend—I think I can guess what he wanted. I'll bet that didn't end on friendly terms. Did he take a poke at you?"

"Uh-uh, just tried to scare me," Johnny said, "but not

the way you think. He said he'd send me to prison if I didn't stay away from Margaret."

"Prison?" Joe's voice was incredulous. "For what? Not the phony robbery?"

"No, taxes. Federal taxes."

Joe whistled. "He's a fed?"

"No, just another hard-on with a briefcase," Johnny said. "But he said he's got a direct line to the D.A. and—get this, Joe—he knew about stuff I was spending money on, like Martha's treatments."

Joe whistled again. "So it's not a bluff—the boyfriend's no lightweight."

"You can say that again," Johnny fired back. "And here's the clincher, Joe. The asshole knows there's a contract with my name on it."

"It's not exactly common knowledge," Joe said. "How would he know? Do you think he's behind it?"

"I used to," Johnny said. "I figured he'd be happy to see me dead because of Margaret and also he hates Jews. But you and me, we can always spot a guy who's connected. And this *zhlob* is definitely not connected, couldn't arrange a contract with an instruction book. The tax thing, though—that's another story. I think he could jam us up. Trouble is, there's something strange about the guy, Joe."

"Strange? What do you mean?"

"The whole time he was talking to me, he was shooting pool— you know, by himself ..."

"You met him in a pool hall?"

"It's a long story, Joe. Anyway, he had all the right moves. Looked like fucking Willie Mosconi, for Christ's sake. But I don't think he sank a ball. Not even one."

"Big *k'nocker*," Joe said with a note of contempt.

"Exactly what I was thinking."

"But he could still put you and me behind the eight ball," Joe said.

34

*T*he buzzer sounded once, twice, a third time.

"All right, all right," the resident manager grumbled. "Hold your horses."

He put his sandwich down and walked across the interior of the dingy apartment. He moved stiffly, with a limp, the result of a wound sustained in France during The Great War. Still chewing, he leaned down to speak into the mouthpiece near the door. "Yeah, what is it?"

The speaker grate above the mouthpiece crackled. "We want to talk to the manager," a man's voice said.

"It's lunchtime, come back in an hour."

Crackle. "Are you going to let us in, or do we kick this fucking door down?"

The manager, shirtless but wearing suspenders to keep his pants tucked under his belly, leaned back and shot a wide-eyed look at the speaker. Then he reached up and pushed the button that unlocked the inside door in the vestibule. He opened the apartment door and waited, listening to the approaching footfalls in the hallway.

"Nice of you to let us in," Mike Greenberg said without sincerity.

"Real nice," Tony Capezio chimed in, stationing his considerable self behind Greenberg's right shoulder.

"We're trying to find a guy," Greenberg said. "We got reason to think he might be in this neighborhood, maybe here."

"Why here?"

"If you don't mind, we'll ask the questions," Greenberg said. "The guy we're trying to find is about five-ten, early forties, brown hair, classy dresser—probably not using his real name."

The manager thought a second. "How about Turner—John Turner?"

Greenberg exchanged a glance with Capezio. "Could be," he said to the manager. "When did this Turner move in?"

"July twenty-sixth, late," the manager said. "Right around ten."

"Bingo, that's our boy," Greenberg said out of the corner of his mouth.

Capezio took a small step to his right, to get a better look at the manager. He had one hand inside his suit jacket. "Seems like you got one hell of a good memory, mister," he said.

"Memory's lousy," the manager answered, shaking his head. "I just happened to check the date. Somebody else was here looking for the same guy—a cop, I think."

"When was this?" Greenberg said.

"Friday night," the manager said. "Maybe it wasn't a cop. A cop would have flashed a badge, right? This guy was flashing dollar bills."

"Fucking private dick," Greenberg groused. "Give me a break. Let's have a room number and a key, old timer. We got business with this, eh, Turner."

"I think you missed him," the manager said. "He's paid through the end of the month. But I saw him and that other guy on Paulina real late Friday night. Turner was carrying a suitcase. His room's been cleaned out."

"Shit," Greenberg said through his teeth, again turning to Capezio, "this was supposed to be easy. Now he could be fucking anywhere."

The manager gave Capezio a once-over. "I guess you fellows aren't cops, eh?"

"Right, not cops," Greenberg said. "I know you wouldn't be stupid enough to lie to us, but we got to take a look at the room. Give me your pass key."

It took less than two minutes for Greenberg and Capezio to check the room. It was empty—closet, drawers, wastebasket, everything.

Greenberg retrieved a long blond hair from one of the pillows on the unmade bed. "Looks like our boy had company," he said.

Capezio looked around and shook his head. "In this shithole? That dame must have been a piece of work. You don't think ... naw, couldn't be."

They left the room and walked down the hall toward the front stairway, their leaden footfalls like thunder on the wood flooring. Near the stairs, Capezio leaned over, grunting, and picked up what looked like a scrap off the floor—the grunt setting off a short, high-pitched fart.

"Jesus, can't you do anything to control that?" Greenberg fussed. "What'd you find?"

Capezio squinted at his hand in the low light. "A card," he said. "Says ... L. Shockey Associates, Confidential Investigations."

"Gimme the card," Greenberg said. "That's got to be the asshole who's ahead of us. I wonder what he wants with Sharansky."

35

*J*ohnny spent his first three nights at the Umber wondering whether the benefits of a fire escape were canceled by the easy access to his room. If the outfit's two palookas discovered where he was, they could punch out the glass and be on him before he got to the window.

Tuesday afternoon Johnny switched to a front room on the second floor of the Umber—almost as shabby as the room on the third floor, only large enough to accommodate a wood restaurant-style chair and a dark-green painted table in addition to the dresser and nightstand. The unpainted dresser was marred by gashes where strips of the blonde wood veneer had been torn away. Grime clung like a 5-o'clock shadow in the corners where the plaster walls met the ceiling.

He knew the noise from Belmont Avenue would keep him awake at night, but the door, unlike the one with the painted glass panel, would offer at least a momentary obstacle. He'd have time to climb out the window, drop to the ground, and get away—assuming he didn't break a goddamned ankle or a leg when he hit the sidewalk.

For a week he used the rear service entrance whenever

he left the hotel, taking the alley east to Fullerton or west to Paulina. He survived on canned vegetables and soups purchased at a small market around the corner on Lincoln.

He found a deck of cards in the one-drawer nightstand and, when he wasn't studying the *Daily Racing Form*, played solitaire, even though he knew he couldn't win because the deck was missing a jack and a trey. Sometimes he just sat in the creaky wood chair, watching the street below his hotel room.

"I can't keep living like this," he told Joe in early September. "I'm going to wind up in the nuthouse."

"Don't talk like that, my friend," Joe said. "We'll find a way out of this. I promise you."

If he wanted to keep his sense of dignity, Johnny knew he couldn't succumb to squalor. It was important to keep up personal appearances—how many times had his Aunt Rose said that? Once a week, he gave dress shirts and other laundry to the hotel's day clerk, whose wife laundered and ironed the clothing for a small charge. He kept his blue suit cleaned and pressed. He never went out without a tie.

And with little else to do, he was still gambling, using Joe as a proxy. Joe reported that Johnny's winnings had long since outgrown the shoebox where he'd been stashing the money.

Johnny was now making his morning calls to Joe from a phone booth in the back of Carmine's Hideaway, a large bar with a jukebox and a dance floor about a block and a half from the hotel. Dark and virtually deserted except for a handful of grizzled drinkers from the neighborhood during the daylight hours, Carmine's underwent a transformation late each evening.

"I hope this doesn't tip you to where I'm calling from," he told Joe on a Friday morning, "but I got to tell you about this place. I came in here to get a drink a couple of nights ago and—get a load of this, Joe—there were guys dancing with each other. And I'm not talking about that Irish crap. These guys were dancing slow."

"Jesus, I don't think they can do that. Isn't that against the law?"

"I don't know, Joe, but that's not all: I think a couple of the dames in here might have been guys."

"You mean they were dressed like women?" Joe said.

"That's what I'm saying."

Joe whistled. "I'm pretty sure that's against the law, too. Let me ask you this—did anyone make a pass at you?"

"No, but I'll tell you, Joe, a couple of those guys ... you know, the ones wearing dresses and makeup, they weren't so bad."

"Holy mackerel, we've got to get you out of there."

For Johnny, Carmine's Hideaway became a refuge. True, the refuge was populated by alien men, outlandish men in some cases, but it was still a refuge—an escape from his 10-by-12 cell of a room with cigarette burns on the furniture, slow drains in the bathroom, and a partial deck of cards in the nightstand.

Carmine's was a place where Johnny could get an occasional drink without worrying about running into someone he knew; a place where no reputable mobster would ever set foot for fear of being labeled a secret fairy and beaten to a pulp, possibly even killed, by his own people. And Johnny could walk to the rear door of Carmine's through the labyrinth of alleys west of Lincoln Avenue without showing his face on any street.

As a night patron at Carmine's, Johnny kept to himself, avoiding eye contact with other male patrons. But it was inevitable that he would be approached. And when he was, he did not handle the come-on with the courtesy normally expected of a visitor in a strange land.

The night bartender, Francis, pronounced frawn-*cease*, as if it were a French name, offered a caution after

Johnny's loud rebuff threatened to start a fight.

"It's OK to say no," Francis told Johnny. "With most of these fellows, that's all you have to say—no. When you call a fellow a cocksucker and stuff like that, you're just going to make trouble. And that's something we don't need here, for reasons I shouldn't have to explain."

Tall and slender with a Salvador Dali moustache, Francis had been born Franklin Bassett in Indianapolis in '04. He had come to Chicago and changed his name to Francis Fornier in 1939 after walking out on a wife and four children in Muncie.

Based on Johnny's choice of reading material, Francis had guessed that his volatile new customer was a gambler. Francis knew better than to ask why Johnny chose to drink at Carmine's, but, as an occasional gambler himself, he was comfortable asking for Johnny's thinking on a race or a ballgame.

Francis took one of Johnny's tips to a handbook on Halsted and walked out seven hundred dollars richer. From that point on, Francis made sure there was a highball and a copy of the *Daily Racing Form* waiting for Johnny at the far end of the bar, in front of the one stool between the wall and the bartender's walk-through, a location intended to minimize interaction with other customers. Whenever Francis noticed anyone giving Johnny the once-over, he'd come out from behind the bar and give the window shopper a silent shake of the head.

One night when Johnny arrived at Carmine's, there was a new deck of playing cards resting on the *Racing Form* in front of his usual seat. "I felt sorry for you," Francis said. "Maybe now you can break your solitaire losing streak."

Sipping a Canadian and water about 9:30 on a rainy Thursday night at Carmine's, Johnny laid his copy of the *Racing Form* on the bar, tipped his head back slightly, and stared up at nothing.

Francis approached the end of the bar. "See something

interesting up there?"

Johnny snapped out of it. "Just thinking—you know, analyzing my case. I'm thinking maybe I should quit the gambling racket and go legit while I still got time."

Francis picked a highball glass off the drain board under the bar and began polishing the rim with the bar rag he carried draped over his shoulder. "You married?"

Johnny instantly switched into clown mode, clasping his hands together over his heart, and speaking as if from a script: "Forty-four years without a bride, and people wonder why my life is so sad and lonely." Just as quickly, the clown mask faded. He put his forearms on the bar and stared at the highball glass in front of him.

Francis smiled. "Like you said, you've still got time. You could have a career, a family—all that. Not that I'm recommending it. But you could do that if you wanted."

"I don't know," Johnny said. "I'm thinking ... don't get me wrong, but I'm thinking maybe I got something in common with the guys who drink in this place."

"You're going over to the other side?" Francis looked surprised but also amused.

"No, no, not that," Johnny said. He took a sip from his highball and looked around the barroom. "What I'm trying to say is, most of the guys in here probably don't fit in so good in certain circles. Maybe they wish they could fit in— some of them, anyway. But they can't. Same with me—to my sorrow."

They fell silent. The juke box, brought to life by someone's nickel, began playing "Shoo-Shoo Baby," by the Andrews Sisters. Johnny drained his highball and put the glass in the gutter. Francis lifted the glass and cocked his eyebrows into a question. Johnny nodded. Francis added ice to the glass. He snatched a bottle of Canadian Club off the back bar and eyeballed a short pour. After filling the glass with water from the pressure spigot near the beer taps and adding a swizzle stick, he returned and put the drink in front of Johnny.

"That one's on me."

"Thanks." Staring hard at the drink, Johnny moved the swizzle stick in a slow circle. He looked up. "Would you say you know most of the fellas who come in here?"

"It depends," Francis said. "These men don't talk a lot about what they do out there, the respectable ones. They want to be known one way in here and another way out there. That's how it has to be. But, yeah, I know most of the regulars. Why?"

"I'm curious about a certain guy," Johnny said. He began a word sketch: curly blonde hair, probably early 30s, medium build, pretty good looking, often wears a blue blazer with brass buttons and a blue handkerchief in the lapel pocket.

"Wire-rim glasses?" Francis interrupted.

"That's the guy," Johnny said.

"Name's Dwight, or at least that's the name he uses in here. Always comes in on Thursdays. Don't know where he is tonight, but it's still early. I imagine he'll be in with the 11-o'clock crowd. I think he works at one of the high-class stores in the Loop. Capper & Capper, maybe. The word around here is he's hung like a horse. What's up? You want an introduction?"

"No, Jesus, nothing like that." Johnny drained his drink, and pushed a dollar bill across the bar. "He looks familiar, that's all. I think maybe he sold me a dress shirt one time. Thanks for the drink; I'll see you tomorrow."

36

Tony Accardo leaned forward in the wooden armchair, took a final drag off the cigarette pinched between his right thumb and forefinger, and crushed the stub into a glass ashtray on the conference table, the last wisps of smoke curling through the dim light from a single shaded lamp suspended over the table.

"So what you're saying is Ricca might as well be in Timbuktu—we can't get information back and forth."

Accardo, wearing a short-sleeve knit shirt, open at the collar, leaned back in his chair and looked to his left toward the only other person seated at the long table in the third-floor loft of the Capri Restaurant on North Clark Street. The restaurant loft, formerly Frank Nitti's headquarters, was used for meetings only occasionally now, Accardo preferring locations closer to his suburban home. He had come to the Capri because it was just four blocks from Charles Turner's law office.

"I'm saying it can't be done without putting Mr. Ricca in great danger," said Turner. "The warden—Sanford— appears to be violently anti-Catholic. He's already making prison life as difficult as possible for Mr. Ricca and the other Chicago defendants. And if he was to find out that Mr. Ricca was continuing to make decisions about his business interests back here, I believe the reprisals would be nothing short of brutal."

Accardo thought a moment. "What if we used a go-between? You know, a lawyer or maybe a police detective. Respectable. This person goes down to Atlanta once or twice a month for legal consultations or questioning or whatever—and this person uses a code ..."

"Very risky," Turner interrupted. "Sanford doesn't miss a trick. I sent a man down there—a private investigator, except we said he was a lawyer. He wasn't even allowed to shake hands with Ricca. And both times they met, a stenographer took down every word—if you can believe it. As far as Sanford is concerned, Ricca has no legal rights."

"So there's nothing we can do."

Turner paused for effect. "I didn't say that."

"OK, keep talking." Accardo twirled his index finger in a speed-it-up gesture.

Charles Turner said the solution would be to arrange a transfer from Atlanta to Leavenworth. Once in Leavenworth, where the atmosphere was less oppressive, it would be a relatively simple matter for Ricca to resume oversight of the operations in Chicago. Turner said he had been in St. Louis several times recently and had learned the transfer could be set in motion through a lawyer there.

Accardo crossed his fleshy arms and leaned forward on the table. "How do we get to this guy?"

"His name's Dillon, and he doesn't like dealing direct. The approach has to be made through a state politician, Brady. Goes by the nickname Putty Nose."

Turner added that there was even a chance Dillon could be used to get the wheels turning on a parole for Ricca—but that would have to come later.

"What's it going to take to make all this happen?"

"A hundred, maybe more," Turner said. "A lot of people would have to be, ah ... persuaded. But I'm just guessing. I'm told Dillon will have a price list once he finds out what we want."

Accardo told Turner to start the wheels turning. "But keep your distance," he added. "If this guy Dillon doesn't deal direct, then you don't either. It's better for you to stay in the background anyway. You need to finish what you're doing on Ricca's tax case. Until that's done, we're blocked on all these other things. I'll get word to our lawyer Humphreys, and we'll have him make the approach to this Putty Nose."

"Since you mentioned the tax case," Turner said. He covered his mouth with a loosely clenched fist and cleared his throat. "Have you made the necessary, ah, arrangements?"

"Yeah," Accardo said. "You'll have the money in a few days."

Turner cleared his throat again. "Good, I'll meet privately with the Bureau and that'll be the end of it. The newspapers will be kept in the dark. The case will just disappear. And I'm sure it's unnecessary to say this again, but the source of the settlement cannot be traceable."

"No problem. We'll have some of Ricca's friends drop by your office and leave cash donations."

"His friends." Turner, his faced drained of expression, stared at Accardo for a long moment.

Accardo looked up and met Turner's stare. "Hey, you want money that can't be traced back. This is the way to do it."

"But ... cash donations?" Charles Turner tugged at his shirt collar. "The U.S. attorney is certainly going to want information about these extremely generous friends."

"Don't worry about it," Accardo snapped. "You won't know any of these guys. And you won't ask. Got it?"

"No questions, right." Turner used a fountain pen to jot notes on a legal pad. He swept the pad off the table and slipped it into the briefcase next to his chair. He returned the pen to the inside pocket of his suit jacket. When he looked up, Accardo was still leaning on the table, arms crossed, only now he was grinning.

"This is some jackpot your daughter's got herself into, eh?"

"You read the papers, Mr. Accardo," Turner said coolly. "She was an innocent victim—held at gunpoint and forced to participate in an act of lawlessness."

"Right," Accardo said, still smiling, "except the fucking gun wasn't loaded."

"A technicality. She had no way of knowing it wasn't loaded. She was in fear for her life." Turner pushed his chair back from the table and stood up. "And as long as we're on the subject, have your people located Sharansky?"

"Still working on it. We did find out that one of our own people was involved. Gave your guy the gun and then tried to blow smoke up our asses. Very, very unfortunate." Accardo tapped a cigarette out of the pack lying on the table and lit it with a chrome-plated Zippo. He inhaled and then continued with his thought, the smoke coming out in little jets and puffs as he spoke. "I'm sure your guy's still holed-up somewhere in the city. He moved out of one place just before we could get to him. Nobody's seen him since. You sure you still want this done?"

"Positive. I'd take care of it myself if I had a chance. And I'd appreciate it if you would stop referring to him as my guy."

"Sure, whatever." Accardo stood, and the two men walked to the elevator door at the back of the dimly lit loft. Accardo pushed the button and they waited. "You know," he said, "I don't want tell you your business, but this thing you're asking, it seems personal. In my line of work, we try to keep personal feelings out of these decisions."

"It's the same in the legal profession, Mr. Accardo. But I'm sure you understand—if a member of your family, your wife or a daughter, had been coerced and humiliated..."

"Sure, sure, I understand," Accardo said.

The elevator door slid open, and the two men stepped into the car.

"Main floor, Sam," Accardo growled, then lowered his voice. "With all due respect, counselor, what I'm saying is if it's a personal matter, I'd try to handle it personally. Maybe you should do likewise—keep our people out of it."

"No," Turner said, "leave things the way they are."

37

*J*ohnny spotted Joe a few minutes before noon, walking along the northern boundary of Vernon Park on what had been known as Macalester Place back when the two of them were growing up in this part of the city.

In those days, this was the only nice street in the Nineteenth Ward. Joe's family had lived here, along with the ward's meager cadre of professionals and politicians. Johnny's family had lived in a tenement on the ward's southern fringe, an area settled by Russian Jews fleeing brutal pogroms in the 1880s.

Spurred by a succession of chilly nights, the elms in the park were making the transition from summer green to autumn yellow-gold. The angle of the sun in the southern sky was more than halfway to its December low, creating long, north-leaning shadows even now in the middle of the day.

Johnny and Joe knew it was risky to meet in public. But Johnny had insisted. He needed to get out, breathe a little fresh air, he said. Besides, they hadn't seen each other in ten weeks, and both of them were growing weary of the phone conversations.

Johnny watched as Joe paused and looked at a row of French-style townhouses across the street from the park— the building where his family had lived, and where Martin, his *schlemiel* of a brother, still lived.

Joe turned and walked into the park. He stopped maybe an arm's length from Johnny. They stared, both of them beaming now. Johnny lifted his arms away from his sides. "Jesus, Joe, what are you doing? Don't just stand there, for Christ's sake."

Johnny took a step and threw his arms around Joe. Joe hugged back. They stayed that way until Joe cleared his throat and pushed gently away. Holding Johnny by the shoulders, he said, "I got to be honest, my friend—you don't look so hot. You've lost weight."

"What the fuck did you expect, Joe?" Johnny's speech was even more rapid-fire than usual. "I been living like a rat in a cage. Eating out of cans, drinking with pansies. I don't even know who I am anymore. But I'll tell you, I'm done with this. I'm ... no, let's sit down. You need to be sitting when I tell you this."

"No," Joe said. "No sitting—just tell me, now."

"All right, listen to this." Johnny dropped into a slight crouch, looked furtively around the park, and brought one hand up to shield his mouth. "No, wait." He lowered his arm and stood straight. "First, I got to give myself a little credit on the Series. Did I call it or what? The Cardinals in six."

"It's not over yet," Joe said.

"Believe me, Joe, it's over," Johnny said. "There won't be a seventh game. It ends this afternoon ... where was I?"

"What I need to be sitting down to hear."

"Right," Johnny said, returning to the crouch. "Big decision, Joe. I'm about to make my move."

Joe leaned back and gave Johnny a skeptical frown. "Where, to Mexico?"

"Not that kind of move," Johnny said. "I'm going to walk out of the dump where I been holed up, start living a normal life again. I'm done hiding, Joe.

"Don't talk like a *meshugener*," Joe said, "it's not funny."

"I'm serious," Johnny countered. "I'll go bughouse if I have to stay on the lam. So here's the story—I think I've got this mess figured out. And I got a plan."

"A plan," Joe said cautiously. "Why am I afraid to ask?"

"Don't get me wrong. There's a few parts that are still ... you know, iffy. But here's the main thing. We're going to go legit, Joe. You and me, like we always talked about. We're going to quit gambling, buy a little business of our own. I even got the business picked out—a bar, far North Side. I can hardly wait for you to see it. "

"Hold on, you're getting way out front of yourself," Joe said, again reaching out to grab Johnny's shoulders. "I want to hear the part of the plan where you don't get killed. And what about the part where your buddy the pool player doesn't get us in trouble with the feds?"

"I told you, Joe, I think I've got this mess figured out," Johnny said.

"All well and good," Joe said, releasing his grip. "But just because you think you know what's going on doesn't mean it's over. Greenberg's still looking for you. Until that changes, you've got to stay under wraps."

"Joe, don't you see?" Johnny clenched his hands into fists and made like he was thumping them on a table. "I don't want to keep on living like a bum. I'd rather be dead. Really—I'd rather be dead. So we buy this bar, you and me. And if something happens to me, then you got a nice little business to carry you into old age, which, if you don't mind me saying so, you're already getting pretty close to."

Joe stared at Johnny for a moment, then walked with measured stops to the bench and sat down, removing his hat and placing it next to him.

Johnny followed, and they sat in silence.

Joe was the first to speak. "What makes you think I'd want to run a business—*our* business—if you weren't around?"

Johnny flashed a bemused look. "Joe, come on, you're not going mushy, are you?"

"I'm on the level," Joe said. "We've been like partners, brothers. Think of all the scrapes we've been through. *Together*. I think I'd ... I don't know how to put it. I think I'd lose interest if you were dead."

Johnny brightened. "You mean you'd miss me?"

Joe closed his eyes and shook his head slightly. "Of course I'd miss you, you *shmuck*. How could I not miss you?"

"Jesus, Joe, that's really ... you know, sweet," Johnny said. "But the odds are eight-to-five you won't have to miss me. I told you I got plan. I think I can make this mess go away. Now here's the deal—I'll come by your place Thursday. No, make it Friday, right around dinnertime. That's a hint, by the way. Between now and then you got to do me a favor."

"Shoot."

"See what you can find out about the federal case against Ricca."

"The extortion rap?" Joe flashed Johnny a look that said, *Huh?*

"No, the thing with his income taxes."

Joe's nose wrinkled. "What the hell does that have to do with anything?"

"Maybe nothing," Johnny said. "Just see what you can find out—tell me on Friday. Then we'll figure out how much money we got between us, and I'll tell you all about the saloon."

Joe swept his hat off the bench and placed it on his head. He sighed. "OK, my friend. As long as I can't convince you to be safe, I'll see if I can do something about the outfit's contract on you. I figure I've got one card left—I might as well try to play it. While I'm at it I'll try to get the straight poop on Ricca's taxes."

38

"*H*ave you and your mother finished the invitation lists for the wedding?" Charles Turner asked, changing the subject to indicate he no longer wished to argue with his daughter over her continuing confinement at home.

Dark squalls were roiling the lake, creating periodic torrents of rain and casting a gray morning light into the east-facing breakfast room at the back of the Turners' Ridge Road home.

Annoyed, Margaret reached across the breakfast table, gripped the handle of the teapot, refilled her cup, and returned the pot to its place on the silver tray.

Charles Turner, his newspaper lowered, observed his daughter over the tops of his eyeglasses. "I believe it's customary to ask the person closest to the tea if he or she would be kind enough to pass it to you," he said.

"There's not going to be a wedding," she said.

Silence fell over the table. Charles Turner straightened his newspaper, creasing it at the fold and placing it on his lap. "Do I sense that you and Brantley have had a quarrel?"

"Nope—no quarrel. I just don't want to get married. I'm not ready for marriage."

Charles Turner scowled. "You are twenty-six years old, young lady. Of course you're ready. Your mother was twenty-three. Have you said anything to your mother about this?"

She said she had not.

"Well, don't," he said. "It would just upset her—and unnecessarily so. This little case of cold feet or whatever it is will soon pass."

"I'm not going to change my mind," she said, glaring at her father.

Charles Turner studied his daughter. "Knowing you as I do, my dear, I'd say you are doing this just to vex me—or possibly to persuade me to loosen the restrictions I've put on you. In either case, you will be disappointed. I am not going to get upset, and you are going to remain grounded. We can discuss the restrictions again after your friend ... rather, your kidnapper no longer poses a threat to your freedom." He started to retrieve the newspaper from his lap.

She put her elbow on the table and leaned forward. "As long as you've mentioned Johnny, when were you planning to give me the money?"

Charles Turner paused. "What money?"

"The money he left in the car. In the paper bag, remember? I believe it belongs to me." She leaned back, stirred the cream into her tea, and laid the spoon her saucer.

Charles Turner flashed a disingenuous smile. "Ah, yes, the proceeds from your little escapade," he said. "I think it's best if I retain custody. Evidence, you know. Besides it was only thirty or forty dollars—didn't you read the paper?"

"It was three *hundred* dollars," she hissed. "Johnny told me."

Her final three words hung in the air for a long moment while father and daughter stared at each other. "When, exactly," Charles Turner measured each word, "did he tell you this?"

She sat up and shrugged. "I don't know ... six, seven weeks ago. I think you were in St. Louis."

"He called? And you didn't tell me?" He was annoyed.

"No, he didn't call. Well, actually he did. From a pay phone. That's how I knew where to look for him."

Charles Turner snatched the paper out of his lap and hurled it on the floor. "Damn it!" he sputtered, "you ... you *saw* him? Where is he? Tell me now."

She pouted. "Awww, you're upset. Was it something I said?"

Charles Turner's face was crimson. "You deliberately disobeyed me. You knew you weren't supposed to leave this house on your own. You *knew* you were not to see that wretched man, and you did it anyway. Now I will ask you one more time—where is he?"

"Go screw yourself."

It was the quickness of his blow, rather than the force of it, that stunned Margaret, although the slap was hard enough to make a sharp pop when it connected. It spun her head to the right, leaving the left side of her face feeling hot and prickly. In the hush that followed, she could hear him breathing.

"Don't you dare talk to me like that—*ever*," he fumed. "Do you hear me? Never again."

With her left hand pressed to her stinging cheek, she reached for the silver spoon near her right hand, and raised her eyes to meet her father's glare. "Even if I told you where he was, it wouldn't help," she said in a level voice. "He was about to move."

"I can't tell you how infuriating this is," he said, his lips drawn tight against his clenched teeth. "I simply do not understand your lack of regard for my counsel and everything I'm trying to do for you." He closed his eyes and massaged his forehead with the fingers of one hand. "Did he tell you where he was going?"

"No, he just said he had to move. Certain people were

getting too close."

Charles Turner's eyebrows shot upward, yanking his eyes open. "Certain people. Which people? This is important—did he say?"

"He didn't have to. I saw them. One of them was that ridiculous private investigator of yours. Shamus, or whatever his name is. I assume he was following me again."

Charles Turner leaned forward. "How did you know who it was? You've never laid eyes on Lloyd Shockey."

"Johnny told me who he was," she said.

"Johnny," he repeated with churlish inflection. "I simply cannot understand ... Where did this happen? Where was Mr. Shockey?"

"In the city," she said. "That little street off Howard with all the bars on it. And he had Brantley with him."

"Brantley? Good grief ... did either one of them see you?"

"No."

He chopped his hand on the table to emphasize his question: "Are you absolutely *sure* they didn't?"

She shot a glance toward the ceiling: "Of course I'm sure. Don't have a cow."

Charles Turner looked away, drumming the fingers of his right hand on the table. "That would have been very difficult to explain," he said before retreating into thought.

The ensuing silence was broken only by the *tink* of Margaret's spoon hitting the sides of her china teacup. Charles Turner continued to stare off to one side. "I'm quite sure," he said after a while, "that Mr. Shockey was on assignment—if Brantley was with him, it was something for the firm."

She snorted. "You're not the least bit worried about this private eye, are you? You're so obsessed with Johnny you can't see the real danger right under your nose. Just think about what that P.I. knows, for heaven's sake."

He turned and glared down his nose at his daughter. "I

am perfectly capable of handling Mr. Shockey," he said, "without your advice."

"Fine, handle him any way you want. I'll enjoy seeing the look on your face when I say I told you so. And I still want my money."

"What?" He reacted as if startled by the change of subject.

"The three hundred dollars—it's mine and I want it, damn it."

Charles Turner shook his head vigorously. "It's far too much money for you to have in your possession—especially since I can guess what you'd try to do with it. For now, we'll consider it a fee for my legal services, and you will remain grounded."

He leaned to the side and picked up the newspaper off the floor, straightening the pages. "And we will talk about the wedding again this weekend, after you've regained your senses."

39

*J*oe drove the Ford convertible to the Loop and paid a call on Frankie Fats Aiello—second time since Johnny went on the lam that he'd gone to Frankie's handbook looking for a favor.

Frankie's connections were impeccable—with good reason. He had worked his way up from bagman to driver to bookie during the regimes of three bosses, and was regarded in the upper echelons of the outfit as a guy who did what he was told and kept his mouth shut.

According to one story, Frankie also had done a stint as a button man, responsible for one or more of the killings in the territorial war of '33. Joe and Johnny never put much stock at that story, though. As Joe put it, "Frankie, he could kill a bottle of Chianti and a plate of spaghetti, but not a human."

Frankie had survived two bombings and a shooting since being put in charge of the North Wabash handbook in '33. A couple of the handbook's regulars swore Frankie could pick up a telephone any time of day or night and talk to someone close, very close, to Tony Accardo.

But Frankie Fats was a realist when it came to his own

connections—which is to say he knew when *not* to make such calls. And something told him this was one of those times

"Why the hell do you want to see Greenberg?" he asked Joe. "I already set up one meet. You still trying to work things out for that crazy pal of yours?"

"Yeah, you could put it that way," Joe said. "I still can't figure out what the hell is going on. That's why I need to see Greenberg."

"What is it with you and Johnny, anyway? I don't get it."

Joe pulled a wood chair away from the loft railing, turned it toward the desk, and sat. "Hard to explain," he said. "Maybe we were brothers in another life, I don't know. So, do I get to see Greenberg again? I'm just looking for information."

"You think you're going to get information from Greenberg?" Frankie shook his head. "You're not going to get shit—not from him."

"I got that impression the first time I saw him," Joe said. "But I thought maybe he could get me a sit-down, nothing major, just a minute or two, with the guy who put out the contract in the first place."

Frankie's eyes narrowed. "You talking about ... the top guy?"

"Right, I thought ..."

"Stop right there," Frankie commanded, tipping back in the groaning swivel chair. "Two things." He held up one pudgy finger, then two. "Number one, Greenberg doesn't have the juice to set up a meet like that. Number two, even if he did, it wouldn't happen. You got a better chance of having afternoon tea with fucking Roosevelt."

"For God's sake, Frankie, when Francesco was running the business, he'd see me in a minute," Joe protested. "Are you telling me that doesn't that count for anything?"

"That's what I'm telling you," Frankie said. "Sure, everybody knew you and Nitti went way back. But he's dead. It's a whole new thing now."

Joe looked away and exhaled, his shoulders slumping. He turned back to Frankie Fats. "What about you? You've got connections all over the place. You must have heard something. Why are they looking for Johnny?"

"Haven't heard one word," Frankie said, raising his right hand as if testifying under oath. "And, OK, I got to be honest with you—that's a little unusual. I mean, you and I know that nine times out of ten these beefs have something to do with business—or maybe a double cross. But this is more like a vendetta or something. What I mean is, when a guy tries to screw the outfit and gets taken for a ride, that guy knows why. And the outfit wants everybody else to know, too. Otherwise the rubout doesn't do anything except get rid of one asshole. But why am I telling you this, Joe? You know all this shit. My point is, if the contract on Johnny had anything to do with business, there'd be some kind of word on the street by now. And there's nothing."

"What about that holdup on Broadway last month?" Joe asked. "You know, the one where that guy got killed. Greenberg tried to tell me the contract had something to do with that."

"Yeah, I heard your pal was mixed up in that," Frankie said with just a hint of a smirk. "Let me answer your question this way—the last time I checked, the outfit was not putting out contracts on guys for—what's your word?—michigans."

"*Mishegas*—right, you can say that again," Joe nodded. He looked away, took a deep breath, and exhaled. "What do you hear about Ricca's tax case?"

Aiello scowled. "Ricca ... why do you want to know about that?"

"Just humor me," Joe said, now looking at Aiello. "I need to know. It's for Johnny."

"For Johnny?" Aiello was still scowling. "I don't get it. But don't explain—since you're a friend of ours, I'll let you in on what I know. You saw the stories in the paper last year, right?"

"Sure," Joe said, learning forward. "The feds were claiming Ricca owed something like a hundred and forty G's in taxes."

"One forty-one," Aiello corrected. "And they wouldn't back off that number. At least that's the impression I got because a lot of us were asked to, ah, shall we say, *contribute* toward the settlement. By now it's probably done. But it's all very hush-hush. You didn't hear it from me."

"Right," Joe said. "Back to Johnny—you must have some idea, some theory about that contract."

Frankie pulled a pack of Lucky Strikes out of his shirt pocket, tapped one cigarette out of the white pack with the red bullseye label. Tipping forward in his chair, he swept a Zippo off the desk and lit the cigarette. "I got shit," Frankie said, tipping his head back and exhaling. "And I know better than to ask questions. Face it, Joe—maybe we'll never know."

"So I'm just supposed to sit and wait? That wouldn't be right. Johnny and I go way back, Frankie. I've got to do something."

"Hey, you and I know how this is going to end," Frankie said. "This is gonna sound a little harsh, but if I were you, I'd start getting used to not having my friend around anymore."

40

Johnny leaned in through the passenger-side window and gave two singles to the cabbie. "Keep it," he said.

He turned, pausing on the sidewalk to scan the industrial-looking building that went with the address he had given the cab driver. He had assumed there'd be a conspicuous sign, probably neon. Instead, a painted-wood rectangle, maybe one foot by two, marked the entrance door in the red-brick facade. Johnny realized this would be the first time he'd ever walked into Carmine's Hideaway through the street entrance.

He looked right and left, pulled his hat brim down low in front of his face, and crossed the sidewalk.

The bar, reeking of clashing brands of cologne, was packed with overheated men, as it usually was late on a Thursday night. Johnny could feel himself being sized up, a discomfort he had avoided, though not completely, when he was entering Carmine's via the alley door. At least he had learned not to take it personally.

Glancing to his left through the crowd, he caught sight of Francis behind the long bar. The barkeep had already spotted Johnny; he held up an empty highball glass and pointed to it, raising his eyebrows in a silent question mark. Johnny waved a wordless no.

He moved along the edge of the dance floor, taking care not to make physical contact with any of the male couples or eye contact with any of the men who might be hoping for dance partners. Reaching the line of booths on the wall opposite the bar he paused for a moment to survey the patrons who were drinking and conversing. He took five quick steps, turned, and slid into a booth already occupied by two men.

"Hey, how y'doing?" he said. A crooked smile creased his face as he looked into Brantley's wide-eyed gaze. "Fancy meeting you in a joint like this."

"How did ..." Brantley was suddenly breathing hard. His face reddened. "You little shit—you can't do this. I warned you, god damn it."

"Yeah, yeah—taxes and jail and all that baloney," Johnny interrupted. "But things have changed. Or maybe you didn't notice." He leaned across the table and lowered his voice, as if sharing confidential information. "You guys have been hanging out in a fairy bar. No kidding. By the way," he shifted his body toward Brantley's companion, "we haven't been introduced. You're Dwight. Or at least that's what they call you, right? They call me Johnny. I heard a few things about you—actually I only heard one thing. But we don't want to get into that. I'm not a cop, I'm just here to have a little conversation with your playmate, and it's kind of, you know, confidential."

"Give us a minute," Brantley said, his voice now level. "It won't take long."

Dwight looked at Brantley and moved one hand under the table. "If you need me, I'll be at the bar," he said. He pursed his lips for an instant, then slid to his left out of the booth.

"All right," Brantley snapped, "what's this all about?"

"Simple," said Johnny. "I want you off my back.

Permanently."

"Or?"

"Or your future takes a turn for the crapper," Johnny said, settling into a matter-of-fact cadence. "Your wedding plans, your house in the suburbs—kaput. Personally, I don't care if you marry the boss's daughter, and I don't care how many dirty little secrets you have on the side."

"There aren't any secrets," Brantley blurted out. "Margaret already knows. We ... we have an understanding. So just forget whatever it is you think you're doing."

Johnny's eyes narrowed. "Nice try," he said after a moment's thought. "I think you're lying. But even if you're not, even if Margaret is all simpatico with you and Eisenhower over there," he jerked his thumb in the direction of the bar, "here's the thing. I got a funny feeling your future father-in-law won't be so—how should I put it?—so accommodating. When he finds out, you can kiss goodbye to your big promotion."

"You little shit—you think you can blackmail me?"

"You're not listening," Johnny said, tipping forward to emphasize the point he was about to make. "This isn't a business transaction. I don't want money, I just want you to get off my case, forget you ever saw me, leave me the fuck alone. If you don't fuck with me, maybe I'll forget how pissed off I am at you—you and that palooka of yours. That's the deal."

Brantley looked away, then snapped back and pointed at Johnny. "One thing stays the same," he said. "You keep your distance from Margaret."

"No, no, no, no," Johnny leaned back in the booth, wig-wagging both hands. "You're not getting the point. We're not negotiating here. You just listen to me and do what I say. You don't get to tell me anything."

Brantley gripped the edge of the table with both hands and spoke through clenched teeth. "You think you're so clever," he said, "but you're forgetting one little detail, Jew boy. There's a contract with your name on it. You're as good as dead—it's only a question of when."

"Don't count on it," Johnny said. "I've been beating the odds for twenty years. That's a hell of a streak, mister. One thing I've learned—never bet against a streak."

Johnny slid to his right on the red plastic seat and got up out of the booth. He looked down at Brantley. "Forget all that shit about getting me jammed up. You sic the feds on me, it's over for you. Got it?"

"Get out of my sight," Brantley growled.

"Gladly." Johnny turned and took two steps, but stopped, wheeled, and came back to the table. "One last thing," he said, placing both hands on the table top and leaning in. "You're going to find this out eventually—or figure it out for yourself. If Margaret was kidnapped, why did she sit in her daddy's car and wait while a holdup was going on inside that store? Think about it, asshole. She *wanted* to be there. I know because I pulled the heist."

Johnny headed back toward the street entrance.

Behind him, Brantley lurched clumsily out of the booth and pitched forward, lumbering into the aura of the blue lights illuminating the dance floor, quickly closing the distance between himself and Johnny.

Johnny heard someone in the crowd of dancers yell, "Look out," and turned just as Brantley tackled him, slamming the side of his face to the dance floor. "I'll kill you," Brantley roared.

Brantley curled an arm around Johnny's neck and rolled, pulling Johnny off the floor. Johnny kicked wildly and scrabbled at Brantley's encircling arm with both hands. Uttering a primal scream, Brantley used his free hand to pull his arm tighter around Johnny's throat.

His face bathed in blue light, Johnny was having trouble seeing. His eyelids fluttered as consciousness slipped away.

41

*J*oe was reading the *Tribune* and listening to "Major Bowes' Amateur Hour" when the buzzer sounded in his apartment, indicating he had a caller.

He tossed the paper on the floor, rose from the armchair, and went to the front window, scanning the street below. The buzzer sounded again. Joe walked to the door of his apartment and, after a brief hesitation, pushed the button that unlocked the inside vestibule door downstairs.

A moment later, he could hear footsteps on the stairway. Definitely one person. That was good. If it was Greenberg, he'd have Capezio with him.

The sound of the footfalls stopped and someone rapped on the door. Without removing the security chain, Joe turned the handle and opened the door about three inches.

"Joe, it's me," Johnny said. "Open up, for Christ's sake."

Joe unhooked the chain. "Jesus," he said as Johnny walked into the apartment, "what the hell happened to you?"

"Bar fight," Johnny said. "Bartender stopped it in the seventh round. If you think I look bad," he sized himself up in a small mirror near the door, "you should see the other guy. The bartender whacked him pretty good—sent him to the hospital."

"What other guy? And why were you in a bar fight? You've never been in a fight in your life."

"First time for everything," Johnny said, walking into the small living room and falling backwards onto the sofa. "And that's the last time for me. Any chance I can sleep on this for a couple of nights? You know, while I'm looking for a place of my own."

"Of course," Joe said. "You mean you're really not going to tell me about this . . . this bar fight?"

Johnny turned on the sofa and lay on his back, feet still on the rug. "Let's just say I had a little talk with Margaret's fiancé. It's all part of my plan, Joe. Which reminds me, can I borrow the Ford on Sunday—I'll probably need it all afternoon."

"It's yours, any time you need it," Joe said, taking a seat in an armchair facing the sofa. "I've got a pant-load of gas coupons, enough to get you to Mexico."

Still lying on the sofa, Johnny turned his head to look at Joe. "Do you think we've wasted our lives?"

"Jeez, where did that come from?" Joe said. "Have you been analyzing your case again?"

"I'm serious, Joe." Johnny turned his head to look back at the ceiling. "The thing with Margaret and me—it was like an alarm clock. 'Wake up, you *putz*—while you were pounding twenty years down a rat hole, here's what you were missing.'"

"OK," Joe said, "so we didn't do a lot of the things that normal people do. We missed out on some things. But we made good money in really hard times, my friend. And we had a lot of fun together. That's not such a horrible way to spend twenty-three years. As long as you're analyzing your case, here's something to think about—maybe you couldn't have had the romance without those twenty-three years."

Johnny scowled. "I don't get it, what are you saying?"

Joe tipped his head back, raised his arm, and moved it in a slow arc, left to right. "I'm saying maybe everything you did in all those years, every good and bad decision you made, every step you took, every screwed-up experience you had, led you to that moment in the Empire Room and got you ready for that relationship. Change one thing—just one—and it doesn't happen."

"What about her?"

"Same deal."

Johnny stared at the ceiling for a moment. "That's deep, Joe," he said. "Where do you come up with this shit? I get a headache just trying to think about something like that."

Joe smiled. "Here's another reason why we haven't wasted the last twenty-three years. How many people go through life and never have a friendship like this one, eh? But here I go, getting mushy on you. We've got business to take care of." He smacked his hands on the tops of his thighs. "So I'll fix you something to eat, and then we'll get started."

"I got a better idea," Johnny said, sitting up. "Let's go up to Howard Street right now. I want to show you the place we're going to make an offer to buy. Let's hope they still got the For Sale sign in the window. After we look the place over, we'll get a bite, and you can tell me about Ricca's tax thing."

"I don't have much," Joe said.

"Tell me anyway," Johnny said, getting up from the sofa. "I'll try to look interested. Let's go look at a bar."

42

"May I help you?"

The receptionist at the desk inside the door to Turner, Barfield, and Moran was a head-turner—her hair a tumble of black ringlets piled high on her head and cascading down the back of her pale white neck, her mouth a crimson smear. She wore a phone operator's headset, a thin chrome boom curling from the single earphone to the small black microphone in front of her pouted lips.

Minutes earlier, Johnny had called from a phone in the ground-floor lobby, asking if Brantley was in the office. He was not surprised when the receptionist reported that Mister Adams had been out sick since Friday.

What a pussy.

Now in the office, Johnny removed his hat and looked around at the dark-paneled waiting area. "I'm here to see Turner," he said to the dark-haired receptionist. "It's about the wedding."

"Miss Turner's wedding?" The receptionist eyed Johnny carefully. He was well dressed, but the bruises and abrasions were clear signs that he'd been in an accident or a fight. "Do you have an appointment?"

"I don't really need one," Johnny said without thinking.

The receptionist explained that Turner—except she called him Mr. Turner—was a very busy man. "Would you care to make an appointment for later in the week?"

"Look, I know he wants to see me," Johnny said, fidgeting with the brim of his hat. "We were going to meet yesterday ... after church. The three of us—me and him and, ah, the missus. But something came up. He'll be sore if we don't get this problem worked out today."

Over the weekend, he and Joe had agreed to make an offer on Apex Liquors, a bar and package store on North Paulina Street. They figured they had more than enough between them to make a down payment. At this moment, Joe was probably opening a checking account at North Shore National Bank. But there was one more piece of unfinished business. It involved Turner. And it had to be put to rest right now.

Johnny was glancing around, shifting his weight from foot to foot. The receptionist eyed him coldly, then pushed a button on the large console in the middle of the desk. "Gladys, there's a gentleman out here, a Mr ..." She glanced up at Johnny.

"What the hell—Sharansky, with a Y."

"A Mr. Shansky, wants to see Mr. Turner—something to do with the wedding ... I know, but this gentlemen says there's a problem. Seems like it might be important."

She pushed the button again, and looked up at Johnny. "You can take a seat over there."

"Thanks, I'll stand."

After two or three minutes, Turner, in a vest and shirtsleeves, stepped into the opening to the left of the reception desk. He looked Johnny up and down, barely concealing his contempt.

"Wedding, my foot," he said. "You are a very reckless man, Sharansky. I can't imagine what you think you're doing here."

"I got a business deal for you," Johnny said. "It shouldn't take long. You want me to spell it out?"

"Not here," Turner said. "In my office."

Turner headed back in the direction he'd come from.

Johnny stepped through the opening, falling in about two strides behind Turner, who continued until he reached a door at the end of the interior hall. He paused in front of a desk to the left of the door. "Gladys, tell Barfield our meeting will be delayed. And I'm expecting a phone call. Don't hold it—put it through."

He strode into the office and headed for an oversize Cuban-mahogany desk in front of a bank of windows. "Close the door," he barked at Johnny.

Turner circled the desk and stopped in front of the east-facing windows, his back to Johnny. "If you've come here looking for money," he said, wheeling to face Johnny, "you're out of luck. The deal I offered expired when you refused to stop seeing my daughter and almost got her killed."

"I don't want your money," Johnny said. "All I want is for you to pick up that phone and cancel the contract."

"What contract?"

"The contract on me, my life—that one."

Turner folded his arms and shook his head. "I can assure you I have no earthly idea what you're talking about," he said.

Johnny walked slowly toward Turner, with the desk still between them. He placed his hat, brim up, on the desk and then leaned forward, palms flat on the smooth wood surface. "Sure, and Dempsey had no idea he was punching Sharkey in the nuts," Johnny said. "Spare me the act. I'm gonna show you how easy it is for a dummy like me to put you in the middle of this jackpot."

"I thought you said this wouldn't take long," Turner said.

"It won't," Johnny replied. "Just be patient. While I was on the lam, see, I spent a lot of time thinking about people who might want to see me dead."

"A long list, I'm sure." Turner cracked a sardonic smile.

Leaving his hat on the desk, Johnny walked to a large red-leather chair, pirouetting into the seat. "No, as a matter of fact, it was a short list. Only two names—yours and your future son-in-law."

"Sheer paranoia," Turner challenged. "Mister Adams doesn't even know you exist."

"Wrong," Johnny barked, leaning back in the chair. "We were introduced by your P.I.—in a fucking pool hall yet. But I'm guessing the shamus neglected to tell you."

"Shockey?" The smirk faded. Turner glared at Johnny. "Did this encounter, by any chance, take place in the vicinity of Howard Street?"

"Could be," Johnny said. "Maybe you're smarter than I thought. Nah, you're not that smart. I bet Margaret told you."

Johnny vaulted out of the chair and strode back to the desk, pointing to the abrasions on the side of his face. "And then I saw your lawyer boy again last week. Not in a pool hall. That's when this shit happened. But that's between me and him. It's nothing to do with you." Johnny went back and flopped into the chair, crossing his right ankle over his left knee.

"So there's two guys who wanted to see me dead," Johnny said, picking up his train of thought, "but they didn't have the connections. So there's no way either one of them could have put out a contract. And they were too hoity-toity to do it themselves. But then—and here's the really interesting part—a little birdie told me you're handling Ricca's tax case."

"That's no secret," Turner interjected. "It's a matter of public record. And it means nothing."

"Wrong again," Johnny said, raising an index finger to punctuate the point. "It means you're connected. And it all adds up, see—you got your reasons to want me dead, you got access to the outfit's top guy, and he's got a way to get the job done. As soon as I heard that, I knew." Johnny stared triumphantly at Turner and jabbed an index finger. "*You're* the sonofabitch."

Turner turned slowly to face the window, his back to

Johnny again. He clasped his hands behind him. "You are delusional," he said smoothly. "To show the absurdity of what you're suggesting, let's say you really are a marked man. If somebody out there wants to help clean up this city by getting rid of you, I can't think of a single reason— not one—why I would want to intercede. So, you see, you've come here on a fool's errand. You are trying to get me to do something I have no power to do even if I wanted to do it—which I do not." He turned back toward the room and gave Johnny a terse smile. "And now I believe our business has been concluded."

"Not quite," Johnny said. He got up from the chair and walked around the desk, approaching to within a couple of feet of Turner's right shoulder. "See, I figure you already put in a call. You did it as soon as you knew I was in the waiting room. So before you get a call-back from Accardo or one of his people, let me tell you why you'll want to cancel that contract. The way I see it, you don't want your old lady to know about the Edgewater Beach, and you don't want her to hear the true story about that heist on Broadway. And you really, really don't want her to find out what a bad boy you've been, right?"

Turner's face hardened. He gripped the back of his desk chair with both hands. "Stop right there," he snarled, head down. "You are playing with fire, Sharansky. My wife is off limits. You will not involve her in any of this, do you hear? Just stay away. If you so much as think about communicating with my wife ..."

"Oops, too late," Johnny interrupted. "I met your wife yesterday when I drove by the house."

"No!" Turner shouted, his head snapping right to look at Johnny. "You did *not*."

"Yeah, I did," Johnny said, leaning in. "She told me you and Margaret were at church."

"You spoke to my wife? At my house?" The veins in Turner's head and neck appeared to be on the verge of exploding.

Johnny smirked. "Don't worry, Chuck, I didn't let any family secrets out of the bag—just told her I was an old friend. Said I'd catch you here at the office. Handsome woman. I think she liked me. And I don't want to split hairs, but it's really her house, right? Not yours."

Uttering a cry between a roar and a growl, Turner heaved the heavy desk chair toward Johnny, causing it to topple on its side with a thud, and forcing Johnny to do a quick backward dance step. Turner reached down, opened the top left desk drawer, and withdrew a nickel-plated .38 revolver. His hand shaking, he pointed the revolver at Johnny.

"You detestable snipcock ..." Turner was breathing hard.

"Are you all right, Mr. Turner?" The voice came from the intercom on the desk.

Keeping one eye on Johnny, Turner leaned across the desk and pushed a button on the black box. "Yes, I have everything under control—thank you, Gladys."

He straightened up, still pointing the pistol at Johnny. "Mr. Accardo told me I should handle this myself," he said. "I had no idea how easy it would be."

"Sure," Johnny said, now edging very slowly away from the pistol, "easy to do. Maybe not so easy to explain, eh?"

Turner answered with a mirthless "Ha." His eyes narrowed. "You seem to be forgetting that you're a wanted man," he said. "Kidnapping and armed robbery. I'll have an entirely plausible story for the police, you can be sure of that."

"There's something you ought to know before you pull the trigger," Johnny said, talking fast now because he hadn't anticipated this turn of events. "If I leave here dead, the world is going to find out about the money you took."

"You're bluffing." Turner cocked the hammer and raised the revolver.

"Pull the trigger, you'll find out," Johnny said.

43

After parking their unmarked Ford in a loading zone, the two detectives angled across the street toward the alley running behind buildings on Clark Street. They pulled their overcoats snug at the neck and held their hats in place against a biting 25 mile-an-hour wind bringing an early taste of winter off the lake.

Even in plain clothes and with their shoulders hunched against the cold, they walked with the indifferent swagger that identified them as cops. The older of the two was a sergeant, Ryan Flaherty, a detective for most of his 24 years on the force; the younger was a patrolman, Nick Longo, recently reassigned to detective.

At the alley entrance the two plainclothesmen shouldered through a knot of onlookers, some of them blowing on their bare hands or stamping their feet to stay warm. A uniformed cop prevented the onlookers from moving any closer to the tarp-covered body that lay in the alley, about fifty feet from the street. Standing around the lump were two more uniformed officers, a man from the county coroner's office, Michael McCarthy, and two guys in coveralls and knit caps who were waiting for permission to load the corpse into a hurry-up wagon parked to one side of the alley.

"You guys took your time getting here," McCarthy said as the two detectives approached the group.

"What've we got?" Flaherty said.

"Could be a jumper," McCarthy said, pointing up. "He came from up there."

Still holding the brims of their hats, Flaherty and Longo tipped their heads back and noted an open window eight floors above the brick-paved alley.

"On the other hand," McCarthy continued, "he could have been helped out the window. Autopsy'll settle the issue. Maybe."

"Any suicide note?"

"Haven't found one yet," McCarthy said.

"How about witnesses?"

"A man out walking his dog, sergeant," replied one of the uniforms. "Said he was crossing the alley just as the body landed. But that's all he saw."

Flaherty looked back at the coroner's man. "Why do you say he might have been tossed?"

"Looks like there could have been a fight or some kind of struggle—you'll see when you go up there," McCarthy said, pointing again toward the eighth floor. "The office looks like a tornado hit it."

"So what are you thinking, robbery?"

"That's your call," McCarthy said. "We just decide whether it was homicide or suicide."

"Did he have a wallet on him?" Flaherty said.

One of the uniforms shook his head: "No, sir. No wallet, no cash."

Flaherty dropped to his haunches and pulled back the tarp. He winced. "Jesus, he must landed head first. Hey, am I the only one here who recognizes this son of a bitch?" He looked up at the shrugs. "I remember the guy from when he was a cop—nineteenth district. This was before your time, kid," he said to Longo. "I'm talking fifteen, twenty years ago, Prohibition. The son of a bitch was a bagman for one of the North Side gangs. Made a pile of money. Allegedly."

Flaherty dropped the corner of the tarp and stood up. "If this was a suicide, I'll eat my fucking hat," he said. "And forget about robbery. This mutt had a real talent for making enemies. One of them tossed him out the window, you can bet on it." He looked at McCarthy. "You said he came from an office—what kind of office?"

"Assuming it was his office," McCarthy said, "looks like he was a gumshoe."

"Well, well," Flaherty said with a smirk. "Patrolman Shockey became a private eye—a fucking private eye—the last refuge of a dirty cop."

44

*J*oe pried open one of the four corrugated cardboard boxes on the counter and ran his left hand over the tops of the half-pint bottles of Seagram's 7 and Corby's blended whiskey, Chapin & Gore bourbon and Gordon's gin, checking his count against quantities listed on the delivery invoice in his right hand.

He counted the bottles in the other three boxes while the driver who'd delivered the boxes leaned on a hand truck and waited. If there was a discrepancy, it was important to catch it before the driver left—a lesson Joe had learned his second week as owner of Apex Liquors. Distributors didn't want to hear about a shortage unless it could be verified by the driver who delivered the goods.

"OK, everything checks out," Joe said. He signed the top copy of the invoice, separated it from the copy underneath, and gave the top copy to the driver, whose name, Walt, was sewn into a patch on the left breast of his green wool work jacket.

"See you next week," Walt said. He rolled the hand truck to the street entrance, turned and pushed his rear end against the door to open it, pulling the hand truck past him to the sidewalk while holding the door with his body.

"Yeah, be good," Joe said.

"Have a nice Thanksgiving," Walt sang out as the door swung closed.

Joe tossed the invoice copy on the desk near the front window, and took a look at his wristwatch. It was a few minutes past four. He walked the length of the L-shaped counter toward the rear of the store and entered the adjacent barroom, separated from the package goods by a floor-to-ceiling partition with doorless openings at the front and rear of the store. Clear Plexiglas panels ran the length of the partition, just above the level of the booths on the barroom side, and each panel was curtained to filter out the harsh fluorescent light from the package store.

Joe stopped just inside the dimly lit barroom. "Red, Earl, you fellows need anything? Another shot of that Irish paint remover?"

The two men at the bar, both wearing U.S. Mail caps and cold-weather uniforms, turned slightly. "Thanks but no thanks, Joe," Red said. "We got to get back to the P.O. and punch out."

Joe returned to the package store, hefted one of the four boxes on the counter and carried it to the storeroom at the rear of the building, then did the same with the other three boxes. As he was lifting the final box, he heard Red call out: "Catch you tomorrow, Joe."

It was past 4:30 when the night bartender, Dexter, came through the front door—late again. "I got tied up at my girlfriend's place," he told Joe. "Lost track of time. Be a pal, would you, and keep an eye on the bar while I shave?"

"Go ahead," Joe said. "You look a little rough around the edges."

Stripping off his coat, Dexter headed back to the men's room.

In the barroom, Joe removed the beer steins and shot glasses from the bar where the two mailmen had been sitting. He cleaned the top of the bar, washed and rinsed the steins and shot classes, and left them to dry on a steel drain board along with glasses used earlier in the days.

The daily chores, remembering what to do and when, had seemed tedious at first. But the routines and details were beginning to take on a rhythm. Joe had to admit he enjoyed the mindless repetition.

He heard the door open on the package side, and glanced at his watch. Four forty-five, right on time, he thought.

He walked through the partition and looked toward the front of the store. Johnny, wearing a camel's hair topcoat and a light brown felt hat, was standing a few feet inside the door, tugging at his leather gloves. Johnny looked up and grinned.

"Hey, Joe," Johnny said, spreading his arms wide as if putting himself on display. "I'm still breathing. What are the odds on that?"

45

*J*ohnny hefted his overcoat onto a coat hook, spun his hat into the booth and slid in after it. Joe, early as usual, was already seated across from Johnny, hands cradling a cup of tea.

It was Sunday, Joe's day off. Come warm weather, Johnny and Joe would almost certainly resume their bench-sitting at Howard Street Beach, but with winter closing in, they were happy to spend Sunday mornings at Ashkenaz Restaurant and Delicatessen on Morse Avenue.

They went through their usual greeting:

"Johnny, how're you doing?"

"Still fooling 'em. How about you, Joe?"

"Everything's copasetic—couldn't be better."

Johnny ordered coffee and a bagel, switching to tea when he was told the restaurant was out of coffee, and then noticed the sports section lying on the table. "If we were still in action," he said, putting his finger on one of the headlines, "do you think we'd be putting money on pro football?"

"Nah," Joe shook his head and made a sour face. "College ball is tough enough to figure, but the pros are a joke. Take that Chicago game today—you'd have to bet eight hundred, maybe more, to win a lousy fifty bucks. They gotta figure out a different system. Even the bookies don't want to mess with those odds. But we don't have to worry about crap like that anymore. Right?" He looked suspiciously at Johnny.

Johnny raised both hands. "Honest, Joe, I've quit. No more bets. But here's the thing."

"Uh-oh." Joe's shoulders sagged.

"No, listen," Johnny said, the words coming in a rush. "What about little bets, say, fifty cents? That would be the limit."

Joe frowned at Johnny as if he were a stranger. "Aren't you the one who always said we had to do this cold turkey—no big bets, no little bets? Nothing. What's going on?"

"For Christ's sake, Joe, we spent half our lives in saloons," Johnny said. "And now we're running one. You know what goes on. Guys are always arguing about a game or a prizefight, always making bets with each other. When one of our customers wants to make a bet, we can't say fuck you, we don't believe in gambling."

"Ah, so you bet the guy a half a charlie."

"Right, just to be sociable. If it was more than fifty cents and the guy lost, he might take his business to Walgreen's."

Joe nodded his head: "OK, we'll change our agreement. Starting now, we will allow fifty-cent bets—but only to promote friendly relations with customers. Now that we've got that settled ..."

Joe paused and looked away. "There's something I want us to talk about," he said. "You know how it bothers me when something's going on with you, something you're not telling me about. I've had a feeling for weeks ..."

"Jesus, Joe, how can you say that? We've always been straight with each other."

"Yeah, what about that *verkakte* holdup?"

"Well, almost always. You know what I mean."

"OK, just hear me out," Joe said. "Then tell me if I'm wrong. Every afternoon you walk into the bar and make it sound like a minor miracle you're still alive. But I'm thinking, Greenberg knows damn well where to find you. He's known since we bought the business. So it's not a miracle, is it? Something happened to that contract."

Johnny gave Joe a pleading look. "Joe, I'll be honest, it's hard ... I don't know if I can talk about it. I'm still having nightmares. But I got to get it off my chest sooner or later." He leaned across the table and lowered his voice. "You're right, there's no contract. I got it cancelled. Except that's not the miracle, Joe. See, Margaret's old man tried to kill me."

"What?"

"I'm serious, Joe, he tried to kill me. But the gun—how would you say? It didn't go off."

"You mean he tried to shoot you and the gun misfired?"

"Yeah, that's it—misfired. It was a fucking miracle, Joe."

Joe, too, leaned across the table. "That's awful," he said, speaking in a half whisper. "No wonder you're having nightmares. But where does the contract come in? Or does it?"

"It was the old man all along," Johnny said. "He's connected. He was the one who took out the contract. But then he tried to do it himself—he pointed that thing right at me and pulled the trigger, for Christ's sake. I was so scared I crapped my trousers. But just a little bit. And then I could see he was losing his nerve. So that was my chance. I told him I knew he finagled Ricca's taxes and took the money for himself."

Joe flopped back against the booth seat. "He stole? From the outfit?"

"More than a hundred G's," Johnny said.

"That huge," Joe said. "How'd you find out?"

"The big *k'nocker* boyfriend let it slip," Johnny said, now whispering and glancing around at nearby booths. "In the pool hall—he was bragging about how his boss settled Ricca's case for pennies on the dollar. But you told me the outfit had to pony up the full hundred and forty-one G's, so I figured most of that went right into the *gonef's* pockets. I warned him—this is after the gun didn't fire, and I was doing some fast talking—I told him the outfit was going to get tipped off if anything happened to me."

"So you had some kind of insurance," Joe said.

"Yeah, my sister would have mailed a package," Johnny said. "I gave it to her that day I borrowed your car. But I almost fucked up, Joe. I never thought the *schmuck* would pull out a gun and try to do it himself. Anyway, now you know why it's a miracle. And when you think about it, it was a miracle for the old man, too. If that gun goes off, he's in the sanitary canal right now."

"And I'm a sole proprietor." Joe was shaking his head. "I can't believe you've been carrying this around since October."

Joe leaned back in the booth and looked hard at Johnny, with just a trace of a smile. "What a morning this turned out to be," he said. "I just want to sit here, look at my business partner, and feel thankful that gun misfired."

46

*J*ohnny saw the story in the paper the following spring.

As he often did after business tapered off late on Sunday nights, he had Sunday's *Tribune* spread out on the counter in the package store, and he was leaning over with his palms on the counter, straddling the paper. He scanned the open pages in front of him, occasionally pausing and leaning closer to read a story, then reaching across with his left hand to turn the page.

He was mostly scanning: two top Nazis commit suicide, U.S. Marines advance on Okinawa, Yokohama damaged in bombing raids. He learned closer to comb through a story on the state's attorney's latest efforts to shut down a Guzik gambling operation, looking for familiar names.

He continued scanning and skipping, moving faster as he paged through the section labeled "SOCIETY CLUBS TRAVEL NEWS FOR HOMEMAKERS."

And then he stopped.

There she was, staring right at him out of a black and white photograph on page 10. Gorgeous in white.

Turner-Adams
By Thalia

Saturday, May 26, was a memorable day for two prominent North Shore families as Margaret Scott Turner of Evanston and Brantley Cheswick Adams III of Winnetka were married at 5 p.m. at First Congregational Church of Evanston. A large reception followed at the Michigan Shores Club in Wilmette.

The Rev. James R. Q. Davies, minister of First Congregational Church, officiated.

The bride, who was educated at Evanston Township high school and Smith college and who made her debut several years ago, is the daughter of Mr. and Mrs. M. Charles Turner of Evanston. Grandparents of the bride are the late Mr. and Mrs. Morgan L. Turner of Kenosha, Wisc., and the Rt. Hon. Lord and Lady Bartlesby Sinclair of London and Crestwick Abbey, England.

The groom, a graduate of New Trier high school, Amherst college, and Northwestern university law, is a partner in his father-in-law's Chicago law firm, and is the son of Dr. and Mrs. Michael B. Adams of Winnetka. Grandparents are Dr. and Mrs. Brantley C. Adams II of Lake Forest, and Mr. and Mrs. Gilford Pechloss of Phoenix, Ariz., formerly of Oak Park.

The bride, radiant in a tulle veil worn by her mother and maternal grandmother at their weddings, was given in marriage by her parents and escorted by her father. Her maid of honor was Gabrielle d'Audeville, of Cherbourg,

France, a close friend and former college roommate, whose presence was made possible by last summer's Allied liberation of her home city.

Serving as the groom's best man was his younger brother, Chauncy Adams, on furlough from his duties at Navy Pier, where he is a radioman third-class.

Johnny stopped reading and raised his head, staring at thin air. He had tried not to spend time thinking about her. But there was always something—a peal of female laughter from the bar, a leggy blonde walking on Paulina Street—that would take him back to all the craziness.

And now all the wonderings and unanswered questions had been resolved. She was comfortably ensconced in her world, galaxies away from North Paulina Street, a world with unspoken but unbreakable membership requirements that would never be welcoming to guys like Johnny or Joe.

"What the hell," he said quietly. "Maybe it's all for the better."

He took a deep breath and exhaled.

"Dexter," he barked. He spun right, striding down the length of the counter and turning left toward the lounge entrance.

"What you want, boss?"

"I need a drink," Johnny said.

47

On June 20, one of those crystal-clear late-spring days Chicagoans wait all winter for, Johnny made his first visit to Wrigley Field since the Sunday he'd sold his clothes.

He stayed until the top of the seventh inning, gave a wave to the jamokes in the top row of the center field bleachers, and caught an "L" to Howard Street.

He walked into the Apex a few minutes before 5 o'clock, stopped in front of Joe, who was writing checks at the small desk in the package store, and announced: "The Cubs stink."

Joe looked up. "You were there this afternoon?"

"Yup, first trip since last spring," Johnny said.

Joe put the pen down and gave Johnny a pained look. "Why didn't you tell me you were going, my friend? You didn't have to leave early—I'd have been happy to stay late. Sounded like a pretty good game on the radio. And the Cubs are in the hunt—not like last year."

"To me, it's the same team," Johnny said. "Except Pafko's having a better season. That's the only reason they're in contention. They were ahead when I left. Did they win?"

"Five to three," Joe said.

"Yeah, wait till July," Johnny said, as if talking to himself. He brightened. "Here's the real news, Joe. I spent all afternoon in the bleachers, sitting there with Izzy and Laughing Larry and all those nothing guys, money flying this way and that way, and," he drew himself up and shifted into stentorian voice, "I did not make—a—single—bet! I wasn't even tempted, Joe."

"That's great," Joe said, rising from the desk chair. "I mean it. How long is it now? Almost nine months? I'm not saying we can relax, but I think we've kicked the habit."

"So does this mean we can start lecturing other people about the evils of gambling?"

They laughed together.

Joe got up from the desk and went back to the coat rack across from the men's room. He returned wearing a grey fedora. Johnny had moved behind the package store counter.

"Anything happen here today?" Johnny asked.

"Not much," Joe said, his hand on the door. "The accountant says our numbers are looking good the past two months—but we already knew that. And we're starting to get a lot of mailmen in the afternoon. They all finish their routes around eleven, eleven-thirty and then drink till the shift's over."

"Dandy little game," Johnny said.

"See you tomorrow, my friend. I'm going down to the lakefront—relax for a while before dinner."

"Yeah, if you see any good-looking dames, send 'em up here."

Joe was almost out the door when he turned: "Oh, almost forgot. There's mail for you. On the desk somewhere."

It was almost 10 o'clock before Johnny remembered. He went to the desk and scrabbled around in the litter of invoices, bills, liquor advertisements, and handwritten notes until he found the square, light-blue envelope. He thought the handwriting on the envelope was familiar, but he wasn't sure. He turned the envelope over to see if there was a return address on the back. Nothing. He pulled a small penknife out of his pocket and used it to cut a slit across the top of the envelope. He levered the blade back into the knife handle and returned the knife to his pocket.

From the envelope he extracted a single sheet of notepaper, same color as the envelope, folded in half. When he flipped open the note he didn't have to look at the embossed letterhead centered at the top of the sheet because he immediately recognized the large, casual scrawl.

Johnny blue eyes,

You owe me one now. I persuaded my father to do something about that nosy p.i., the one who was following us around. He won't bother us again. And I still get to pick my own friends. Call me soon, Windsor 0521— same rules as before. Missing you.

Margaret

He hardly had time to react before the package store door swung open and a man and woman, both in their late 20s or early 30s, he in a sailor's uniform, each with an arm around the other's waist, careened into the store. Johnny guessed they'd been drinking elsewhere. He refolded the note, folded it a second time, and slipped it into his shirt pocket. "How can I help you?" he said.

"How much is a half-pint of Seagram gin?" the man asked.

Johnny stretched up to the third shelf and brought down a large bottle. "The quart's your best buy, sir," he said, holding the bottle in his right hand and rubbing away any traces of dust with his left. "This stuff doesn't spoil, you know."

"Thanks, just the half-pint today."

Johnny rang up the sale. The couple left, laughing about something, or maybe just happy to be with each other.

He removed the notepaper from his shirt pocket, unfolded it, and read the message a second time.

Almost a year later, it was easy for him to look back and see how selling his wardrobe had set in motion a chain of events that compounded faster than a juice loan. There had been times early in the spiral when he might have walked away before things went out of control. But he had been in love—he was sure about that now. Sure, maybe she was too young for him. And maybe she was out of his league, like the big-shot pool player had said. But it didn't feel that way at the time.

Hindsight.

The hand holding the note dropped to his side. He ran the fingers of the other hand through his hair, and stood there, shoulders sagging.

"She wants to start doing that tango again," he muttered, shaking his head. "What are the odds? What are the fucking odds on that?"

He read the message one more time, his lips silently forming the words. He crumpled the notepaper, and dropped the wad into the trash barrel next to the beer cooler.

"Dexter," he yelled, "pour me a Canadian and water. *And make it a goddamned double.*"